TELL US
NO SECRETS

TELL US
NO SECRETS

A Novel

Siena Sterling

wm
WILLIAM MORROW
An Imprint of HarperCollins*Publishers*

HarperCollins books may be purchased for educational, business, or sales promotional use. For information, please email the Special Markets Department at SPsales@harpercollins.com.

FIRST EDITION

Designed by Diahann Sturge

Classroom photo © BlurryMe / Shutterstock, Inc.

Library of Congress Cataloging-in-Publication Data has been applied for.

ISBN 978-0-06-316180-1

22 23 24 25 26   LSC   10 9 8 7 6 5 4 3 2 1

To my brother:
Hang on Sloopy.
You are the yarest.

Karen Mullens

Abby Madison

Cassidy Thomas

Zoey Spalding

Prologue

2018
APRIL 12

She sent me a Friend request. Usually I get stupidly excited by one of those—someone out there wants to get in touch. At my age, anything unexpected that doesn't involve disease or death is a relief. So unless it's from some random weird person, a Friend request is a plus.

But when I saw her name I winced.

Why had she contacted me after all this time? Almost fifty years had passed since I last saw her. I know that school ties, especially at a boarding school, are strong ones. We spent four years together in classrooms, on sports fields, in dormitories. Four years seeing each other every day and every night. Four teenage years cooped up like chickens in a pen. We all got to know each other much too well.

Yet our class has been a ghost class: it's been as if we never existed. Not for us the "are you married/do you have children/what job do you have/you're looking great" staples of school re-union banter. The Stonybridge School for Girls graduating class of 1970 never had a class reunion. We effectively disappeared ourselves.

We all wanted to forget. So why look me up on Facebook? Why now?

She didn't have a photo of herself, just one of those shady out-lines. I stared at her name. What did she want?

Trying to envision her as a sixty-six-year-old woman, all I could see was the girl in the blue-and-green-plaid uniform and those heavy brown lace-up Oxford shoes.

I saw her in the classroom, in the gym, in the dining hall, sit-ting on the bus as we went off to a dance or a school excursion.

Whatever had happened to her, she was, in my mind, still at Stonybridge and still a teenager.

It felt as if a laser beam had focused on the part of my memory that contained those years, shining its light, releasing all those particular neurons, and setting them flying. I was back in New England. I was back at Stonybridge School for Girls.

Our campus was on the outskirts of Lenox, Massachusetts, a typical small New England town that would have been indistin-guishable from other small New England towns if there hadn't been a famous classical music festival held there every summer. Tangle-wood was renowned and drew cultured visitors from all over the country, though because it was only a two-and-a-half-hour drive from Manhattan, it was an especial favorite of New Yorkers. Set in the midst of the Berkshire Mountains, Lenox was the perfect place for classical music lovers gathering on a warm summer evening to hear conductors like Leonard Bernstein make their magic.

Stonybridge itself was smallish with its hundred and twenty students and looked exactly as a boarding school for girls should look. Redbrick buildings covered with ivy surrounded a court-yard that had a square of grass and a tree in the middle of it. One of the redbrick buildings had been converted into a gym. Another was designated for classrooms; a third for the dining hall, school offices, and Senior Room; and the fourth for dorms and an infirmary. It was a self-contained organism with students constantly crisscrossing the courtyard.

The only time we left during the week was to go to the sports fields, which were a few minutes' walk away, or to go into town.

Because it came alive in the summer, Lenox had a few shops most small towns didn't. There were two clothes stores, a pharmacy, a coffeehouse aptly called the Café, and a record store that stocked the Beatles and Jimi Hendrix as well as Brahms and Beethoven.

Girls at Stonybridge were allowed to go into town on weekends and two weekdays after sports, provided they signed out, went in pairs or larger groups, and stayed only an hour before signing back in.

One weekend every two months we could go home if we chose to, but we also had a required number of school outings on Saturdays—expeditions to a place of historical or geographical interest. And once every six weeks or so we'd be shipped off in a bus to a boys' boarding school for a dance.

In town we'd hang out in the Café or the record store, feeling a little liberated and a touch more adult. If a dance was on the horizon we might try the shops for clothes, but they were aimed at women, not teenagers, so generally we made fun of the clothes and left quickly.

Academic excellence was not a requirement. You went to Stonybridge if you couldn't get into a school like Madeira or Miss Porter's, or if your mother had gone there and it was a family tradition. It wasn't a Swiss "finishing school"; we weren't taught manners or how to walk with the right posture, but we weren't supposed to worry about our future careers either. Careers were for men.

Our class entered Stonybridge in 1966. At that time boarding schools for girls were supposed to be havens of respectability for the entitled: a WASP variation of Catholic schools run by nuns.

What our parents didn't take into consideration was the sixties and the legacy of the sixties that hit the seventies and just kept running.

They weren't prepared for the generational seismic shift that was happening. Girls weren't getting their hair permed and wearing bobby socks anymore. Teenagers had become rebellious and hungry for experience. And suddenly there were a lot more experiences out there to be had.

So the parents of Stonybridge girls might have thought their daughters were safely tucked away, but they had no idea what kind of trouble we could get in.

But then again, neither did we. Not one of us could have foreseen the doom heading our way.

The Class of 1970 considered ourselves a special class, one that played on the edges of the rule books and got away with it. One with a shared sense of humor, a cohesive group that should have kept in touch over the years because we were different. We were memorable.

There had been that morning in May of our senior year when someone had put Aretha Franklin on her stereo and blasted "Chain of Fools" out over the courtyard. Everyone in our class jumped up on the wall separating the courtyard from the classrooms and danced our hearts out as the lower classes looked at us with what we knew was admiration.

They'd miss us when we were gone. So would the teachers. Everyone would miss us.

I remember thinking then that we should do the exact same thing on our tenth reunion. Get up on the wall and re-create the joy, the spirit, the beautiful abandon of those minutes dancing in the sun.

It would have been a perfect way to celebrate a tenth reunion. Or any number reunion.

But the Class of 1970 was never going to get back up on that wall and try to re-create the past.

How can you link arms and dance when you don't know which person in that chain of fools is a murderer?

PART ONE

Chapter 1

1969
SEPTEMBER 10
FIRST DAY OF SENIOR YEAR

Karen Mullens

Karen wandered into the Senior Room looking for a place to hide. She needed to get away from the dorm, from the sound of Cassidy Thomas and Abby Madison and a whole gang of girls on their first day back, discussing their summer vacations. At Assembly that afternoon, Miss Adams had done her usual "Welcome to Stonybridge, or welcome back to Stonybridge" speech, then made some announcements, one of which was to tell them about the Senior Room, where seniors could get together and talk and smoke, and what a privilege it was for them to have it.

Creating a smoking room was the kind of weird thing Miss Adams would do. She wasn't a normal headmistress. Yes, she was a middle-aged spinster with short gray hair and watery blue eyes, the type of woman you'd think might be heading up a boarding school for girls, but she had a totally bizarre mania for all things French.

She'd spent time in Paris when she was young, so she used French phrases and talked about "Les Beaux Arts." The bookcase in her office was stacked with Michelin Guides, and once she even showed up at the

morning Assembly wearing a beret. She must have seen all the girls snig-
gering because she never did again, but she probably wore it to bed at
night.

So over the summer Miss Adams had created the Senior Room so she
could pretend she was sitting in a café on the Left Bank or something.
Maybe French people didn't get cancer.

Karen wasn't a smoker, so it wasn't a big deal to her, but at least the
Senior Room was in the largest building, and if anyone else was there they
wouldn't think she was pathetic and hiding. They'd think she had gone to
check it out.

What she saw was a louche den with a green shag carpet, two battered
leather sofas, a few chairs, and a noticeboard. Sitting on one of the sofas
was Zoey Spalding.

Karen debated whether to walk straight back out, but where would
she go then? Back to the dorm? To the torture of listening to everyone
raving about their summers?

"Hey, Karen—" Zoey waved her cigarette in the air. "I didn't know
you smoked."

"I don't." She sat on a chair across from the sofa. "I just wanted to see
what this room looked like. What was it before? Some kind of office?"

"Yeah. I think they stored all our grades and stuff here. I wonder
where they've moved it all. Maybe we got lucky. Maybe they burned all
our records."

"Yeah, maybe."

It was better, when Zoey Spalding was around, not to say too much:
What was the point of offering up conversation only to have it batted
back with a sarcastic smack?

"So . . ." Zoey leaned back. "Tell me. Are you feeling lachrymose?"

That was Zoey Spalding. She got terrible grades, but she had a vocabulary that put the rest of them to shame, and she never hesitated to use it.

"Lachrymose. Tearful—are you feeling tearful, Karen? You're certainly looking woebegone. You coming in here now; it's fate, isn't it? Synchronicity strikes. The losers meet up."

"What?"

Zoey had a rapid-fire way of talking that made Karen nervous. In fact, everything Zoey did made her nervous. There was an edge to her that had always made Karen steer clear. She was so impatient and restless—and hard.

"You and I. The losers." Zoey shrugged, brushed back her long black hair, then let it fall again. Her face looked birdlike, but not like a robin or a sparrow; more an eagle, because her eyes were slightly hooded and her nose was long. It wasn't an unattractive face, though. It was a striking one. In a scary way. If she cut that messy black hair short, she could have been a man riding a stallion in some country like Hungary or Mongolia.

"What do you mean 'losers'?" she asked.

Zoey was the one who had come up with and organized the "lampoon the teachers" play the year before. She'd gotten the class together and said she'd written a play with all the teachers as characters and they had to perform it for the school. It had been hysterical. So funny that the entire school had given them a five-minute standing ovation at the end.

Karen could still picture Zoey, as Miss Adams, wearing a beret and singing, "Thank Heaven for Little Girls," while constantly tripping over one of those long, floaty types of French scarves Miss Adams always wore. They'd made fun of every single teacher pretty ruthlessly. And gotten away with it. Karen didn't know if that was because Zoey's dad was a famous film director or because her mom was on the school board of trustees. Or because the teachers realized they'd look pretty stupid if they complained.

Whatever the reason—it was hard to believe Zoey could think of herself as a loser.

"Come on, Karen. Don't pretend you don't know what I'm talking about. We're the ones who got well and truly ditched by our best friends last year. Cassidy ditches me, Abby ditches you, and what do you know? We end up here together. You're avoiding the dorm too, right? You don't want to listen to them either. All their first-day-back-from-summer bullshit.

"Hey, maybe they're even comparing tans. Don't want to miss that, do we? Anyway, in case you weren't feeling bad enough already, you should know Cassidy went and stayed at Abby's for a whole month this summer. In Abby's family house on Long Island. The Bobbsey Twins on vacation. No, wait, it's worse than that. They're so close it's like they're sharing every available organ. The Siamese fucking Bobbsey Twins."

"Abby wasn't my boyfriend, Zoey. I wasn't ditched." A sliver of pride made her say this. She could at least attempt to stand up to Zoey.

"No shit she wasn't. And Cassidy wasn't mine. But don't pretend we both didn't get ditched. We were ditched. By our best friends. Who then became best friends. That's cute, right? It's almost poetic."

"I don't—"

"Know what to say," Zoey interrupted, leaning forward. "You're flummoxed. Because I said what you've been thinking. You're still angry and hurt by what Cass and Abby did. Like me. Except I'm better at not showing it. You've put on even more weight this summer."

"Jesus, Zoey—"

"Hang on. Sit back down. Don't get offended and leave in a huff. I was trying to help, to tell you you shouldn't care so much, or at least not show it. I'm sorry if my words wounded you."

They'd wounded her all right. Stabbed her right through the heart. She wanted to run away from Zoey, from everyone, go to her room and bury her head in her pillow. Zoey saying "I'm sorry" stopped her, though. She didn't think she'd ever heard Zoey apologize to anyone.

"Good. You're staying." Zoey leaned back, took a drag of her cigarette. "Thank God they've let us smoke in this fucking hellhole. Thank God I packed my cigarettes. I feel like kissing Miss Adams."

Staring at the smoke rings Zoey had blown, Karen was overwhelmed by a sense of confusion. Because Zoey had said everything she'd been thinking. Which was both painful and strangely comforting. Was it good or awful that Zoey felt the same way, the way she'd been feeling for almost a year now?

From the first day of freshman year when her parents had left her at Stonybridge, Karen's friendship with Abby Madison had made school bearable for her. Abby had been her assigned roommate, and they'd immediately clicked.

Karen, walking into their room, had seen this girl turn and put her hands behind her back.

"Hi, I'm Karen," she'd said.

"I'm Abby."

Her hands were still behind her back, obviously holding something. Was it a bottle of vodka? Was her new roommate a teenage alcoholic?

"Um . . . sorry. But I have to ask. What are you hiding behind your back?"

"Oh shit." The girl named Abby brought her hands in front of her. "Look, I know. I'm too old for this. It's sad. OK? I know that."

It was a stuffed kangaroo. With a cute little pouch.

Dragging her suitcase over to one of the beds and hoisting it up, Karen then unzipped it, pulled out her own stuffed animal—a little tiger with luminescent green eyes—and showed it to Abby.

"Me too," she said, and Abby started laughing. Maybe it was because of being so nervous on the first day away from home, maybe that was why they had laughed so hard they ended up sitting on the floor together practically crying. It didn't matter. Whatever the reason, their friendship was sealed.

Jumpy the Kangaroo and Harvey the Tiger were placed on the windowsill of their room, and every day Abby and she would give a rundown of their classes to them. Which also almost always ended up in hysterical laughter.

Karen had been dreading coming to Stonybridge. When her parents first talked to her about going to a boarding school, she'd hated the idea. They'd talked on and on about how she'd meet the right kind of people and how she'd "get a lot out of being in an all-girl environment." As far as she was concerned, sending her away was proof that they didn't want her at home.

Because they didn't want to look at her.

At least her mother didn't.

Affronted: that was a word Zoey might have used. It was the one that perfectly described her mother's state of mind whenever she saw her only daughter.

How could this overweight, unattractive girl have appeared from her womb? It made no sense, not for a woman who was a blond bombshell, even in her forties, one who thought the world would collapse if she got on the scale and saw it tip over a hundred and fourteen pounds. The woman who wore short skirts and loved dancing and whose first child, a son, was tall and blond and *thin*.

At mealtimes, Karen would see her mother frown as she ate. So she ate more. And asked what was for dessert.

It had occurred to her when she was about eleven that she had been adopted. Why else would she look so different from her parents and her brother? If she found her real parents, she could go live with them and eat as much as she wanted without upsetting anyone. That idea lasted until she realized that her mother wouldn't be so embarrassed by her if she weren't her real daughter. She'd say, *Oh, this is my adopted daughter, Karen*, when she introduced her to anyone, making sure everyone knew she wasn't hers.

Sometimes, thinking she was being subtle, her mother would leave all these medicines on her pillow, potions that were supposed to cure acne. Saying Karen had yet another problem without actually saying it to her face. That didn't feel very subtle to her.

Besides, none of them worked.

Weirdly, though, the worst moment in her life had been on account of her father. Normally they got on well; she knew he was proud of her excelling at school. But on the night of her thirteenth birthday, he had come into her room to say goodnight, lingered by the door on his way out, and announced: "You know, looks don't count, Karen. It's what's inside you that counts."

She knew he was trying to be nice. She also knew she'd never forgive him for pitying her.

Maybe when she was older she wouldn't avoid looking in the mirror. She was smart enough at math that she might be a real brain and win a Nobel Prize. But right then the whole cliché about looks not counting was a huge, not funny joke.

Surprisingly, though, it was a little less of a joke at Stonybridge. It turned out no one paid any attention to how much she ate at mealtimes there. Which might have been why, for those first couple of years, she hadn't put on any more weight. Her acne hadn't disappeared, but it had migrated to her forehead so her bangs covered the spots pretty well.

And while the other Stonybridge girls always complained about their uniforms, she loved them. Back at home when she'd been at day school the girls could wear what they wanted, and of course they started to compete to look the best. It was pretty hard to compete when everyone was wearing the same thing.

Besides, it was clear from day one at Stonybridge that it would be absolutely pointless to compete when there was a girl like Cassidy Thomas at the school. The first time she had seen Cassidy, she decided there wasn't a female alive who wouldn't have done a deal with the devil to look like this girl, even if only for ten minutes.

Karen hadn't seen anyone more beautiful, not in the movies, not on TV, not in magazines. It wasn't fair that a fourteen-year-old could look like that. But then it wasn't fair that anyone could look like that. A dark-haired version of Julie Christie, Cassidy Thomas was like some Greek goddess who had offended Zeus because she wouldn't sleep with him or something and as punishment had been expelled from Mount Olympus and sent to this tiny town in western Massachusetts.

It was obvious that everyone in the school was wowed by her, including the teachers. Who doesn't recognize a goddess in their midst?

So a dreary uniform didn't matter to Cassidy Thomas. She would look astounding in a paper bag. But the rest of the Stonybridge girls blended in the same mass of plaid skirts and blue shirts. Which made day-to-day life a whole lot easier.

And for Karen, being put in a room with Abby Madison that first year had been like getting the perfect present for Christmas. Along with having the same sense of humor, they shared being good academically. They competed for grades, but they never got upset when one of them beat the other. Abby would say, "I'll get you back in math next term," and Karen would reply, "No chance," and it was all harmless teasing.

Abby wasn't boy crazy like a lot of the girls already were; she didn't care about clothes or makeup. So they talked to their stuffed animals, they put on funny little skits sometimes at Assemblies, they hung out with each other constantly freshman and sophomore years. Karen felt protected. It didn't matter that she was overweight; it didn't matter that she didn't have the latest Marimekko dress to wear to a dance because she looked even fatter in them than other ones. Abby and she would always find something to laugh about.

Plus she'd loved going to stay at Abby's house. Their big family made everything fun, and she especially liked Abby's older brother Jeb. The truth was, she had a huge crush on him, but she knew it wasn't ever going to come to anything, so she was happy just to be in his presence the times he was around.

Sending her to boarding school had turned out, strangely, to be the best choice her parents could have made. Because she got good grades, they assumed she'd get into a more academic boarding school like Miss Porter's. When Stonybridge, their last choice, was the only one to accept her, they hadn't understood.

That was because they weren't at the interviews, those painful, horrible interviews when she'd sat there like a lump, unresponsive, practically mute. "Why do you want to go here?" each headmistress had asked, and each time she'd kept her eyes glued to the floor and said: "I don't know."

Miss Adams hadn't cared. "You don't need to know, dear" had been her response.

So, OK, maybe she wasn't 100 percent happy at Stonybridge—the only way she'd be 100 percent happy would be if someone gave her a new body and a new face—but she was as happy as she could be, as happy as she'd ever remembered being. Because of Abby.

She would have stayed happy if the absurdly beautiful, absurdly popular Greek goddess Cassidy Thomas hadn't wrecked her life.

Cassidy and Zoey Spalding had been put in the same room freshman year just like she and Abby had. Cassidy and Zoey had become best friends too. The whole class had managed to work out who was best friends with whom from the beginning of their time at Stonybridge, and nothing had happened to change that. It had worked. Somehow no one had been left out, and there were no cliques.

Maybe if Cassidy and Zoey hadn't been best friends from the very start of their time at Stonybridge, all the girls would have competed to be the one by Cassidy's side. But Cassidy was taken. She and Zoey were as close as Karen and Abby.

Freshman and sophomore years had breezed by without any problems. Once, she overheard a teacher, Miss Gambee, tell Miss Adams she'd never seen a class that got along as well as the Class of '70.

And then, out of the blue one afternoon in November of their junior year, Cassidy Thomas walked into their room, and Abby said: "I'm helping

Cassidy with her Latin," and Karen felt suddenly sick. As that afternoon went on, she felt sicker.

Abby and Cassidy started to joke with each other. Karen, sitting at her desk pretending to do her math homework, would glance over occasionally and see Abby's lit-up face, the way she'd look at Cassidy with an awed expression.

At one point Cassidy looked over at her and said: "How's it going, Karen?" and Karen felt like a dog being thrown a bone. *Sure, I'll acknowledge you, but actually I don't give a fuck.* That was how it came across.

Even worse was the fact that, when Cassidy finally left, Abby didn't say a word about her. As if she were hugging this secret happiness, keeping it in her heart the way Karen kept her crush on Jeb.

"So," Karen had said. "The incredible, amazing Cassidy Thomas has graced us with her presence. That's a real honor. Maybe I should dress up next time she comes. What do you think, Abby? Would a tiara look good on me?"

"It was one afternoon of Latin homework. You don't have to be so mean about her."

No laughter, no smile. A rebuke.

Karen shut up.

If only it had been that one afternoon. But of course it hadn't been. Cassidy came for Latin help; Abby and she studied and joked around, and neither of them really included Karen. They made the occasional feeble effort, but that was what it always was: feeble.

Without saying a word to her, a week later Abby had invited Cassidy to her house for Thanksgiving. Karen only found out about it when she heard a girl in the gym locker room asking Cassidy what she was doing for Thanksgiving and Cassidy answering: "I'm staying with Abby and her family."

She could have confronted Abby, but it would have made her seem so weak, so pathetic and jealous: *You've always invited me to Thanksgiving. Why didn't you invite me? What's wrong with me? Why don't you like me anymore?* So she stayed quiet, while Abby spent more and more time with Cassidy and less and less with her.

After a while, when Cassidy came to their room, Karen left and went to the study hall to do her homework. Not once did Abby say, *Don't be ridiculous. Stay here. It's your room too.*

In a short space of time, they'd gone from being best friends to being passing acquaintances who happened to share the same room.

The real clincher came when Abby took Jumpy off the windowsill and put him in the closet. Again, without saying a word.

It was as if they'd been happily mountain climbing together when suddenly Abby had cut the safety rope binding them—and she hadn't even bothered to look back as Karen fell.

Now, in senior year, Cassidy and Abby were rooming together while she had been stuck with Debby Garrison, who spent all her time talking about her horses.

And now, on the very first day of senior year, she'd learned from Zoey that Cassidy had spent a whole month that summer with Abby on Long Island.

The summers after freshman and sophomore years Karen had spent a week there.

Of course. She should have known. But it still hurt so badly, she didn't know what to think or say or do.

Zoey was right. They'd both been ditched. They were both the losers. The more she thought about it, the more she decided it was a really good thing that at least *someone* understood.

"You want one?" Zoey offered her a cigarette.

"I told you. I don't smoke."

"Really? Come on, be a devil, live a little."

"OK." She took it, put it in her mouth, and Zoey lit it for her.

"Don't inhale too deeply. You'll just cough and choke. Take it easy with the first one. By the twentieth you'll be fine."

Concentrating on not inhaling too much, she puffed. The taste was disgusting. She kept puffing.

"I'm so bored with this place." Zoey sighed. Her foot was busily bobbing up and down. "One more year and we're out. Anyway, I was sitting here before you came, thinking. What could I do to liven things up, make this year a little less boring? For all of us. Put some of that ash in the ashtray."

Karen did.

"And I saw that class list on the bulletin board over there—see it?"

She glanced over at the board and nodded.

"We could have some fun with that."

Karen was trying to figure out when she'd puffed enough of the cigarette to put the whole thing in the ashtray when she realized Zoey had said "we." *We* could have some fun.

Zoey wasn't Cassidy Thomas, but she wasn't a boring nobody either. In fact, if Cassidy Thomas hadn't existed, Zoey would probably be the most powerful girl in the senior class. Not the most popular, not even close, but the most powerful.

"What kind of fun?"

"We'll make a different kind of class list. Jesus, put out the cigarette, will you? You'll burn your hand."

Chapter 2

Zoey Spalding

Zoey watched as Karen put out the cigarette. She wished she could start this whole day over again. Instead of getting in the car with her mother for the drive from Manhattan to Stonybridge, she should have walked off down the street, hailed a cab, and told the driver to take her anywhere. *You choose,* she would have said. *Uptown, downtown, Zanzibar. Get me the hell out of here.*

She could have ended up bound and gagged, struggling for breath on the back seat while the driver decided how best to kill her, but hell, she was effectively bound and gagged in this shithole of a school anyway.

An entire academic year would have to pass before she escaped Stonybridge. That might have been palatable if she were still hanging out with Cassidy Thomas. Instead she was sitting opposite Karen Mullens.

Karen, who had protested that she hadn't been ditched. That was a riot. The minute she'd walked into the Senior Room, Karen had looked like a boxer who'd been KO'd in the first round. Which is how she'd looked most of junior year too.

Dumbstruck. Defeated. Depressed.

Abby Madison ditching her best friend Karen Mullens in order to be the best friend of Cassidy Thomas made sense. Trade in a wholly unremarkable girl for the most popular girl in the school? Only the best kind of person wouldn't have made that switch. And Abby Madison—well, she wasn't some saint, she was normal, unrelievedly normal, so obviously she was going to leave Karen in the dust.

But that was what had hurt so much—the fact that Abby Madison *was* so normal. A normal, preppy girl who did normal, preppy things and would probably end up with some Harvard man and live in the suburbs with three kids. A typical Stonybridge girl.

Zoey had known from the start that Cassidy Thomas wasn't a typical Stonybridge girl, and not just because she was so fucking beautiful. That set her apart, obviously, but Cass wasn't part of the whole Stonybridge WASPy world either. To begin with she was from Minnesota, not the East Coast. No one Zoey had ever met was from Minnesota. Plus Cass was Catholic, and she wasn't rich either. Her father sold insurance for a living. He wasn't a lawyer or a banker or a stockbroker.

Cass's mother had died; she hadn't had a privileged life, but she didn't complain, and she sure as hell wasn't going to be like Abby Madison and end up in a fucking suburb.

"So what brought you to this dump?" she'd asked Cass the minute she had walked, suitcase in hand, into the room freshman year—not even bothering to ask her what her name was or to introduce herself.

"My mother died. And I was starting to get into trouble so my father thought I should come here."

"My parents got divorced. And I've always been in trouble," Zoey stated. Then added: "How'd you get to be so ugly?"

Cass had stared at her, and Zoey had laughed and said: "I bet no one in the world has ever said that to you, right?"

"You're weird."

"Yeah, but you'll get used to it. Who's your favorite? John, Paul, George, or Ringo?"

"Mick Jagger."

"I'm Zoey." She put out her hand. "And I am superlatively happy to meet you."

"You're *really* weird. I'm Cassidy. Cass." She shook Zoey's hand and smiled. "I think I'm happy to meet you."

"You better be. We're stuck with each other for a year now."

"Maybe not. I could kill you."

It had been a long time since a girl her age had made Zoey laugh.

The fact that they'd been put in the same room together that first day had helped cement their friendship, but Zoey knew it would have happened anyway.

They weren't the typical Stonybridge girls. They were the different ones.

Because Cass lived so far away, she'd always come to Zoey's house for their free weekends and Thanksgiving too. They'd wander the streets, roaming around Manhattan, visiting Chinatown and Little Italy, once even going way up on the West Side to a diner on the edge of Harlem. They'd explored the city and had a blast doing it.

Or they'd hang out in Zoey's bedroom at the top of her brownstone, listening to the Rolling Stones.

So why had Cassidy suddenly attached herself to Abby Madison? Tomboy Abby, the Chevron Queen. Stonybridge girls got pale blue felt chevrons sewn onto their dark blue sports shorts if they were part of a sports team that competed against other schools. Zoey didn't have any. Abby had so many there was practically no space for another.

At first that previous November, Zoey hadn't been concerned about Cass spending time with Abby. "What's this new thing with the Chevron Queen?" she'd asked.

"Abby's helping me with my Latin," Cass had answered. Then she'd paused before adding: "Abby's actually really cool."

Abby Madison cool? Not in a million years.

"Uh-huh. Sure she is."

It wasn't until a few days later that the bomb dropped.

"Abby's invited me to her house for Thanksgiving," Cass announced just as they were going to dinner.

"And you're going?"

"Yeah. I thought it would be different. You know, something different." And then a pause before: "You never cared about Thanksgiving, Zo. I mean, you hate those Thanksgiving lunches your mother does. Remember last year you wanted us to skip it and go out somewhere?"

She hadn't replied. It had never occurred to her that Cass might not come for Thanksgiving.

"Anyway, I can come to New York again on one of our free weekends. You know, some weekend soon."

"I'll see you every weekend," her father had said when he'd sat her down and told her about the divorce. "I'm getting a house a few blocks from here, and you can come over and spend every weekend with me."

Zoey remembered thinking that that had sounded like a perfect future. Whole weekends with her father without her mother around. And a divorce would mean there wouldn't be any more horrible arguments to listen to. That would be amazing.

She hadn't been like the other twelve-year-old girls she knew whose parents were divorced or getting a divorce, those girls who were crying and miserable. Her overriding emotion had been relief. If she could have lived with her father the whole time it would have been even better, but she knew that wasn't a possibility because of his film work. Every weekend, though. Every single weekend with him on their own.

They had been sitting in the living room, and he looked at her as though he'd delivered terrible news: an earthquake, a nuclear explosion.

When she'd shrugged and said, "That's cool," he'd smiled his killer smile.

"You're something else, Zoey. You're independent, aren't you? Different. You defy expectations."

She had basked in those compliments, knowing how much her father liked independence, how often he'd said: "I hate Hollywood. It's a factory there. One that stamps out all creativity and independence."

Sometimes she tried to pinpoint when exactly every weekend turned into every other weekend. Maybe after the first couple of months? And how soon before every other weekend turned into a weekend a month? After six months?

She did remember the exact date when he'd first canceled one of their once-a-month weekends: Because, he'd said, "I won't be at home this weekend. I have to go away for a shoot. Sorry about that. It's work." December 11, 1965. That was the Saturday she'd left her house, walked the six blocks to his house at 6:00 p.m., and seen all the lights on. There were a lot of people in the front room. Her father was one of those people.

"I can come to your house again on one of our free weekends," Cass had said.

Zoey wasn't about to say, *Which one? Which weekends will be my weekends, and which will be Abby's? If you have a great time at Thanksgiving, will there be any weekends in New York at all?*

Instead she said: "If you really think Abby Madison is cool, you've got big problems." She was staring at Cass straight on.

"Yeah, well, you've always had big problems, Zo."

That was how they talked to each other: they gave each other shit and had fun doing it. This time, though, it was different. Zoey could feel it in the space between them. Abby Madison was, effectively, in the room with them. And Zoey sensed she wasn't going to leave.

It turned out she was right. There weren't any more weekends in New York together, not after Thanksgiving, not at all.

Karen Mullens might pretend she hadn't been ditched by Abby, but that was all it was: a woeful pretense, especially as Karen had spent the better part of junior year hanging around school looking like a lost puppy dog.

Whereas Zoey had thought: *Fuck this. Everyone thinks I'll be suffering because of Cass and Abby's new best friendship. But I'm independent. I defy expectations. And I will keep defying them.*

She'd written and acted in the "lampoon the teachers" play, which had been so successful that the minute she'd come off the stage, everyone was begging her to write another. In fact, she'd been so fucking good playing Miss Adams that if her father had seen her, he would have hired her for one of his movies.

There wasn't a chance in hell that any of the other Stonybridge girls pitied her. Not Zoey Spalding.

And as shitty as this senior year was doubtless going to be, she'd keep showing them she didn't care. She might wear the same uniform, but she was different.

"So, Karen, here's my plan." She took another cigarette out of the pack, lit it. "I think we should put a star beside the name of any girl in the class who isn't a virgin. When you lose your virginity, you get a star. Obviously if you've already lost it, you get a star right away. And . . . wait . . . here's another brilliant idea. You get to rate the experience. From one to five, five being the best. OK, I know, it's hard to judge, it being the first time and all, but girls know what they expected, right? At least kind of. So they rate it against their expectations. Just how much did the earth move? That kind of thing. And we quiz them afterward, to make sure no one is fabricating the experience. The way I see it, I'm starting another Stonybridge tradition that we can hand over to the next bunch of seniors when we leave this shithole."

"Zoey!"

"Why not? It would be entertaining."

She offered Karen another cigarette. Karen took it.

"That way everyone gets to know who has done it. And no one else in the school will see the list because it's here, in the Senior Room. It's just for our class."

"That's . . . I mean, people won't want to say."

"Are you kidding? Of course they will. What do you think they're talking about in the dorm right now? The war? The cost-of-living index? Spinoza?"

"It's embarrassing."

"Why? What's wrong with having sex?"

"It's private."

"Really? We talk about it all the time. Everyone asks each other anyway. Have you been to first base, second base, third? Come on. You know everyone wants to know. This way, no one has to ask."

Karen was silent, but Zoey could see her mind whirling away.

Cass had gone off with Abby and left Zoey alone in the dust. There was no one else in this stupid school she gave a fuck about. Or who gave a fuck about her.

But here was Karen Mullens, sitting there, manically puffing away, staring at her with frightened hope in her eyes. Definitely giving a fuck.

Karen Mullens, the loser. Was she an inconsolable loser?

"Hey, is 'consolable' a word?"

"Consolable?" Karen gave her a quizzical look.

"Yes, consolable."

"I think it's a word, yes. Why are—"

"How would you use it in a sentence?"

"Um . . . let me think for a second . . . OK. 'They thought she would never stop crying during dinner, but when the chocolate dessert came, they knew she was consolable.'"

"Not bad." Zoey laughed, thinking maybe she had to revise her opinion of Karen. It was possible that Karen Mullens might not be Karen Dullens. In fact . . .

"Listen, Karen, you know how we can switch roommates at the beginning of the term if we arrange it so it works out OK? Who are you rooming with now?"

"Debby."

"Cool. Because I'm with Linda. Debby and Linda like each other, right?"

"Yes."

"So we switch. You and I room together. They'll be cool with that."

"I don't know." She paused. "I mean, it would look like . . ."

"The ones who got ditched got together? So what? And we could have a good time. You're smart. You know, I'm smart too, even if I don't get grades like yours. As far as I'm concerned, good grades are for the make-believe girls. The make-believe girls get good grades and they get into a good college and then they end up getting married to a jerk who's also from a good college and that jerk won't give a shit about having an intelligent wife. It's all just make-believe. All the make-believe girls sell out in the end."

She was a little surprised at herself for talking so much. When she'd say things like that to Cass, Cass would raise her eyebrows and say, "So when are you going to run for president, Zo?"

Karen looked intrigued.

"Anyway, Debby and Linda aren't exactly smart, are they? Debby talks about horses all the time, and Linda talks about makeup. Who wants to talk about horses and makeup for a year? Really?"

"Yeah, but . . . this list thing. I don't know."

"Because it's not ladylike? Come on, it's women's lib time, remember. We're all equal now, and I bet boys do stuff like this all the time."

"Probably. Yes, I think you're right. They probably do." Karen nodded.

"So now we get to too. Anyway, how about it? How about switching with Debby and Linda?"

"You really want to room with me?"

"Yeah, why not? What do you say?"

"Yes." She nodded again. "Yes, that would be great."

Zoey watched as Karen Mullens smiled a consoled smile.

Chapter 3

Abby Madison

What the hell? How had it happened? Karen and Zoey were friends now? They'd started that awful List *together*?

Abby couldn't figure it out. It made no sense at all. In fact, it was crazy.

On the second day of school, when Zoey had first gathered all the seniors together in the Senior Room before dinner and told them about the List, Karen was right beside her. Not only that, Zoey had said: "My new roommate, Karen, and I have a new game for our class. We're going to make it a tradition we hand down to the juniors at the end of the year. We think it will be fun."

We? Since when were Karen and Zoey a *we*, much less roommates?

As soon as Zoey had explained how the List worked, Cassidy had laughed, gone straight up to the board, made two marks, then turned around to face them all.

"So there's my star," she stated. "As if you didn't know already. And I'm giving it a three. That's like a B, right? I mean there was room for improvement. He needed to concentrate on his subject a little more."

Everyone else laughed too, and then they all started looking around at each other: Who was going to go next? Who wasn't going to go?

"Hold on." Zoey raised her hand. "Of course I know Cassidy isn't a virgin and deserves her star. Howsoever, it occurs to me that some of you might decide to lie. Therefore, after you go up and put a star beside your name and give a rating, you have to swear to us on . . . let me think . . . what would mean the most to all of you . . . all right. Swear on the life of your firstborn child that you're telling the truth. That should take care of the lurking fabricators."

"Lurking fabricators": Does Zoey ever take a break? Does she have to show off like that all the time?

And why, Abby asked herself, *am I still scared of her?*

Two other girls went up to the board and put a star and rating beside their names. They tried to be funny about it as well, comparing it to grades in class the way Cass had. And then they both went over to Zoey and swore on the life of their firstborn child.

Karen looked pleased with herself as she stood beside Zoey.

It was certifiably nuts. Karen was a virgin; she should have been as uncomfortable with this whole List thing as Abby was herself. Neither of them knew anything about sex. Karen hadn't even kissed a boy, or at least she hadn't when they'd been best friends. It didn't seem likely that that would have changed.

Besides, Karen had always been afraid of Zoey too. Back in the old days they'd talked about Zoey and laughed about how scary she was. "It's like she's from a different planet," Karen had said. "Full of wild, scary aliens."

Abby had gone further than Karen—she had kissed a boy. But only once. At a party. On the lips, that was all. Nothing more. So it had been bad enough listening to girls talking about the "bases" they had been to when they were all comparing their summers that first night back at school. But having your virginity—or non-virginity—up on a bulletin board for everyone to see? How could Karen, the Karen she used to know, think that was "fun"?

That wasn't the end of it either. After math class that morning Karen had waylaid her, grabbed her by the arm and taken her down the corridors away from the others.

"You know what Zoey calls you, Abby? She calls you the Un Girl. She used to call you the Chevron Queen, but she said she's sick of that so she's switched to the Un Girl. Underwhelming. Unprepossessing. Unbelievably Unexciting. Zoey has a way with words, doesn't she?"

Abby was so shocked she couldn't think of a reply, and anyway Karen had walked off, leaving her standing there in the corridor.

During the rest of her classes, during sports, during dinner, those words stayed with her: Underwhelming. Unprepossessing. Unbelievably Unexciting.

Even though she figured it was Karen's revenge, getting back at her for her friendship with Cass, that knowledge didn't help. She wished she could have thought of a stinging retort right off the bat. Something like: *And you think Zoey is hanging out with you now because you're so prepossessing? Think again.*

Zoey and Karen were the most unlikely pairing of personalities Abby could imagine. But then the other girls in their class probably thought that about her and Cassidy. Their friendship had surprised everyone. And if she was totally honest about it, she'd have to admit it had surprised her too. And if she was totally, *totally* honest, she was still surprised.

The thing about Cassidy, what set her apart from any girl Abby had met before, was that she didn't have to try. She didn't need to wear makeup or cool clothes or padded bras or anything fake. She wasn't self-conscious about her body either. It was as if she knew she was wildly gorgeous and sexy but she didn't particularly care. While every other teenage girl limped around full of self-doubt and angst, Cassidy strode easily, unbothered. She really was from another planet: the planet Cool.

Whereas she, as she'd just been told, was from the Underwhelming, Unprepossessing, Unbelievably Unexciting Planet.

Karen knew how much a comment like that would hurt her. They'd had plenty of conversations about their families when they'd roomed together: Karen had talked about her mother, how disappointed she was in having her as a daughter, while Abby confided that she felt the odd one out in her family.

Peter, her oldest brother, was head of the law review at Yale; Jeb, the next one in line, had already had a short story published, and he hadn't even graduated from Yale yet; while Jennifer, her younger sister, was a musical prodigy on the piano. And Abby? She had no major talents. Yes, she was president of the senior class, but that was just because she was top of her class and that meant she was automatically class president. She didn't have to do anything. It wasn't really a job, just a title. It was nothing special.

She was nothing special.

Which wasn't a great thing to be, but she was used to it.

So she never knew exactly why she'd gone up to Cassidy one afternoon after Latin class junior year and asked her if she'd like some help. Yes, she'd seen her struggling with the ablative absolute, but so were a lot of other girls.

Maybe it was because Cassidy had looked as if she really wanted to get it right, that doing well mattered to her. Abby had never considered that Cassidy Thomas would care about anything as boring as grades, much less a grade in the most boring subject in the world: Latin.

Whatever had prompted her offer of help, she definitely hadn't expected Cass to say, "Thanks, Abby, that would be great. Could I come by your room this afternoon?"

The prospect that they would then end up best friends? That never came within a million miles of her brain. Zoey Spalding was Cass's best friend and always would be.

Yet that all changed when a while after they'd started studying together, Cass had said, "God, Virgil's a drag." Then: "Shit, Thanksgiving's coming up. I always go to New York with Zoey. But Zo hates Thanksgiving. She keeps wanting to skip it, forget the whole thing. It's crazy. I love turkey."

And Abby had pounced. "We always have a huge turkey and pies. Mountains of food. And then we go out and play touch football on the lawn. If Zoey hates it, maybe you could come to my house this year."

"Sounds great. Yes, I'd love to, thanks."

Hearing that "Yes" had felt like sinking a game-winning shot from midcourt just as the buzzer went off. Cassidy Thomas at her house, not Zoey's? Cassidy Thomas choosing her? OK, she was good at sports, she got good grades—which wasn't exactly hard at Stonybridge—and she knew how to drive a stick shift. But that was the sum total of her accomplishments. Whereas Cassidy Thomas was this shining star, the girl everyone in the school wanted to be.

Abby knew then that she'd always remember the moment when Cass had said "I'd love to, thanks." It was the first time she'd ever felt like she counted.

The thought of what Karen's reaction might be to Cass coming for Thanksgiving hit her about five minutes later, and for a second she considered inviting her too. But it wouldn't work. Karen was already jealous of the time she and Cassidy spent together; a whole Thanksgiving break would be unbearable.

If Karen had been cooler with Cass coming to their room from the beginning, maybe it would have been OK, but she'd been bitchy from the start. She'd shot menacing looks at Cass from across the room. After Cass left, Karen had made that comment about wearing a tiara, and then she'd had this wounded, accusing face, as if she'd been stabbed or something. It wasn't fair.

Besides, the two previous Thanksgivings with Karen hadn't exactly been fun. The problem with Karen was that she tried *so* hard, and she mooned around Jeb like some Beatles fan who was in the presence of Paul, and she was *so* uncoordinated. There were times when they'd be playing touch football and Abby had wanted to shout: *Can't you run? Can't you catch a pass from two feet away?*

After sophomore year Thanksgiving, her mother had pulled her aside and said: "It's so nice of you to invite Karen. She obviously needs a friend like you."

Her mother pointing out that Karen needed help made her *think* Karen needed help, which made her look at Karen a little differently.

It wasn't as if she didn't want to be a nice person, but there was being nice and then there was being friends with Cass, and if she had to choose . . . and Karen had done that, made her choose . . . then what was she supposed to do?

She'd had the best Thanksgiving ever with Cass. It had deepened their friendship to the point they hung out with each other all the time, not just occasionally. So everything shifted, and it became "Cass and Abby," not "Cass and Zoey" or "Abby and Karen."

In a way, it made sense for Zoey and Karen to team up together senior year, but it was still strange, as if someone were doing a science experiment, mixing together two elements that should never have been in the same test tube. And the result was this crazy List.

If she'd never asked Cassidy whether she needed help in Latin, Abby knew she would be sitting with Karen right now, moaning about the List together. Instead, she was freaking out about being called the Un Girl.

Getting up from the bed, she went over to the desk and started to look through record albums. Seniors were allowed to play records for an hour after dinner on weekdays and all day—from noon onward—on the weekends.

It was another senior perk, like being able to drink coffee at breakfast and now to smoke in the Senior Room. Abby loved coffee; she hated the smell of smoke. But she'd spent time in the Senior Room anyway because Cassidy sometimes smoked and it was a cool place to hang out. There weren't enough chairs or places to sit, but the shag rug was actually pretty comfortable, so when there was nowhere else to sit, they'd sprawl out on it, lying on their backs, looking up at the cracks in the ceiling.

"Are you cool with Simon and Garfunkel?"

"Sure." Cass, who had been sitting at her desk studying math, turned and smiled. "Why not? 'Feelin' Groovy.'"

Abby had thought that she'd get used to Cass's looks after a while, the way she guessed people who stood around in museums guarding the paintings must grow tired of those beautiful water lilies or whatever they saw every single day on display. It hadn't happened.

"Karen told me today that Zoey calls me the Un Girl. Underwhelming, Unprepossessing, Unbelievably Unexciting." She placed the record on the turntable, switched it on, and put the needle down on the first groove.

"You don't take Zo seriously, do you? That's the way she is. She's called me a thousand things a lot worse than that."

"But it's different. I mean, you know, she's kidding with you, not with me."

"Don't sweat it, Abs. Zoey's making trouble. That's what she's good at."

"Right. OK."

She shouldn't sweat it. Because here she was, sitting with Cass, and Cass wouldn't hang out with an Un Girl.

Everyone at school had started treating her differently as soon as it became clear she and Cassidy Thomas had become best friends. No one said anything, at least not to her face, but they paid more attention to her. They asked her opinion about things like new bands or new albums. They even looked at her differently.

She wasn't an Un Girl. Not anymore.

She was special.

Chapter 4

Cassidy Thomas

Cassidy was humming along as she and Abby listened to Simon and Garfunkel. They were both sitting cross-legged on their single beds. All the beds in the school were the same. So were all the desks. And all the closets. Girls tried to make their rooms look better by putting up posters on the walls. Some had posters of Chairman Mao, some had Jean-Claude Killy, some had the Beatles or Rolling Stones. Zoey had had a print by some artist Cass had never heard of. It was called *The Scream* and it was ugly as hell.

Abby had a poster of a basketball player with the number 17 on his green-and-white shirt.

Cass's own poster wasn't really a poster. She had Scotch taped the album cover of the *West Side Story* soundtrack onto the wall above her desk. A few people had asked her why she had it. She had said, "Because I like it," and left it at that.

Abby was wearing blue-and-white-striped pajamas. Her dirty blond hair came down to her shoulders, and she had bangs slanted to the left side. She looked like the athlete she was but not as much of a tomboy as she'd been the first couple of years.

That "Un Girl" comment of Zoey's had freaked Abby out, and so had Zoey's List. She was so innocent. Sitting there on top of her bed in those pajamas, she looked about ten years old, and from what she'd said, she hadn't experienced more than a kiss. Sometimes Cass thought she should have done a swap. While Abby helped her learn Latin, she'd help Abby learn about sex.

"I can tell you're still thinking about Karen and Zoey, Abs. Forget them, OK? Let's talk about something else. What were people talking about at your table at supper?"

"Nothing interesting. Connie was saying she was going to start planning her coming-out party."

When she'd first heard the words "coming-out party," Cassidy thought they were parties for homosexuals who were coming out of the closet and she couldn't understand why so many girls would be talking about them. Luckily she hadn't made any comment, so she'd learned, without embarrassing herself, that they were big bashes for debutante girls.

Apparently, to begin with you were "introduced to society" at what was called the Cotillion, and then you gave a huge party for everyone else you knew who had been "introduced" too.

They might as well have been speaking in a foreign language when it came to this stuff. And she was the only one who didn't understand it. Most of the girls at Stonybridge were there because they were East Coast preppy types who did this whole "debutante" thing, whose parents had also gone to boarding school, who had summerhouses on Long Island or Cape Cod, who were in some special book of all the good old East Coast families.

Not her. She was at Stonybridge because her mother had died when she was twelve and her father didn't know what to do with her and he'd taken out a second mortgage on their house and, together with all her aunts and uncles, had pooled every extra cent they had to afford a school more than a thousand miles away from home because one of her aunts knew someone who had a cousin who had gone there and liked it or something like that.

It was true that she had been misbehaving a little. She'd started talking back to teachers. And going out with Terry, whom her father hated. And hanging out with a crowd of kids who got in trouble. Still—what had her father been thinking? Did he and the rest of the family really believe that she'd come back from Stonybridge like it was some Swiss finishing school and start acting like Eliza Doolittle after Henry Higgins had done his best?

She didn't belong in this school. The only way she got away with being here was because she was so different. The preppy girls all thought it was far-out and groovy that she actually had a job in the summers instead of going to some snazzy camp or taking a vacation in Europe. They treated her as if she were a rare breed of animal. When she came back to school after summer vacation, they all ran to her room and gawked at her.

"What did you do, Cass? Tell us everything."

They wanted to know what it was like to actually have a job and earn money. As if working at HoJo's was some prize. And they were amazed that she lived in this city somewhere in the Midwest where they'd never been—which was more foreign to them than Paris or Rome—called Minneapolis.

For some reason it was a plus for them to meet a girl from the wrong side of the tracks.

They were a lot younger than she was too. The girls in her class might be the same age, but nothing really bad had come their way so they behaved like kids, talking about all the good stuff that had happened or was going to happen to them. When they'd moan, it was about not having enough of an allowance or some boy not liking them enough.

It wasn't their fault they had everything they had, so she didn't blame them. She just couldn't understand why they didn't understand how much they had.

When she first arrived at Stonybridge she used to imagine what it would be like to have the kind of family lives they talked about. Big houses. Great vacations. No money worries. Brothers and sisters they played games with.

A mother.

So many times they'd complain about their mothers.

Shut up, she wanted to yell at them. *You have a mother. Your mother is alive. Shut the fuck up.*

"You know something? I can't wait," her mother had said once when they were driving to school. Cass must have been nine or maybe ten years old. "I can't wait to go to your high school graduation. I can't wait to see you fall in love. I can't wait for the day when I go wedding dress shopping with you. I can't wait to see your face when you have your first child."

"Mom—"

"I know, I know. It's all a long way off, but I love to see your happy face, Cass. And I can't wait to see how happy that face is at all the big, happy events that are coming up."

"What if I flunk out of school and never fall in love and never get married and never have a kid?"

"What if you tell me what you want for supper tonight?" her mother had said, laughing. "Then I'll get to see your happy face when you're eating it. That will do for now."

"You're crazy."

"Yup." Her mother reached over, turned up the radio. "Come on, it's Buddy Holly."

They'd sung along together to "That'll Be the Day."

She could tell that the girls at Stonybridge knew about her mother dying because they never asked her any questions about her parents. Death made them nervous and afraid. The only person she ever talked to about her mother was the science teacher, Mr. Doherty. He understood. In some ways, he was the only person she could really be herself with there. She never told anyone about talking with him as much as she did, though, because no one would get it. They'd make it into something it wasn't.

In the first couple of years at Stonybridge, she had been buddies with Zoey partly because Zoey had been through some shit too, so she didn't have that whole entitled outlook on life. Her parents had divorced, which meant she had some sense that maybe life wasn't always a piece of cake.

But when Cass would go stay with Zoey in New York on weekends it turned out to be depressing. Most of the time they just roamed the streets. The rest of it they spent in Zoey's bedroom on the top floor of her brownstone on the Upper East Side. Zoey obviously hated her mother, and Cass had never met Zoey's father, the famous film director. The atmosphere in that house was always tense.

Still, Zoey made her laugh, and Cass admired how unafraid she was. Of course they would get on each other's nerves sometimes, but they had been friends from the start, and it felt like they'd be friends forever.

Until November of junior year, when everything changed. Cass had been struggling in Latin class, and Abby had come up to her afterward. "Would you like me to help you out on Latin sometime?" she'd asked.

She had never paid much attention to Abby Madison before. She was athletic, came first in most of her classes, and hung out with Karen Mullens. The two of them used to put on skits in Assembly—silly little things that were supposed to be funny but struck Cass as pretty stupid. Still, she wasn't going to turn down help, not from the smartest girl in Latin.

Sure, she'd like some help. How about that afternoon?

Even now, at the beginning of senior year, most of the girls in school couldn't figure it out. How had she and Abby become best friends? Why was Cassidy Thomas spending all her free time with Abby instead of Zoey?

The thing of it was, she felt more comfortable with Abby. Zoey was definitely cooler, but Cass had a weird feeling she could never really let her guard down when they were together. That she could never show any weakness or take anything at all seriously.

It was a lot more than that, though. About a week after Abby started helping her with her Latin, she invited Cass to her house for the Thanksgiving weekend. They went by bus to Darien, Connecticut, and Abby's mother picked them up in a black station wagon. She was friendly and asked Cass lots of questions about school and about Minneapolis. Unlike Zoey's mother, Mrs. Madison wasn't dressed up or wearing makeup. She looked normal, but classy normal.

As they turned and drove up the driveway, Cass had to stop herself from laughing out loud. There it was: everything she'd imagined. A huge white house with chimneys and a weather vane, set in acres of land, and—off to the side—a group of young people playing touch football on an equally huge lawn.

Jesus, this really does exist, she'd thought. *The perfect family in the perfect house.*

"The ones in jeans are my brothers, Peter and Jeb, and the other boys are a couple of friends of theirs," Abby said, pointing them out. "And that's my younger sister, Jennifer. We all play touch football when we can." As she got out of the car, she added: "But you don't have to play. You don't have to do anything you don't want to do this weekend."

Cass wanted to play. She wanted to do everything the Madisons did. So five minutes later she was out on the lawn, joining in, trying to throw a spiral pass, trying to intercept passes, doing her best to be a part of this fun. She noticed that Jeb, who was on the opposite team, was always the one guarding her—and the one who teased her the most when she'd fumble or drop a catch.

He had sandy blond hair down to his shoulders, dark blue eyes, was thin and tall, and would have looked like he was straight out of a catalog of perfect preppy guys if his jeans hadn't been torn and dirty and his front tooth hadn't been chipped.

"Hey, lay off the newcomer," the oldest brother, Peter, shouted at him.

"She can take it," Jeb answered, then nudged her with his elbow. "You can take it, can't you? I bet you have a Swiss Army knife in your pocket."

Abby had told her all about her brothers and sister before. Jeb Madison was a junior at Yale while Peter was at law school there. The younger sister, Jennifer, was at a day school but was going to go to Stonybridge—natch—when she was old enough. Mrs. Madison had gone there: it was a family tradition.

It turned out their family was as different to Zoey's as it was possible to be. They joked with each other, they teased each other, they actually enjoyed each other's company, she could tell. Except at dinner that Wednesday night when the subject of Vietnam came up.

Peter and Jeb got into a huge argument with Mr. Madison. They were against the war; he was for it. While all the females at the table sat quietly, the male voices got louder and louder.

"This is an immoral war, Dad," Peter said. "What right does the United States have to be in Vietnam? And it's pointless. All these people dying—Vietnamese and Americans for no reason. You're supporting an immoral war, an immoral, pointless war."

"Pointless? If you really want the world to be overrun by Communists, fine," Mr. Madison yelled. "Invite them all here. I'm sure you'll all have a wonderful time together. And that's just terrific. That's what we fought World War Two for—so our children could grow up and burn the American flag."

Mr. Madison was a lawyer and looked like one—tall and thin with short graying hair. His face was thin too, and he had sharp blue eyes. When he shouted at his sons, his voice was full of angry authority.

"What about freedom of speech, freedom of action?" Jeb retorted. "The protestors have a right to protest, don't they? Isn't that what America is supposed to be about? Freedom?"

"Freedom to spit on your own country? Freedom to go to the streets and shout, 'Ho, Ho, Ho Chi Minh, NLF are gonna win'? That's not freedom, that's treason."

"Calm down, Teddy." Mrs. Madison finally spoke. "I truly wish we could avoid the topic of politics at family dinners."

"You can't agree with them. Don't tell me you do, Julia."

"You know how much I hate arguments. Besides, we have a guest. I'm making a rule now. If I don't tell the boys they have to cut their disgusting long hair, you won't argue with them about politics. No one will argue at this table. It's Thanksgiving tomorrow. Let's not forget that."

"So what are we supposed to talk about?" Peter asked.

"Football," Abby said quickly. "Basketball."

"Turkey," Jennifer piped up. "Are we going to have that vegetable thing with marshmallows on top? And can we please have apple pie instead of pumpkin? Pumpkin pie is so gross."

"We'll see, Jennifer. Cassidy—that's an unusual name." Mrs. Madison turned to her.

"It was my mother's maiden name."

"It's distinctive." She smiled.

Cass knew enough about manners to get up and help clear the table, even though Mrs. Madison told her she didn't have to.

"I'd like to help," she said, picking up plates and heading to the kitchen.

Jeb was behind her, carrying plates too.

She turned to face him and said: "I do have a Swiss Army knife, you know. It's upstairs in my bag."

Her father had given it to her before she went to Stonybridge that first year.

"Cassidy," Jeb said, stepping back. It was all he said, but he said it in a way that made her step back too.

They stood there, five feet away from each other, with plates in their hands, eyes locking together so tightly she felt as if their hearts had jumped out of their chests and locked on to each other too.

A hundred years of dating, a thousand years of loving each other, was in that look.

The world stopped.

She didn't cry when her mother died. Not when the teacher

at school told her, not at the funeral. Not until a month later, when she bought the soundtrack to *West Side Story*. It was the first movie she'd ever seen; her mother had taken her when she was nine years old. She'd fallen asleep in the middle but woken up when Rita Moreno was belting out, "I like to be in America." Looking over, she saw the smile on her mother's face. "Isn't it great?" her mother had whispered. "I love it."

Sitting on her own, listening to the album in her bedroom, she wept. Finally. She thought she'd never stop weeping. Until she felt her mother's presence, her mother sitting there beside her. And she heard her mother saying, as she had when they'd watched it together: "Don't cry, sweetheart. I know it's a sad ending, but they loved each other so much, Maria and Tony. That kind of love—it's what everyone should have. I want you to have it. The moment when they see each other and the world stops."

Jennifer burst into the kitchen then, bringing the world back with her. But Cassidy knew. Her life had changed. Everything was different. Jeb Madison. Jeb Madison had made the world stop.

Dinner ended, and they all sat around in the huge living room talking. Cassidy stayed quiet, occasionally looking over at Jeb. He was doing the same thing.

They talked about their relatives, some cousins who lived in California, about a book Mrs. Madison had just read, anything except politics.

"I'm tired," Abby announced. "Come on, Cass. Let's go up to our room."

The end of the unbelievable day. Cassidy lay in bed replaying every second of it. The first time she'd seen him on the football field, how he'd joked around with her as she tried to play, every single instant she could remember.

"I bet you have a Swiss Army knife."

His chipped front tooth.

The kitchen.

That moment.

Jeb Madison. She wanted to fall asleep saying his name.

The next day was Thanksgiving. Another touch football game was scheduled for after lunch, but before lunch Mrs. Madison told everyone they should go out for a walk and leave her alone to organize things.

"I can get it done better by myself. And you can sit and read while the children are out, Teddy. Take a break."

Peter and Abby and Jennifer went ahead; Jeb hung back, then walked by her side.

"You have a choice, Cassidy," he said. "Which one would you like to go to? Paris or Venice?"

"Can't I say I'd like to go to both?"

"You can say it, but it will be hard for us to get married in two cities at the same time."

She stopped. He stopped.

"Don't tease me, Jeb."

"I'll always tease you." He hip-checked her. "But not about our wedding."

"You're crazy."

She walked ahead looking down, her heart pumping. How was this possible? *Was* it possible? Was he actually joking? What the hell was she supposed to do? She was staring at the ground and tears were starting to fall down her face and she felt so unbelievably happy and so unbelievably scared.

"I'm not crazy." He'd caught up with her. "I'm not teasing either. I mean it. I would have proposed back there in the kitchen if Jennifer hadn't interrupted us. What's happened between us

is permanent. I knew it the minute you got out of the car yesterday. Not because of the way you look. You're beautiful, but
that's not it. *You're* it. *We're* it. Together. I'm certifiably sane.
And desperately in love. And I'm proposing to you. So what's
your answer?"

Wiping her cheeks with the palms of her hands, she finally
looked at him.

"OK" was all she could say.

"OK? Well, that's romantic. That's something we can tell our
children. 'When I proposed, your mother said, "OK."'"

"Jeb—"

"We're going to get married, Cassidy. If you want to, I mean.
So—what do you say? Shake on it?" He held out his hand.

"You're crazy."

His hand was still outstretched. They were looking at each
other, sharing that same look they'd shared in the kitchen.

"OK." She shook it. She laughed. "OK."

"OK. Whew. We better catch up with the others now. But I
don't think they're ready to hear our news. You're younger than
me, you're Abby's friend. I thought about it last night, and I
think we should wait to tell them about us being in love until
you graduate. Are you OK with that?"

"Yes." She nodded. *Us. Love. Us.*

"But it's a deal, right, Cassidy? I'm serious. It's a deal. You
shook on it."

"I shook on it. Right. It's a deal." She hip-checked him, and
he laughed too.

For the rest of the Thanksgiving weekend, she and Jeb could
act normally around each other, because they had their deal.
Any time they exchanged a glance, it was there. She could
spend time braiding Jennifer's hair or playing Monopoly,

hanging out with Abby. She and Jeb didn't have to talk to each other or go hide in corners. All they had to do was be near each other. It was there.

She could help Mrs. Madison in the kitchen, clear the table at meals, talk to Mr. Madison about Minneapolis, where, amazingly enough, he'd been. When he'd mentioned a museum he'd gone to there, she'd nodded, but she wasn't stupid; she didn't say she'd been there and try to fake her way through it. And it turned out he watched all the same old black-and-white movies her mother had loved, which made conversation easy. All she had to do was mention *Top Hat* and he'd be off on a monologue about Fred Astaire.

But she was careful too not to spend too much time talking to him. She'd always turn to Mrs. Madison quickly and ask her questions about what she liked.

"You're the perfect guest, you know," Abby told her on the Friday. "Everyone thinks you're amazing."

"I think your family is amazing," she replied. Which was true.

All of them were amazing, in different ways. As a family they were as amazing as she could imagine any family being.

But Jeb wasn't just amazing.

Jeb made the world stop.

By chance, before they left on the Sunday, Jeb and she were left alone together in the living room.

"I don't want to make you lie," he said. They were sitting across from each other in two big green armchairs. "But what we have—"

"It's between us." She finished his sentence, staring at him, nodding. "I know. I get it."

He smiled, leaned over, reached out, brushed her hair back from her face.

"I'll call you tomorrow. At six—that's a good time, right? If I call Abby, that's when I call."

"Right. I'll be by the phone."

He kept smiling his chipped-tooth smile.

"Cassidy Thomas. How'd I get so lucky?"

"Jeb?" Mrs. Madison called out. "Where are you? I have your laundry."

"I'm coming, Mom." He stood up. "Six o'clock."

"Six o'clock."

"Here." He took off his watch and handed it to her. "This will help you keep track of the time."

"But I have a—"

"Take it. It will tell our time. OK?"

"OK."

And he was gone.

Ten months had passed. They were as in love as they had been from that moment in the kitchen. Abby didn't know; no one did. They'd managed to keep it to themselves.

"Until you graduate," he'd said.

She could wait.

Besides, she wouldn't have talked about it to anyone anyway. Not even Abby. What had happened between her and Jeb was private. The idea of sharing details, the way girls did with each other, would have made what they had together something common. Jeb wasn't her boyfriend. He was the love of her life. She'd had boyfriends before and done all the stupid things young girls did with boyfriends. This was different. She wasn't about to go into the Senior Room and blab about things the way the other girls did. It wasn't a teenage crush. It was real.

The only thing that worried her sometimes was the fact that

they came from such different worlds. The Madison house was light-years away from her father's apartment in Minneapolis. Her father was an insurance salesman, not a lawyer. Jeb had grown up with such a privileged background—not that he acted that way, but still, how would it work when the Madisons did find out about them? What would they think?

She'd find out pretty soon because now graduation was only nine months away. They would tell everyone about their relationship in the summer and her real life would begin then. She wouldn't be sitting on a dorm bed, listening to Simon and Garfunkel. She'd be with Jeb Madison. Forever.

"Connie's talking about coming-out parties? I wouldn't mind going to one," she told Abby.

"Really?" Abby gave her a quizzical look. "I can't imagine you at one of those things."

"Why not?"

"I don't know, I just can't."

Abby might be her best friend, but in the end she wanted her to be what everyone else wanted her to be. The supposedly streetwise, tough girl from the wrong side of the tracks. What *would* Abby think when she found out about her and Jeb?

Haven't you ever read "Cinderella"? she wanted to ask her. *Don't I get a chance to go to the ball?*

Chapter 5

Thomas Doherty

It was yet another sign that Stonybridge was deteriorating. A Senior Room for smoking: How much more ludicrous could it get? He had opposed the idea from its inception at the end of the previous year. Veronica Adams, the headmistress, had decided then that the seniors deserved a room of their own, with perquisites attached. They could gather there, talk among themselves, and—all importantly, it seemed—smoke cigarettes.

"That's so unhealthy, Veronica," he had protested.

"If they don't smoke there, believe me, Tom, they'll smoke in their rooms and try to hide it and they'll end up setting fire to the school," she'd replied. "They're old enough to decide for themselves about smoking. After all, we allow them to drink coffee when they're juniors."

Coffee isn't going to give them cancer, he hadn't replied. He knew Veronica Adams too well. She wouldn't give in once she had decided on something. And she liked to think of herself as a touch avant-garde. Her two summers in Paris in her midtwenties were the topic of many of her conversations. She hadn't been a tourist: oh no, she spoke French perfectly and knew which cafés to frequent and which art exhibits to see; so yes, indeed, she had an artistic, slightly bohemian side that manifested itself in her attire with a flurry of floating scarves and, at Stonybridge, with certain fads.

Art was not a minor subject. She'd even installed a photography lab, taking over a classroom at the top of the school. Of course French was required, but she'd also hired a Spanish teacher and, the year before, had attempted to hire a Russian one. The Stonybridge board of trustees had nixed the Russian, but Veronica had waged a fierce battle.

There was no point in continuing to argue against a Senior Room, he had decided, unless he wanted a long, drawn-out debate he'd lose anyway, because she was the headmistress and he was a mere science teacher.

So the Class of 1970 was the first one to have this Senior Room, and he very much hoped it would be the last. He'd heard from the faculty grapevine that some parents had already objected; if enough did, she'd have to cave in. She'd make it seem as if it had been an experiment she was always going to end. What she wouldn't do was admit she'd been wrong or foolish.

It was a silly, dangerous experiment, one she should never have been allowed to make, and it was emblematic of the decay seeping into the school's spirit. Veronica didn't deserve to be headmistress; did she feel no responsibility for the girls in her charge?

Why did he care so much? Other teachers came and went, discussed students in the faculty lounge, but not with the same amount of feeling he had. They didn't seem to truly care about these girls either. And no one, not Veronica, not any other teacher, kept in touch with graduates the way he did.

Tom Doherty made a point of following up on their lives, and for the most part, they reciprocated. He had pictures of his ex-students' weddings, their husbands, their children. He'd never understood how you could teach a girl and then forget her. When he went to the graduation ceremony each year, he'd think of the girls as setting off in little boats, each on her own ocean, and he needed to know where they sailed to and how they had landed.

In nine months' time, he'd be watching the Class of 1970 graduate, the class that had meant more to him than all the others. He was proud of these girls. They were good girls: the best, the funniest, the most sensitive he'd ever taught. Yes, they wore too-short skirts and they swore more than any others, but they were a standout class.

Cassidy Thomas was far and away the most outstanding.

By chance one afternoon three years before, when Cassidy was a freshman new to Stonybridge, he'd run across her in the music room. He'd gone in to find a hymnbook, as he'd had to choose the hymn for the Sunday evening service.

She was sitting on the piano bench, crying. It was mid-September of her first year at Stonybridge; most of the faculty was still surprised by and talking about her beauty.

"It's Cassidy Thomas, yes?" he'd asked, knowing full well it was. She nodded.

"You're upset. Is there anything I can do to help?"

"No, thank you. Not really. I miss my mother. She's dead. And I miss my father. He's in Minneapolis. I don't know what I'm doing here. I wanted to cry. But there's almost no place I can cry where no one can see me."

"I'm sorry I interrupted you."

"It's OK. I was almost through crying."

Even her tears were quite beautiful, he thought. Running slowly in perfectly formed droplets down her face. She wasn't sniffing or brushing them away. The way she cried so quietly was in keeping with the room, which had a grandfather clock in one corner, a harp in another, and a large antique Persian rug. It was the nicest room in the school, dark and slightly mysterious. At that moment Cassidy Thomas didn't look like a teenager, she looked like a sad heroine in a nineteenth-century tale of woe. If there'd been a chaise longue, she would have been reclining on it. And he would have knelt in front of her.

"My mother died too." He sat down beside her on the piano bench. "Many, many years ago."

"Do you still miss her?"

"Every day."

"Do you cry?"

"Sometimes."

"I was thinking about how I used to watch my mother getting dressed up when my dad and she would go out at night. They didn't go out a lot. They weren't, you know, like the parents of the girls here. But when they did, she'd put on a dress and some jewelry and then she'd say: 'Always remember: put on your jewelry and then take one piece of jewelry off. Never forget that.' She must have read it in a magazine or something. She was always reading magazines. She liked looking at people. She gave me pearl earrings for my twelfth birthday. Just before she died. I know they're fake, but they look real.

"But I'm making her sound like she cared more about stuff like jewelry and dresses than other things, and that's not right. What she really cared about was love. I mean, you know, people falling in love, being in love. Loving each other. That's what mattered most to her."

"She sounds wonderful, Cassidy."

"She had a heart attack. No one has a heart attack when they're only thirty-eight."

"Not many people do, you're right."

"I don't think about it. I wipe it out of my brain. Except sometimes I can't. Like now."

"It's good to remember."

"Really?" She looked up at the ceiling, then back at him, her brown eyes full of an emotion: yearning. That was what it was. A heartbreaking yearning.

"You know, she loved *West Side Story*. We saw it together. She told me she hoped I'd fall in love like that, the way they did when the music stopped and the whole rest of the world disappeared. I have the album cover taped on my wall. It's a memory. There will never be enough memories. Sorry." She looked down at the floor. "I'm talking too much."

"No you are not."

"Really? No one wants to talk about her. Sometimes it feels like she's disappeared for more than forever, you know, I mean that she's more than dead. I don't know, I can't explain it."

"You just did explain it. She hasn't disappeared forever, Cassidy. She's in your heart. And any time you want to talk, come find me. We'll come here and chat. About your mother, about whatever you want to chat about."

"Really? I'd like to talk about her. My mother. With you. If that's OK."

"I'd be honored if you did."

"Thanks." She nodded, picked up her book bag from the floor. "You're a nice man. I mean, teachers aren't always nice, you know?"

"I think most of us would like to be."

That first year, she'd find him once a month or so and they'd go to the music room and sit on the piano bench. All she ever spoke about was her mother, and he began to get a picture of her. A woman who'd married fairly young, was very much in love with her husband and with romance. "You need to have a passport," she'd told Cassidy. "You should always have a passport. You might end up in Europe, in a beautiful European city. I'd love to go to Europe sometime with your father. Maybe on our twenty-fifth anniversary."

"She loved movies," Cassidy had told him in her serious voice. "Especially ones with dancing. Fred Astaire and Ginger Rogers. She liked Gene Kelly too, but not as much as Fred Astaire. *West Side Story* was her favorite. But her second favorite was *Roman Holiday* with Audrey Hepburn. She said Audrey Hepburn was the most beautiful woman in the world. And she was sure Audrey Hepburn had fallen in love with Gregory Peck when they were making that movie."

"I agree with her," he'd said with a nod, smiling. "On all counts."

Their meetings became more sporadic over the years, but she would still seek him out every now and then and they'd have their chats in the music room. He never told any of his fellow teachers about their meetings, and he guessed she hadn't told any of her fellow students either. Strangely, however, their meetings didn't feel clandestine, only private.

He discovered she was a Catholic like him. One night at home in bed, he wondered whether he could give her a necklace with a cross for Christmas but decided against it.

If he were honest with himself, he was a lot less strict about grading her papers and tests than he should have been.

If he were even more honest, he'd acknowledge that the other students, the ones from the past with whom he exchanged Christmas cards, doubtless thought of him as a kindly ex-teacher, an old-fashioned man for whom they felt enough of a patronizing fondness not to cross off their lists.

When the Class of 1970 graduated, he knew he'd feel bereft. Cassidy Thomas had stirred his sad soul.

Chapter 6

I was supposed to be organizing an evening out with my oldest son. When he was around eight years old, he suddenly announced that April 14 was his favorite day. A totally random choice, but I decided it would be fun to honor it, so every year on April 14 we do something special together: a fun ritual. This year I was late figuring out a plan of action. I should have been searching the web, looking up plays or movies or restaurants.

Instead I sat staring at that damned shaded profile.

You can spend years forgetting the past. Now I was stuck in my chair, spending hours remembering.

Stonybridge School for Girls liked rituals too. My favorite was the one that took place when Christmas vacation began. The juniors all had to get up early and go from room to room, waking up the other girls and lighting candles for everyone. A silent candlelit procession ensued, down the corridors, out and around the campus, before heading for the dining hall, where we took our places at the tables and Christmas carols began. Everyone was excited, knowing we were about to go home, waiting for release, and digging into a special breakfast: instead of cereal or runny scrambled eggs, we had popovers with butter and honey.

Maybe the other girls' boarding schools had similar rituals. If they did, we would have defended ours as the best. Stonybridge had to be the best at something. Academically, it was on a lower tier than the other East Coast girls' boarding schools, and when we played other schools at sports, we always lost. But we were brilliant at rituals.

At the end of every year the seniors handed challenges down to the junior class that they had to complete if they wanted to then hand challenges down themselves. They were silly things: Wrapping the flagpole in the middle of the quad with tissue paper. Sticking a message reading "Meow" on a teacher's back while she was at the blackboard. Dumb little tests some senior class must have made up years ago that had continued on and become a tradition.

The List was a whole different ball game.

The beginning of that fall term we were all talking about it among ourselves. We'd all go look at it constantly; we were all quizzing each other. "You put a two up. Was it really bad?" someone would ask a self-proclaimed Star while other girls wondered who might be lying about their status. "I don't believe Debby is. And I don't believe Harriet isn't" were just some of the comments whizzing around the Senior Room.

The sexual revolution had begun: long make-out sessions didn't stop before they went too far anymore, and it wasn't clear whether that was because girls were feeling free enough or pressured enough not to stop them.

Not long ago I read an article saying that because so much emphasis was put on parenting these days, people were overlooking the importance of peer groups in terms of influencing the development of children.

I could picture it: the scene in the Senior Room, where shy, introverted Allison Munroe sat silently on one of the leather sofas, discreetly waving smoke away from her face, trying as hard as she could not to look shocked or out of place as the talk became raunchier and raunchier. No one ever stood up and protested when the Stars would tease the girls who weren't and ask when they were going to "join the club." No one wanted to be ostracized.

And it never occurred to us that behaving like teenage boys in a locker room wasn't liberating or that this kind of equality with the male sex wasn't something to be proud of.

Losing your virginity turned into a class competition. And whatever doubts anyone might have had when they heard about the List for the first time quickly dissipated as everyone played the game, which could have been called Bully Sex.

A whole different take on #MeToo.

Chapter 7

1969
OCTOBER 11

Abby

Every year on the second Saturday of October, Stonybridge had what was called the Foliage Day Out. The entire school went on a compulsory hiking trek through the Berkshire Mountains, whatever the weather. They'd set off at nine in the morning and hike all day, stopping only for a big picnic at lunchtime.

Their sophomore year it had been raining so hard they had come back soaking and one of the girls had ended up in the infirmary with pneumonia. This year it was one of those fall days New England was famous for. The trees were bursting with color, all shades of reds, oranges, and yellows, and the air was crisp and clear.

Abby would have been happily hiking up the pine needle–covered path if it hadn't been for the fact that somehow it had worked out that she and Cass and Zoey and Karen had ended up beside each other on the climb. Which was the worst possible combination, but it wasn't as if any of them could suddenly break into a run and race ahead.

At least Mr. Doherty was there with them, Abby thought. So Karen wouldn't come out with any bitchy comments again. They hadn't spoken to each other since Karen had called her the Un Girl.

Hiking along, she stayed silent. She didn't want to say a word in case Zoey came up with some stinging comment about how boring she was.

"Girls." Mr. Doherty pointed upward. "The trees aren't going gently into the night, are they? Look at those stunning colors. They're raging."

"Wow, quoting Dylan Thomas, Mr. Doherty. I thought you were a science teacher, not an English one," Zoey said, proving what Abby knew already: Zoey was smarter than the rest of them, knew more poetry, read more books, but never applied that to the classroom.

"There is poetry in the workings of nature too," he replied. "I'm interested in many different subjects. No one should have a one-track mind."

"Did you know that Dylan Thomas left school when he was just sixteen?"

"That doesn't mean you should, Zoey."

"I'm seventeen, Mr. Doherty. I've already lost the chance to do that."

Karen laughed and shot Zoey an appreciative glance.

Abby still couldn't believe this unlikely friendship of theirs. Lately there'd been rumors going around: when Zoey and Karen went off campus in the afternoons, they'd go get stoned somewhere. Karen had never smoked before she'd met Zoey, much less smoked dope. Not only had they started the List—which had to have been Zoey's idea—now Zoey seemed to be leading the way in drug-taking as well. And Karen was in her slipstream.

"Hey, no one's leaving Stonybridge, Mr. D." Cass laughed too.

They all called Mr. Doherty Mr. D. behind his back. Cass was the only one who could get away with calling him that to his face.

"We love Stonybridge too much. We never want to leave. Next

year at Foliage Day Out time? I'm going to be weeping. I won't get
to hike all day. It's tragic."

"Cassidy, you really shouldn't joke so much. You should be looking at this glorious foliage, taking in the beauty of nature. Because
when nature is beautiful, it lifts the spirit."

"Absolutely, Mr. D." Cass stared up at the trees. "Wow. Nature.
It's far-out. I can feel my spirit lifting." She looked down. "So now
can we get going and finish this walk? My spirit might be floating,
but my legs are killing me."

She started walking at a brisker pace. They all followed her.

"Hey—" Abby caught up to her quickly. "You're coming to my
house for Thanksgiving again, right?"

"Yes! I mean, I'd like to. Yes, please."

"I got a letter from Jennifer yesterday. I forgot to tell you. She
wants to know if you want pumpkin pie or not. Obviously she's hoping you say you don't."

"Pumpkin pie?" Cassidy smiled, bent down, picked up a pile of
fallen leaves, and threw them up and over herself. "Gross."

Abby would have loved to have a picture of Cassidy at that exact
moment: the leaves falling down around her as her smile turned
into a laugh. Hers was as natural a beauty as the stunning foliage.

And she's my best friend, Abby said to herself. For about the mil-
lionth time.

Chapter 8

Zoey

She'd made a calendar counting the days until she got out of Stony-bridge for good. Each time she crossed off a day, she felt a little rush of pleasure. Which was then canceled out by sitting in those class-rooms listening to the boring teachers, then sitting in the Senior Room listening to everyone talk about shit. She was even bored by the List. At first it was fun seeing girls coming back from a weekend away, striding up to the List, and putting a star beside their name, but it was, basically, tedious. Like almost everything was.

The afternoons after school when she and Karen went over to Racetrack's place had been OK, though. Getting stoned without getting so stoned they couldn't handle themselves at school later was a trip. Racetrack was ugly and a loser, but he had access to good weed and a decent record collection, so it was worth listening to him talk endlessly about the horses he was betting on. She didn't think any of them won, but he made enough money selling dope, so he managed to survive in his one-bedroom apartment with a moody sofa and a broken wooden chair he'd found on the street.

She and Karen had met him when they were sitting in the Café one afternoon. He appeared at their table, his dirty hair falling down to his waist, wearing bell-bottom jeans and a stained hippie Indian shirt. Just as she was about to tell him to get away, she saw him drop a piece of paper on the tabletop. He flashed her a peace sign, then disappeared.

"If you want a good joint, come see me," it read. Underneath was an address. She showed it to Karen, who frowned and said: "He looked like a tramp. And he smelled."

"Sure, but a smelly tramp with something to offer. You just told me you have bad cramps. Some pot will fix that for you."

"But we'll get caught. And it might be a trap. I mean to find out if we'd do it."

"Listen, Miss Adams would never think we'd do something like this. We're good, well-brought-up girls, remember? That's what's so great. They let us come into town because they assume we're so thrilled to be able to get into town, we'll never do anything bad. We can get there, smoke some weed, and be back in time to sign in."

"This isn't a good idea. I mean it, Zoey. I've never smoked dope."

It took Zoey maybe two seconds to figure out the sentence that would convince Karen to go along with her: "You're just like the Un Girl. A rule-follower."

No one checked where they went when they got into Lenox, and it was easy to find his apartment, which was on Main Street above a newspaper shop. All they had to do was make sure nobody was around or could see them when they rang his bell.

That first afternoon was a little tricky, though, because when they got back and then went for supper, Karen was giggling and eating so much it was really suspicious. But no one said a word, so Zoey just made sure from then on Karen didn't have more than half a joint.

Still—someone must have overheard them talking about it because there were rumors going around.

She'd told Karen they should stop going to Racetrack's. The rumors were bound to spread further and someone might investigate them, so she told Racetrack one afternoon that they weren't coming anymore.

He couldn't have cared less.

"It was fun hanging with you, but if you gotta split, you gotta split. But, hey, if you gotta have a spliff, I have a spliff." He laughed so much and so inanely at his own joke, Zoey found herself wondering if what the boring adults said was true: Did too much pot really destroy your brain?

On the Sunday night after the Saturday foliage hike, Zoey started down the stairs from her room, heading for the Senior Room. As she was going down, she noticed that one of her shoelaces on the revolting brown Oxford shoes they had to wear was loose, so she sat down to tie it.

"Jeb, I can't get out next weekend. I can't get out until Thanksgiving. But I'm coming then, you know. And I told Abby no pumpkin pie."

Cass was on the phone at the bottom of the stairs. She was talking quietly, but Zoey could hear every word. The stairwell turned at each floor, so Zoey, on the landing one floor above, was invisible.

"No, listen, I know Abby doesn't have any idea about us. I know . . . I know. I wish I weren't trapped in this place too. But it's almost over. Less than a year to go. Anyway, we'll have some time at Thanksgiving. Yeah . . . I know . . . OK . . . I have to go now. But I'll talk to you day after tomorrow. Me too."

Luckily Cass didn't come up the stairs when she hung up. She continued down the hall and out the door to the courtyard.

Zoey stayed sitting. Jeb? A Jeb who would be at the Madison house over Thanksgiving? Was there a Jeb Madison? Abby's brother? It had to be. She had a flash of a memory: Abby talking about her brothers one day in the Senior Room.

"They're both at Yale. Actually, Peter graduated from Yale and is at Yale Law School. Jeb's still an undergraduate," she'd said—hadn't she? Yes, she had—because Zoey remembered her adding: "It's so cool that Yale accepts girls now. I was thinking of applying myself, but I'd be so embarrassed if I didn't get in."

If she did apply and get in, Little Miss Goody Two-Shoes Abby could hold hands with her brothers and they could all sing, "Bulldog! Bulldog! Bow, wow, wow," together. Yet another example of total inanity—college students getting together singing silly, shitty songs.

Which meant . . . Cass was with the younger brother—Jeb Madison. And clearly Abby didn't know this. That was interesting.

But, Jesus. Cass was with a Yale boy?

She'd already sold her soul to the bourgeois preppy Madisons, and now she was selling her body to them too.

Chapter 9

Karen

She was getting used to Zoey's moods. Abby had always been fairly easy-going, but Zoey could suddenly turn from being seemingly OK to mute and brooding in one second flat. Living with this had been hard at first, but now she knew just to leave Zoey alone when she went into one of her funks. Today, however, she saw Zoey in a mood she'd never seen before: joyful.

The reason for this happiness turned out to be a package she'd received from her father in that morning's mail. They were in their room after classes had ended when Zoey unwrapped the brown paper parcel, cutting off one of the strings with her teeth.

"Wow!"

She actually screamed with delight when she pulled out the long afghan coat.

"Look at this! It's amazing!"

Jumping up from the bed, she put it on over her uniform.

"And it fits perfectly."

Twirling around, she tried to see all angles of herself in the tiny mirror above the dressing table.

"I can't believe it. Dad actually remembered. He's even two days early for my birthday. Wow! This is so cool."

Zoey's looks reminded her of that saying "You can never step in the same river twice" because they constantly shifted. Sometimes she resembled a bird of prey; other times she made Karen think of a French student, a tall, dark-haired Parisian girl with a haughty air and a cloud of smoke enveloping her, ready to hop on the back of a motorcycle and ride off to a café, where she'd sit and discuss Jean-Paul Sartre. Or shoot up.

However the angles of her face presented themselves, there was always a tinge of aggression to them.

But not now, because the childlike delight on her face made her look actually pretty. And almost vulnerable.

"It really is a cool coat," Karen said. "Your father forgets your birthday sometimes?"

"A lot. Yeah. He's busy. You know, with his movies."

Karen had never seen any of Zoey's father's movies, but she'd definitely heard of him. He was a director and made independent films. One of them, *The Way Home*, had been a huge hit, so he'd obviously made a ton of money and before long he'd probably win an Oscar.

She guessed he was one of those "hip" parents, so unlike her own father; she'd been wildly curious to find out all about him. Up until now, though, Zoey would change the subject any time Karen asked a question about either of her parents.

"Right. I bet he's really busy. But he didn't marry again after he and your mother divorced, did he?"

"No. Not yet. He's got a girlfriend. Shelley. She's a bitch." Zoey rolled her eyes.

"Does he . . . I mean, does he know Hollywood stars?"

"Hollywood's a dump. That's what he says. That's why he lives in New York. He hates Hollywood."

"Oh. Right."

"Sometimes—times like this—he does the perfect thing." Opening the drawer of her bedside table, she pulled out a framed photograph. "Sometimes . . ."

Karen stared at the photo Zoey had now placed on the bedside table. A younger Zoey—she might have been ten or eleven—was standing beside an incredibly handsome, tall guy with wild, curly dark hair. He was wearing a leather jacket and jeans and looked about twenty years old. His hand was up on his forehead, shading his face from the sun.

"That's not . . . ?"

"My father? Yes, it is. And don't say it. I know he looks young, OK? That's just the way he is. Everyone thinks he's my brother."

"I bet." Karen kept staring. What would it be like to have a father who looked like that? She couldn't imagine her father ever putting on a pair of jeans.

"Did he make you do your homework when you were growing up?"

Zoey shot her a look of disbelief.

"I mean, you know, was he a normal father?"

"He wasn't around a lot. He could be—" She paused and looked at the photograph herself. "Magical." Then she looked away, out the window. "When he bothered. Anyway, come on, let's take one of our afternoons into town now. I want to wear this coat. It's cold enough. Look, it's even started to snow."

So they signed out and went into town, but Zoey wasn't walking, she was skipping and dancing down the sidewalk to the Café, and in the falling snow, she began to look magical herself. One birthday present from her father had transformed her.

As they sat sipping their coffee, Karen pictured Zoey as a little girl at Christmas, hyped up about the tree, her presents, the whole thing. And none of it jibed with the person she'd been living with since September.

For the past six weeks, Karen had followed Zoey's lead and done things she would never have imagined herself doing. She'd started smoking cigarettes, she'd started smoking dope—in a seedy apartment with an older man who sold marijuana and bet on horse races. She'd been Zoey's right-hand man, so to speak, and a part of her had been terrified while another part was thrilled that she could take the risks and experiment and do things her parents would have had heart attacks about if they'd known.

This coat thing was strange, though, because Zoey didn't normally care about clothes. One reason Karen was really beginning to enjoy hanging out with her was the fact that Zoey didn't give a shit about her appearance. She rarely bothered to wash her hair; she never shaved her legs. And she wasn't obsessed with boys. After that first comment in the Senior Room about her gaining weight, Zoey had never remarked on Karen's figure and never looked even remotely disapproving when Karen pulled out a packet of potato chips and munched through them.

Even though Abby hadn't been overly into boys, clothes, and makeup, toward the end of their friendship she had been beginning to change. She had stopped talking about sports so much and started in on boys she had seen that she thought were cute or what kind of haircut she should get. And she'd started looking at herself in the mirror a lot more often.

Zoey was a stranger to mirrors—until she got that coat.

"When I was younger, Dad used to give me a lot of presents," Zoey said as she sipped her coffee. "They were all cool."

"It must be weird. I mean, you know, he's pretty famous."

"He took me to the set of one of his films when I was ten. It was a real trip."

"I bet."

"Then, I don't know . . ." Zoey started playing with her spoon, stirring the coffee one way, then the other.

"He must be really busy. My father works in a bank. Nine to five."

"Listen—" She stopped stirring, looked up. "Would you like to come to my place for Thanksgiving? We'd have to stay at my mother's, but maybe my father will be around too. I can call him tonight. I have to call him anyway, to thank him for this." She stroked her coat. "Maybe this Thanksgiving we could go to his house, instead of my mother's."

"That would be great."

She couldn't stop herself from wondering whether there'd be anyone famous there. Someone she could then say she'd met. *Oh, you know, I had Thanksgiving lunch with Robert Redford.* That was what she'd love to say to Abby. Drop that neatly into a conversation, then watch Abby look impressed. And jealous.

Plus—New York City? Her parents lived in a suburb of Boston—Newton. They'd taken her and her older brother to New York once, to see the Empire State Building and the Statue of Liberty, but that had been like a school trip. This—New York with Zoey—would be a blast.

"Let's go back now. I should call my father right away."

The snow had stopped. When they got back to school, Zoey headed straight for the phones and Karen went back to their room and stood looking out the window at the tiny bit of white covering the courtyard.

Supper was in ten minutes. Every week a chart was posted on the school bulletin board, telling them which table they were assigned to. This week, she was at Miss Rutgers's, the nurse's, table, sitting with six other girls, one of them Zoey, but no Abby or Cassidy.

So far she'd only had to sit at Abby's table twice and Cassidy's once: when faced with either of them, she decided the best policy was to stay silent and try to look bored. It was an effort, though. Because she wanted to do what she'd done outside that classroom a while ago: tell Abby what an asshole she was.

And tell Cassidy she might be beautiful, but she was dumb. But if she'd been sitting with one of them tonight, she could have mentioned her trip to New York. And Zoey's father. It just might have made them a little less smug.

Zoey walked back into their room, threw her precious coat on the floor, and stomped on it.

"Your coat! What are you doing?"

"It's not my coat." She kicked it, and it went flying, landing beside the window, looking like a wounded animal.

"What do you mean, it's not your coat?"

"It's not my coat. It got sent here by accident. My father bought me a scarf and his girlfriend this coat from the same store, and he sent the wrong ones to the wrong people. This is Shelley's coat. Can you believe it—Shelley's as fucking tall as I am. And almost as young. He wants me to send it back."

"You're kidding."

"No. The bitch gets my coat." She sat down on her bed, her face full of fury.

The bell for dinner rang out then. Karen could hear girls leaving their rooms and heading for the dining room. Zoey didn't move.

"Maybe the scarf is really beautiful."

"Fuck the scarf. I don't want a fucking scarf."

She grabbed the photograph and shoved it back into the drawer.

"At least he remembered. I mean, at least, you know, he remembered your birthday."

Picking up a pillow, Zoey put it over her face.

"Zoey? Are you all right?"

She sat there with the pillow over her face, her chest heaving.

"The dinner bell just rang. Maybe we should go down."

She put her hand up, waved Karen away.

"OK, listen, I'll go to supper and I'll say you're sick. But I'll be back as quickly as I can, all right? I'll be right back. I promise."

Miss Rutgers wanted to know exactly what was wrong with Zoey, so Karen said she had an upset stomach and that she felt one coming on too. That they'd eaten an odd-tasting cake at the Café in town and it must have been that.

"If it's all right, I'll go back, Miss Rutgers. I don't want to throw up in the dining room. Zoey's already thrown up twice." She tried to look as if she were about to get sick, making an anguished face, but not overdoing it by clutching her stomach.

"All right. Come see me in the infirmary if it gets any worse."

"I will. Thanks."

As she ran back across the courtyard, she wondered what she could possibly say to Zoey, how she could help her feel better. The only experience with heartache she'd had up until now was her own. And she had no idea what it would feel like to have a father take back a present and give it to his girlfriend instead. That was really fucked-up.

Her parents would never forget her birthday, but then if she'd been given an afghan coat by them, she would have known right away there was some kind of mistake. First of all, her mother would have never given her anything to wear; she wouldn't have wanted to go into a store and buy a large size of anything.

Secondly, they were resolutely ordinary: her father was a banker, her mother a housewife. They played golf and belonged to a country club. But it was a second-tier country club. Not the kind of country club Abby's parents belonged to. Theirs was a nice house in the suburbs, but not a big, sprawling house in the suburbs. And when they went away for the summers, they did go to Cape Cod, but they rented a cottage, and it wasn't right on the water, and it wasn't some big pad on Long Island.

Karen knew her mother wanted to move up one more rung on the social ladder, which may have been yet another reason she'd been sent to boarding school. Her mother didn't want to look at her, but she did want to use her to up their social status. Which seemed unbelievably pathetic to her.

Now, though, she didn't think they were quite so pathetic. They weren't divorced, her father didn't have a young girlfriend, they didn't tell her to send back presents.

And they'd be furious if they found out she'd been smoking cigarettes, much less dope.

It seemed as if Zoey's parents wouldn't care even if they knew everything she was doing.

When she got back to their room, she saw Zoey sprawled out on her bed, facedown.

"Are you asleep?"

Zoey shook her head.

"I told Miss Rutgers that we ate something bad at the Café and we're both sick to our stomachs. Listen . . ." Karen sat down on the edge of the bed. "I'm really sorry. You deserved to have that coat."

Zoey sat up, and when she did, Karen saw her tear-wrecked face.

"It doesn't matter," Zoey said softly. "I should have known anyway."

"No, that was really wrong of him."

"I was stupid." She pulled her knees up to her chest, shook her head. "I can't believe I was that idiotic, that I believed he'd give that to me."

"You weren't stupid. He was."

"Yeah, well." Straightening up, she wiped her eyes with her palms. "I'm never going to be stupid again."

"You weren't stupid."

"I'm not five years old. I'm almost eighteen. I shouldn't fucking care. I *don't fucking* care."

Karen was at a loss. Zoey was still wiping away her tears, and now she looked like a kid who'd just been told there was no Santa Claus.

"Listen . . . how about . . . I don't know . . . maybe we could do something really fun for your birthday."

"Like what?" Her tone was pleading.

"I don't know. Hey, maybe we could ask Racetrack where the nearest racetrack is and go bet on horses."

For a second she thought she'd said the absolutely wrong thing.

Then Zoey laughed, reached out, and squeezed her hand.

And Karen thought: *This is my real friend. This is my friend for life.*

Chapter 10

Thomas Doherty

Janet Lee had roped him into refereeing this field hockey match, and he was loathing every minute of it. Not only that, he was a hopeless referee. He didn't understand the rules, and he hated all the running up and down the field, especially in the rain.

"We need you, Tom," she'd said. "Miss Harrington has a cold, and there's no one else."

He very much doubted that. There had to be someone else, but he couldn't call her a liar. Nor could he think of a brilliant excuse when after the match, as they walked back to the school from the sports fields, she asked him if he'd like to join her for dinner.

"I can't. I'm so sorry, Janet. I have a huge amount of homework to grade."

It was a lame excuse, just as most of his excuses to decline her invitations were lame. She didn't give up, however. She plowed right on asking, in much the same way she plowed on as she ran up and down the field blowing her shrill whistle.

Janet Lee was a big-boned woman. Absolutely made to be a sports coach at a girls' school. She had arrived the spring before, a replacement for the old sports coach, Miss Park, who was getting too old to have such a physical job. He guessed Janet's age as early forties, but she might have been younger. She was wide, heavily muscled, with short dark hair and a flat, broad nose.

Yet her eyes, an unusually bright blue, turned so pale and disappointed when he'd rebuffed her once again, he couldn't help but relent.

"But I could do a coffee, Janet. I can meet you at the Café at five, if you'd like. I'll need a cup of coffee before I grade all those papers."

"Wonderful," she replied. "Coffee it is."

At ten to five, when he entered the Café, he saw Cassidy Thomas and Abby Madison sitting together, and for one moment he was embarrassed that Cassidy would see him having coffee with Janet Lee. He should have thought of that: of course there would be some students here. Miss Adams's policy of two afternoons in town a week for the girls was another freedom he was a little dubious about, but it wasn't as harmful as the Senior Room. Getting off campus, he supposed, was a good idea in some ways.

"Mr. D.," Cassidy called out, beckoning him over to her table. "Hi! Come sit with us."

"I'm afraid I can't, Cassidy. But thank you for the invitation."

"Aha! You're meeting someone, aren't you? Let me guess . . ."

"Cassidy. You and Abby continue with your conversation, please. I'll sit over there."

"It's Miss Lee, isn't it? I bet it's Miss Lee. Wow, Mr. D. . . . ."

"Cassidy. Enough." He strode over to the corner of the Café, sat down, furious at himself for blushing. If he could have left without being rude to Janet, he would have.

Because this was so clichéd. The elderly bachelor science

teacher meeting for a coffee with the spinster sports coach. And of all people to witness it, Cassidy Thomas.

Cassidy kept sneaking smiling glances at him, and he couldn't help but smile back. She had on one of those coats he normally found disgusting, some afghan thing that was all the rage now. On her, though, it looked resplendent.

Whereas Janet, when she came in, looked like a bulldog wrapped in a bulky raincoat. A brown bulky raincoat. He saw Cassidy's eyebrows raise and an "I was right" grin spread across her face.

"Janet, sit down." He stood up. "I haven't ordered yet. Would you like some coffee?"

"Yes, thank you." She plonked herself in the chair opposite him.

He knew that she felt the same way as he about Stonybridge going downhill, how Veronica had been letting things slip badly, but for reasons he couldn't explain to himself he didn't want to discuss it with her. What *were* they going to discuss, though? Agreeing to meet her had been a mistake.

"I'll signal for a waitress."

Just as he put his hand up, he saw Zoey Spalding and Karen Mullens walk through the door. Yet more students. What had he been thinking choosing this place?

"Where'd you get that coat?" It was Zoey, suddenly shouting. "Where'd you get it from, Cass?"

"My aunt gave it to me. She found one in a thrift store. Why?"

"Because you shouldn't be wearing that coat, that's why."

"Zoey." Karen Mullens put her hand on Zoey's arm.

"Really? Why shouldn't I be wearing it?" Cassidy asked.

"It's too long for you. Is it you? Not Shelley?"

"What?"

"Have you been sleeping with my father?"

He leapt up, headed toward their table. This was outrageous.

"Wow, Zo—are you on drugs or something?" Cassidy laughed.

He reached Zoey just in time to grab her hand and stop her from slapping Cassidy.

"Get out of here, Zoey. Right now," he barked. "I'm going to have to report you for this, you know."

"But it's my coat." Struggling to wrench free from his grip, Zoey glared at Cassidy. "It's my coat."

"Hey, Zo—" Cassidy stood up. "If you want it so badly, here—" She took off the coat. "Take it."

But he was already leading Zoey out of the Café and onto the street, Karen following behind.

"Get back to school now, both of you. I'll deal with you later, Zoey."

"She's upset, Mr. Doherty. You don't understand."

"I understand she almost struck another student, Karen. Now both of you go. I'll be back in a few minutes. And we'll deal with this with Miss Adams. Go."

"Are you all right, Cassidy?" he asked when he went back in.

"I'm fine. Honestly, if she's so hung up on this coat, she can have it."

"You don't mean that," Abby said.

"It's a coat." Cassidy shrugged, then put it back on. "It's not an engagement ring."

Back at the table, Janet sat stony-faced.

"That Zoey Spalding is bad news," she said. "The sooner she's gone from this school, the better. I know everyone loves this Class of 1970, but I for one will be happy when they graduate. They're not good for the school. And that includes Cassidy Thomas. They have too much power."

"I'm afraid I have to get back now, Janet. I need to talk to Veronica about what just happened here."

"Right away?"

"Yes, I'm sorry. Another time."

Taking his own coat off the back of the chair, he left.

He knew it was terrible of him, but he still felt a little relieved that Zoey Spalding had caused that scene when she did.

Chapter 11

Cassidy

Zoey and Cassidy were on the ground beside the sports field, both substituted in a field hockey game. After the business with the coat, Zoey had had to apologize to her formally and she was also given a month of detention. Which meant she couldn't go into town and she had to go to study hall before dinner to do her homework rather than staying in her room. So Zoey was looking grumpy and not talking to her, and Cass thought the whole thing was ridiculous.

"Listen, Zo. Whatever that coat thing was about, let's forget it, OK? I'm sorry you got detention. That must be a bummer. I know how much you like getting out."

"It's not so bad." She shrugged a typical Zoey shrug. "I'm not going to apologize to you again."

"You don't have to. But, whoa. Thinking I was sleeping with your father? That's crazy."

"Yeah, I know." Zoey picked up a leaf, crumpled it in her hand. "So are you going to the Un Girl's for Thanksgiving again?"

"No, I'm going to Abby's for Thanksgiving. Enough with the Un Girl, Zo."

"Oh, sorry. I forgot. Abby's a bundle of excitement. A veritable—"

"Zoey—"

"Anyway, there must be a lot of people there, right? I mean, she has a big family, doesn't she?"

"Two older brothers and a younger sister."

"Older brothers . . ." Zoey picked up a blade of grass and put it in her mouth, sucking on it as if it were a cigarette. "Is one of them named Jeb?"

"Yes, how did you know?"

"That's so freaky. My mother was just talking about a Jeb Madison, and I wondered whether it was the Un . . . oops . . . I mean Abby's brother."

"Your mother?" Cass turned to face her. "Why was your mother talking about Jeb Madison?"

"You know how she talks about social stuff all the time? She wants me to be a debutante, all that crap. Anyway, I think she was trying to convince me by telling me her friend's daughter is going to the Cotillion in New York with some boy named Jeb Madison. You know how deluded she is. She thinks if her friend's daughter is going, I will too."

"Jeb Madison? Are you sure? Not Peter?"

"Yes, Jeb. I remember."

Jeb? It couldn't be.

"You're sure?"

"Yeah. Why is it so important? Do you have a crush on him?"

"No. No." She needed to calm down. "I didn't know Jeb was dating anyone, that's all."

"I don't know if they're dating per se. Maybe they're just old friends. But my mother said something about her being a real 'catch.' Can you believe it? A catch? As if she's a baseball."

"What's her name?"

"Melinda. I think. Why do you care?"

Zoey narrowed her eyes, and Cass willed herself again to keep her voice neutral.

"I don't care. I love all those WASP names, that's all. Isn't there a Melinda in a Shakespeare play or something?"

"No. That's Miranda."

"OK. Yeah."

"Anyway, I don't know her last name. She's not really my mother's friend's daughter—she's her stepdaughter, and I can't remember the mother's new married name. She got divorced and remarried."

"OK. It doesn't matter." Cass picked up a blade of grass as well, put it in her mouth, clenched her teeth.

"He's a Yale boy, isn't he? Typical that he'd be going to a cotillion."

"Yeah."

She looked out over the playing field, at these girls whacking a field hockey ball, running up and down as if it were important. She wished Miss Lee would substitute her back in so she could go whack balls and run as fast as she could and try to forget what Zoey had just told her.

Melinda? Melinda who? Jeb had never mentioned any Melinda. And she couldn't grill Zoey any further or she'd get suspicious.

Can he really be going to a party with another girl?

Whenever she went with Abby to stay at her house, Jeb would make sure he came back from Yale so they could have some time together. They had a routine. During the day they'd be nice to each other, but not too nice. At night, she'd sneak down the corridor into his room. She'd always wait until 2:30

in the morning, and she'd always leave at 4:30 to be safe. Two hours together wasn't enough, but it was better than nothing.

They hadn't had sex, not yet. They'd lie together in his bed and talk and hug and kiss. "I want to wait until we're not hiding anything. I want it to be special, somewhere special," he'd said. "It's killing me, but with you and me, Cassidy, everything is different."

He was different, so different from the boys she knew in Minneapolis, especially her last boyfriend, Terry, who had dropped out of high school and was working at a garage. She and Terry talked about TV shows or movies or the people they knew in common from the neighborhood. But mostly they spent their time having sex.

Jeb and she talked about their childhoods, their dreams, their future together.

Melinda who?

He'd once mentioned an old girlfriend named Sally, but he'd never said a word about any Melinda.

Unlike Terry, he was polite and gentlemanly. And unlike Terry, who had never written a letter in his life, she was sure, Jeb sent her amazing letters. They talked on the phone every other day, and he wrote to her too. Letters she hid in her drawer, alongside his watch. He'd write about the books he was reading, what his professors were like, and little things he thought she'd like to hear.

"There was a squirrel running across the yard today. It looked like he was late for a class."

The kind of little thing that made her laugh. They laughed a lot, so much so that sometimes when she'd be lying beside him at night, she'd have to cover her face with a pillow to stop from laughing so loud it might wake someone up.

At times like that she'd think about having sex with him and wonder if they'd laugh during that too.

Having sex with Terry had been simple. It just happened. She liked him, he liked her, they had some fun. She hadn't worried what he thought about her. And losing her virginity hadn't seemed very important.

Everything with Jeb was important.

She loved him with a passion that scared her.

In bed, lying in his arms, she'd find herself thinking: *It's OK—I can die right now and it will be OK.*

What wouldn't be OK was if she lost him. She couldn't take that feeling again, how everything changed when the person you loved left and all you wanted to do was talk to them and they weren't there. And the whole thing got even more screwed up because they weren't there and your dad was looking at you like you made him even sadder and he ended up sending you away and you still couldn't talk to the person you wanted to talk to more than anything in the world. Because they were gone.

If she had Jeb's arms around her, closed her eyes, and never woke up, she could die without ever feeling that feeling again.

He was strong, he was smart, he was funny, he was handsome. He had a way of teasing her that made her feel loved and happy. But he also took her seriously. Once, he'd put his hand on the top of her head and said: "What worlds are you going to conquer, Cassidy Thomas?"

It had never occurred to her that she could conquer any world.

Enough people had told her she was beautiful for her to think that maybe she was, at least sometimes. But there were other attractive girls, girls who were beautiful all the time. Not only that, they were smart. No one had ever called her smart. And there were beautiful smart girls who also knew the social rules like which fork to use when and what words not to say.

There were all these secret, crazy little ways these people recognized each other, like those Masons who gave special handshakes. How was she supposed to know you weren't supposed to say "drapes" or "couch"? They might all dress like hippies and give each other the peace sign, but in the end they stuck together.

Melinda had invited him to the Cotillion thing. Melinda was one of them. And she was a catch.

Is Jeb going to disappear too?

"Cass—" Zoey waved her hand in front of Cassidy's face. "Where are you? Are you OK?"

"I'm fine, Zoey. Just thinking about our math exam tomorrow. I'm going to flunk it."

"No, you won't. Miss Gambee loves you. Like Mr. Doherty. It doesn't matter how badly you do. Neither of them would ever flunk you."

"That's not true. They don't have to help me like that. I'm not that dumb. Why does everyone assume I'm stupid? Maybe I don't get great grades, but I'm not an idiot."

"Hang on." Zoey held up her hands. "You're the one who said you were going to flunk."

Luckily Miss Lee blew her whistle, the game stopped, and she motioned for Cass and Zoey to get back on the field.

I'm not stupid, she told herself.

Jeb thinks I'm going to conquer worlds. And I will. With him. But whoever the hell Melinda is, I'll fucking kill her first.

Chapter 12

Karen

She was standing in the goal watching them. What were they talking about? Zoey wasn't supposed to like Cassidy now. She'd almost hit her that day in the Café, which Karen had to admit had made her feel triumphant. But there they were, talking away on the sidelines. Like best friends.

The ball whizzed by her into the net.

"Jesus, Karen. You didn't even try to stop that," Debby yelled.

It can't happen again. It won't happen again.

Zoey wouldn't do that to her. She couldn't. Not after everything they'd been through together.

She was the only one who really understood Zoey. No one else knew how vulnerable she was. Zoey had actually cried in front of her. She'd asked her to room with her that first day in the Senior Room. They hadn't been put together randomly, not like she had been with Abby. This was a best friendship that *meant* something.

If Cass took Zoey away, she'd fucking kill her.

Chapter 13

Abby

They were on the bus from Lenox to Darien when Cass asked her if she knew a girl named Melinda.

"Melinda? No, I don't think so. Who's she?"

"Nobody. I thought you might know her, that's all."

"But why? Melinda who?"

"I don't know. Forget it, OK?"

"Is she a friend of yours?"

"No. I thought she was a friend of yours. Or Jeb's."

"Jeb?" Abby was puzzled, racking her brain for someone named Melinda and coming up with no one.

"I heard Jeb had a girlfriend named Melinda, that's all. Forget it, will you?"

"Who'd you hear that from?"

"I can't remember."

"That's really weird. Jeb's last girlfriend was named Sally. She was great, but she went to college in Colorado and they split up. I don't think he has a girlfriend now. I would have heard if he did."

"Why was Sally so great?"

There was a strange edge to Cass's tone. Did she have a crush on

Jeb? Like Karen had had? No, Cass would have told her if that were the case.

"Sally was really nice and fun. Everyone loved her."

"Your parents loved her?"

"Maybe not love, but they liked her a lot."

For a minute or so Cass was silent, then she asked:

"So is Sally's family in that book that has all the good families in it? What's it called? *The Special Register?*"

"*The Social Register*—and it's ridiculous. No one pays attention to it, no one our age, anyway."

"But is Sally's family in it?"

"Cass? I don't get it. Why do you care about Sally's family? You've never even met her."

"I don't care. I was just asking. Forget it."

She turned away and stared out the window.

Of course. This was all about the whole social thing. Abby often forgot how different Cass's life had been to her own growing up. Of course she'd be curious about the privileged WASP world and ask questions about it. She couldn't have felt jealous, though. The thought of Cass being jealous of anyone or anything was a joke.

Just like cotillions and all that bullshit had become a joke to most people their age. There was a war going on. Besides, women dressing up in white ball gowns like vestal virgins and being introduced to society was outdated anyway. That whole way of life was changing. She remembered Peter and Jeb in yet another argument with their father, saying he should cancel the membership of the country club they belonged to because it didn't accept Black or Jewish people.

She'd even had the guts to pipe up and say she agreed with them, at the same time secretly hoping her father wouldn't cancel the membership because she loved the swimming pool there. She wanted to go to coming-out parties too, but there was no chance she'd ever admit to any of that. Peter and Jeb would have been horrified. She was horrified by herself for having those thoughts.

In a way Cass was lucky because she didn't have anything like that she had to give up.

Abby looked out the window too and saw a Volkswagen Beetle overtaking them. Someone in the back seat put their hand outside the window and flashed a peace sign. Cass flashed one back.

"Are you a hippie now?" she asked her.

"Nope. I hate brown rice and macramé, so I'm not a hippie. But peace is always a good idea."

Thinking of her family and the escalating arguments over the dinner table, Abby sighed and said: "Peace is a groovy idea. Sometimes I wish we could go forward in time and the war would be over and everybody could be happy again. I can't wait for the future."

Chapter 14

Zoey

"She's not an attractive girl, is she?"

"Is that all you have to say about her, Mom? Have you even talked to her since she's been here?"

"Yes, of course I have. I was only making a remark, that's all. It's noticeable, you have to admit. Especially after your friend Cassidy. Cassidy could be a model. She should be a model."

"I thought you always said comparisons are odious."

"Don't be difficult. I was making conversation."

"You're the one being difficult."

"I'm not in the mood to have a fight with you, Zoey. The Lewises are coming for Thanksgiving lunch. And the Rathbones. I'd appreciate if you dressed normally—and your friend did too."

"What's wrong with what I'm wearing now? What's abnormal about it?"

"If you were a beatnik I'm sure that black getup would be entirely appropriate. In Greenwich Village. But not here. Honestly, I've bought you enough pretty dresses. Wear one of them. And go take a bath."

"Where should I take the bath? Where do you think the bath would like to go? The Bahamas?"

Her mother sighed an exaggerated sigh Zoey knew well. Just as she knew how much her presence in that house irritated her mother. She didn't fit in, not with the gleamingly polished antique furniture, the floral-patterned covered sofas, the pale pink velvet curtains, the crystal vases full of pink roses. She didn't look immaculate, and she didn't care about this house or the Lewises or the Rathbones or what the caterers were cooking in the kitchen.

Every conversation with her mother turned into an argument, just as, leading up to the divorce, every conversation between her mother and her father had turned into one.

How had her parents ever fallen in love in the first place? She didn't believe in that whole opposites-attract concept. In her parents' case, they definitely should have repelled. Her father was artistic. He was gifted and interesting and curious about life.

For a long time, he'd been curious about her too. He'd taught her how to take photographs, even given her a Hasselblad camera for Christmas when she was twelve years old.

"I'm trusting you with this," he'd said. "You're young for it, I know, but I know you'll take care of it and use it wisely. And I hope wonderfully."

Two months later, he'd left. Now he was with Shelley—Shelley, who had the afghan coat. Shelley, who might be tall and pretty but who was, like the rest of them had been, ordinary and insipid. And who was around twenty-five years old.

In a way her father was a lot like Cass. He'd abandoned her for a cardboard cutout too.

Yet she still missed both of them so much. That was the real killer. There was a part of her that hated them, but she couldn't stop missing either one of them.

The Hasselblad was up in her room, sitting on a shelf. There were times when she thought about taking photographs again, but then she'd decide not to. What was the point? They'd never be good enough to impress her father.

Zoey looked at her mother, sitting straight-backed on one of the sofas. It was only 9:00 in the morning and she was already in her makeup and high heels. One foot was bobbing up and down impatiently.

This was going to be a dire Thanksgiving. The only joy she'd have was thinking how upset Cass would be about the fictional Melinda and the nonexistent cotillion date. How would she and Jebby Boy work that one out? It was a small satisfaction, but one she hadn't been able to resist.

"All right. I'm leaving. But I'm not going to take a bath and I'm not going to put on a dress. Maybe Karen and I will go down to Greenwich Village for Thanksgiving. We'll go find some beatniks."

As she left the room, she heard her mother say:

"There's not a thing I can do with you, is there?"

Chapter 15

Karen

When Zoey insisted that they couldn't have Thanksgiving lunch at her mother's house, that they had to go out and find something else to do, Karen was actually relieved. Mrs. Spalding scared her. When she'd first arrived and was introduced to her, she saw her look her up and down and judge, and it wasn't a good judgment. She knew she didn't fit whatever pattern Mrs. Spalding wanted her daughter's friend to fit into.

Yet again, she could hear her father saying "Looks don't count." Whoever first said that was a bullshitter. Probably an ugly bullshitter trying to pretend she didn't care how ugly she was.

She did her best to be polite, but Mrs. Spalding was intimidating, and Karen knew for a woman like her, manners were important but not everything. Just like for her own mother, appearance counted for a whole hell of a lot.

Karen already knew that Zoey and her mother didn't get along, but she hadn't realized how deep the problems between them were until she saw them together. It was as if they couldn't stand being in the same room. They barely looked at each other when they sat down to have dinner on Wednesday night, a dinner served in a fancy dining room full of Chinese objets d'art.

The conversation wasn't stilted: it was, after the first few questions about school life, which Zoey barely responded to, nonexistent.

When they'd finished eating, Zoey and she went out into the garden at the back of the house and Zoey pulled out a pack of cigarettes, gave her one, took one for herself, lit them both.

"Nice, right? My mother's so much fun."

"Has it always been like this? I mean, you know, you must have loved her when you were little."

"Really? Must I have? Must she have loved me? Is that written down somewhere? Is it in the Bible? Or the Constitution?"

Their combined smoke coiled upward through the freezing air, and she thought how different living in Manhattan was to living in the suburbs of Boston. Her family didn't have a huge yard like Abby's, but they had half an acre, while everyone in the city was cramped in side by side.

And yet these brownstones were supposedly worth a fortune. Her mother had told her that when she'd asked whether she could go to Zoey's for Thanksgiving.

"A brownstone in New York City," she'd exclaimed, and Karen heard what she always longed to hear in her mother's voice: approval. "They must be incredibly rich."

There was no "they" in this house. It was beautifully decorated, just as Zoey's mother was impeccably dressed and made up. But it was a house that reeked of loneliness.

"Come on, Zoey. Of course it isn't written down anywhere that you must have loved her, it's just . . . Anyway, your father lives in a brown-stone too, doesn't he? Is it near here?"

"About six blocks. And yeah, he made a lot of money from *The Way Home*. And he comes from an old rich family too. But they didn't care as much about all that as my mother does. And his house doesn't look like this one—on the inside, I mean. He has amazing black-and-white photographs all over the walls and furniture that doesn't match or go together but somehow it works and looks cool."

"You love him a lot, don't you?"

"You really don't get it." She shook her head. "Your parents aren't divorced. My mother hates me because I remind her of my father, and my father doesn't want anything to do with me anymore, probably because I remind him of my mother. It doesn't matter what *I* feel. What *I* feel is irrelevant."

She took a drag, then threw her cigarette on the ground.

"Let's go upstairs and listen to some music."

The next day, when Zoey told her they were going out for Thanksgiving, she figured there had been an argument.

"Is any place going to be open?" she asked.

"We'll find somewhere. And if we don't, we can just walk around 'til late in the afternoon and then come back and raid the fridge for leftovers. I can't cope with one of these lunches. It has nothing to do with family or giving thanks. It's all social shit."

In the end they found a diner open in Midtown where they bought a couple of turkey sandwiches and Cokes. It was freezing so they stayed sitting in a booth as long as possible, then walked around aimlessly, then went back to the diner and had coffee and stretched that out for another couple of hours. They must have gotten through two packs of Marlboros.

And all the while, Zoey was weaving a magic spell. She began by talking about the immorality of the war, then moved on to poetry, getting so excited about some man named Ferlingsomething, her expressive hands almost knocked over her cup of coffee. Karen listened, entirely entranced.

No one else she knew had such depth or cared so much. And no one else took such brave stands. Zoey didn't believe in marriage or women giving themselves up for men. She scorned the normal social conventions.

She was incredibly passionate, but not about a basketball team or some teenage boy.

Karen found herself wishing she had a notebook with her and could take down what Zoey was saying, keep it word for word so she could go over it all again on her own.

By the time they finally tramped back to the Upper East Side, it was 6:00 in the evening. As they headed uptown, Karen vowed to herself that she'd start to read poetry, learn more about the war, understand everything Zoey cared about, and be in a position where, next time, she could join in.

On the way to Zoey's on Wednesday, she'd worried that she'd be wondering what Abby and her family and Cass were probably doing, how much fun they'd all be having in Darien. Now she couldn't give a shit.

Even though they hadn't had lunch with Robert Redford or met Zoey's father and being with Zoey's mother in that house was tense and depressing, she didn't care. She'd rather be cold and hungry in Manhattan than cozy and warm and safe in Darien with Abby.

Because she'd rather be with Zoey.

Anywhere with Zoey.

Chapter 16

Thomas Doherty

He lived in a little cottage that used to be the caretaker's for a family estate. The big house had a hundred acres and a farm, a swimming pool, a tennis court, and maids' quarters, but it had been sold ten years before and the estate had been broken up into parcels.

Often he would think of the glory days that must have been: a luxurious lifestyle catered to by servants, all set against the backdrop of the beautiful mountains.

Now there was no farm and no caretaker and no servants. The people living in the big house were nouveau riche types whose taste was highly suspect and who never acknowledged him when they saw him on the road or in town.

Although he had sympathy for those who protested against a system that depended on people catering to their every whim, people who were paid almost nothing, he still had a hankering for the elegance that same system often produced.

He'd filled his cottage with books, so many of them that it had begun to resemble a womb, or perhaps a tomb. The tiny square living room was reserved for classic novels, the little study for science books, and his upstairs bedroom was his philosophy room.

The spare bedroom housed all the old Stonybridge yearbooks as well as communications from former students.

Living alone, having Thanksgiving alone, was the norm. His parents had both died: his mother when he was twenty-five and his father when he was forty, and his younger sister lived with her husband and two children in Santa Fe. It was a long trip to take, and when he'd done it before, he'd found the family life they lived chaotic and exhausting.

It was far preferable to sit in his cottage by the fire on a cold Thanksgiving Day, reading. If he felt like it, he could rustle up some lunch, perhaps even watch a program on TV if there was anything decent on.

Just as he was deciding what he might cook for himself, his telephone rang.

"Tom? It's Janet. I was wondering if you were busy later today. I'm on my own for Thanksgiving, and I thought you might be too."

"Janet. It's nice of you to call. But I have some family over and I'm just about to get the turkey out of the oven."

"Oh. Well, I'm sorry to interrupt you. I didn't know you had family here."

"I don't. I mean, they don't live here. They've come to visit. Cousins."

"That's nice, isn't it? Distant cousins?"

"Not very distant."

Who, in their right mind, would call someone at 1:00 p.m. on Thanksgiving Day?

"I see. Fine. Well, I'm around all weekend, if you get any time."

"I'll keep that in mind, Janet. Many thanks again for calling."

Her persistence was remarkably irksome, he thought as he hung up. What could he say to get rid of her? If he invented a lady friend, she'd doubtless cross-examine him, or perhaps even follow him to establish whom her rival might be.

Being put in this position of having to lie to her was horrible. He hated fabricating stories. What did he keep telling his students? That truth and beauty existed in the world and it was important to keep hold of them both. He was routinely denying the truth with Janet—which made him a hypocrite.

If she kept pushing him, he'd have to tell her to her face he wasn't attracted to her. Which would make school life awkward. But would it be better than being a hypocrite?

Still—women weren't supposed to pursue men so relentlessly. There were unwritten rules about these things, or at least there had been.

But the world was changing at such a rapid rate he had difficulties keeping up. All the old values were being questioned, which he, as a lover of philosophy, welcomed, but only to a certain extent.

The young were growing up too quickly, taking on adult personae before they had the knowledge or the wisdom to handle the adult world. Luckily, however, the girls at Stonybridge were still children and sheltered from the Sturm und Drang of this decade.

They were his shelter as well. When he despaired of what was happening in the world, or when he questioned how he'd managed his life and what he'd accomplished, he thought of them. Especially the Class of 1970. When he branched off from science and tried to teach them what was important in life, they actually listened. They understood about sacrifice and having a moral vision. "You will have base instincts," he warned them. "That's human. To be truly human, however, is to deny them. There is a unique beauty in renunciation."

Occasionally Cassidy might say something like: "You're getting a little heavy here, Mr. D. We get the picture." And they'd all laugh, including him.

There was a purity to their playfulness, and he felt sure they would find their way through this morass of troubled times with their heads held high. Cassidy once told him that she wanted to be a nurse, which had pleased him to no end. And the academically gifted Karen Mullens could very likely become a university professor.

As he put another log on his fire, he brushed aside all disagreeable thoughts about Janet Lee. She would get the picture too.

If not today, then soon.

Chapter 17

Cassidy

Thanksgiving at the Madisons' had been far-out. Beyond far-out. She'd been so nervous and hurt about Jeb and whoever Melinda was that she had avoided him all Wednesday afternoon and not even gone to his room at 2:30 in the morning the way she always did. On Thursday she woke up at 7:00, couldn't get back to sleep. Putting on a pair of jeans and a sweater, she went down to the kitchen. She noticed, as she always noticed, the beautiful round wooden kitchen table. The whole house was beautifully furnished. Which made her think of her mother, who would have loved sitting here at this table, a cup of coffee in her hands.

Her mother would have loved Jeb; she knew that in her heart. Did Melinda's mother love Jeb? Melinda's mother wouldn't have died. Melinda and her mother would be able to go shopping for a wedding dress together. Cass could picture it all. Blond Melinda wearing an expensive wedding dress, smiling as she walked down the aisle . . .

"Cassidy—"

She jumped, spilling some of the coffee she'd made for

herself as she pictured the wedding, the party afterward, a honeymoon somewhere exotic . . .

"What's going on? What's wrong? Why won't you talk to me? Why didn't you come to me last night?"

She didn't know what to do or say, sat there mutely trying not to cry.

"Cassidy—"

"I—"

"Aren't you two up early? Whereas I'm late. There's so much work to do." Walking into the kitchen, opening the fridge, then peering inside, Mrs. Madison turned to them. "Darn, we've run out of milk. Maybe we don't need it, though. I could probably do without."

"I'll get some, Mom. Cassidy, you'll come with me to keep me company, won't you?"

"That's very thoughtful of you, Jeb, but I'm not sure there will be any store open."

"We'll find one. Come on, Cassidy." He'd grabbed her by the elbow. "Be nice. Keep me company on my thoughtful quest for milk."

How could she say no with Mrs. Madison there?

But she wouldn't speak to him in the car. Until he pulled over into a deserted parking lot.

"You have to talk to me, Cassidy. Whatever I've done wrong, whatever is happening, you have to tell me."

Then she did.

And he burst out laughing.

"I can't believe you thought I'd take someone to a cotillion. First of all, I'd never go to a cotillion, and secondly, well, maybe not secondly, actually firstly, I love you. What the hell would I be doing going anywhere with any other girl?"

"You don't know anyone called Melinda?"

"No. Jesus, Cassidy. Look at me, will you?"

When she did, he pulled her to him, pulled her hair back, kissed her on the neck, then on the lips, and then they couldn't stop kissing, and after about five minutes, she said:

"Please, Jeb, don't stop. Please don't stop." And they moved to the back seat of the car and made love for the first time.

"I'm so sorry," he'd said, after they'd finished. "I wanted it to be special."

"But it was." She took his face in her hands. "It was, Jeb."

And it had been. Every single minute of it.

That night, when she snuck into his room, he was sitting cross-legged on the bed.

"Will you sit down opposite me?" he asked. "I want to talk a little seriously, and I don't want to get distracted by having you too close."

"OK." She hopped on the bed, sat cross-legged too.

"You know I love you. And I want to make plans for our future together. If I had the money we'd get married today. But we've talked about what we want. I want to be a writer, and you want to be a nurse. And that's going to take time. I'll have to get a job of some kind to support myself while I'm writing and you'll have to get a nursing degree, and we have to hang in there, Cassidy. Until we can stand on our own four feet together. Because I can't take money from my father. You understand that, don't you?"

"Of course I do."

"I know I argue with Dad about the war, but I want him to respect me. He respects Peter. You know, the whole law school thing, of course he respects him. But I'm studying English, and he won't respect me if I say, 'Oh, by the way, can you fund me and my wife while I write the next great American novel?' I have to prove myself to him, to you, to myself. As soon as I graduate from Yale and you graduate from Stonybridge, we can stop sneaking around. But I can't marry you until I can afford to. Obviously, all of this is assuming the war will be over by then and I won't get drafted."

She hated the war; she hated politics. Her father was a Republican, and she loved him; Jeb was a Democrat, and she loved him. She didn't give a fuck about Ho Chi Minh or Henry Kissinger.

"Don't say that. You're not going to war, Jeb."

"You know." He smiled. "I think you believe that if everyone would just stop talking about it, the war would go away."

"Maybe it would."

"No chance of that, kiddo."

"Well, talking about it doesn't help, does it? It's like death. These days dying people are supposed to come to terms with dying, right? They are supposed to talk about it and say goodbye to their loved ones before they've even died and it's all supposed to be OK because they've talked about it and come to terms with it. That's bullshit. No one ever comes to terms with dying or losing someone they love. Never."

"Come here—" He held out his arms, and she moved into them. "Listen. You're right. I'd never come to terms with losing you. Never. And we won't talk about the war. I'll stop being so serious. Just please say you'll wait for me to get my act together. You won't disappear on me."

"I'll never disappear on you, Jeb. Never. I promise."

"Shake?"

"Shake."

"It's a deal."

"It's a deal."

Leaving him after that Thanksgiving weekend was hard. And Christmas vacation back in Minneapolis was going to be hard too; being so far away from him for so long was torture, but she could still hear him saying "I love you" on the phone. That was all she needed. Meanwhile she could go to the school college counselor, Miss Hanley, and ask about colleges in Connecticut she could apply to. And she might even start studying really hard for the SATs. Jeb wanted to prove himself to his father.

She wanted to prove to Jeb that he was right, she really could conquer worlds if she put her whole heart into trying.

PART TWO

Chapter 18

2018
APRIL 12

I decided to accept her Friend request. Refusing it or ignoring it would have seemed defensive. Obviously she knew I was alive. It would have been odd not to respond. Besides, I was curious. What had happened to her in these intervening years? There were no photos on her page, no information at all. Only her name. Had she married, had children? Where did she live now?

Should I write her a note as well? Probably a good idea. "Hi. Great to hear from you! How are you doing? What are you doing?" Something simple. Then she would reply and I could get a sense of why she had contacted me. She was probably curious too. Nothing wrong with that. I typed the note, pressed Send.

My cell beeped, and I saw a message from my daughter, with a picture attached. She and her husband and daughter had gone to a hotel for a weekend break. "Look, the hotel made little crowns of flowers for me and Samantha. How cute is that? Or is it too Gwyneth Paltrow?"

I looked at the picture of my daughter and granddaughter posing with wreaths of flowers on their heads.

"It's cute. VERY cute," I texted back with a smiley emoji at the end. I almost added "A little Gwyneth, but more Scott McKenzie" before realizing she wouldn't know who Scott McKenzie was, wouldn't know the "If you're going to San Francisco, be sure to wear some flowers in your hair" song that had been close to an anthem for my generation.

San Francisco, Haight-Ashbury, the Summer of Love. So many young people who were idealistic, full of love and goodwill and peace.

We were also self-righteous, selfish, smug.

One of the hippie slogans was "Don't trust anyone over thirty." Not only did we not trust them, we trashed them. Because anyone over that age was boring and conventional and didn't understand. They didn't understand our music or our values, our clothes or our politics. All of which were, of course, enlightened. We were so wonderfully enlightened.

We had revolutions going on all fronts. We'd march against the war in Washington, we'd sleep with anyone we wanted to sleep with, boys would grow their hair long, girls would wear miniskirts, some would burn the flag, some would take LSD, some would rage against capitalism, but everyone was absolutely certain that we deserved to take over the world. Peace and love went along with a giddy sense of entitlement, a generational solipsism.

During our Stonybridge years we played at being political and hip: we might dream about being old enough to go on marches in Washington, but in real life, 99 percent of us took allowances from our parents, were hoping to get cars for our eighteenth birthdays, were obsessed with boys, and would go on to be debutantes.

We took what we wanted from the system even as we ridiculed it.

I typed "Scott McKenzie" into Google.

He died in 2012.

We didn't have Google or cell phones or iPads or iPods or apps or Facebook back then. It's hard to imagine now a world without computers, but we lived in one. We made telephone calls and wrote letters and didn't always know where anyone was at a given time. We were able to live with some degree of privacy.

The technological revolution has turned out to be the biggest revolution of our time.

But there was something else we didn't have back then that turned out to be more important than computers in the short run, and in the long run too.

We didn't have DNA testing.

It was a whole lot easier then for someone to get away with murder.

Chapter 19

1969
DECEMBER 6

Abby

Abby held out the blue dress, then the green one. Which one should she wear? Not that it really mattered. It wasn't as if a dress could make a big difference. But days before a dance everyone got excited anyway. And on the day it was going to happen, some girls spent literally the whole afternoon putting on makeup. In the end, it was pretty much always a disappointment. They'd spend hours driving to some boys' boarding school on a bus, arrive, and disembark like dolled-up cattle, only to stand in a large hall and be paired off according to height with the guys standing opposite them.

So the tall girls always got the tall boys and the short ones ended up with the shrimps. The girls who were medium height had the best chance of being surprised and finding someone good-looking and funny, but surprises were rare.

They'd fast dance to Motown hits or Sly and the Family Stone, slow dance to Donovan. If anyone looked around the gym and saw couples dancing to "Catch the Wind," they'd see most of the girls desperately trying to keep space between themselves and the lunging, grabbing boys. The others would be locked with their partners in bear hugs, their feet barely moving in a kind of stationary swaying.

Occasionally a dance would result in letters between the schools winging back and forth, but they usually petered out pretty quickly. Normally the best part of going to a dance was the bus trip back and forth, all of them singing along to the radio.

But everyone still hoped. And Abby was one of those everyones.

The day before, Miss Chase had told them about Richard Nixon's Silent Majority speech in their civics class and asked for comments.

"If they're all silent," Cass was the first to volunteer, "how does he know they exist? Or what they're thinking?"

"They take polls of public opinion," Miss Chase responded.

"So if they say in the polls what they think, then they're not silent, are they?"

"You know what President Nixon is saying, Cassidy. Many people aren't as vociferous as the young these days about their beliefs. So they are overlooked."

"They can vote. Count the votes. Whoever wins wins. What's the problem?"

Abby had thought it was a really good point, but Miss Chase just sighed and rolled her eyes.

Aside from Mr. Doherty, all the teachers were old, unmarried women. The school line was that they were unwed because their fiancés had died in World War Two.

Miss Chase wore caked, powdery makeup that would have looked right on a corpse. She dressed in tweed suits in all seasons and had a walking cane with an ivory handle.

"Maybe those soldier fiancés are better off dead," Zoey once commented.

Everyone who heard her had laughed.

Abby wished she could come up with some funny comments that

made everyone laugh. Was she Unfunny too? Probably. She was definitely Uncool.

What exactly did it take to be cool? If it had to do with the right clothes, she could try to figure that out and buy them. She knew, though, that that wasn't it. That to be cool you had to not care about being cool. You had to be naturally cool. Were people born cool? Was coolness genetic?

If she could get a vial of coolness, she'd inject it and maybe, just maybe, she'd meet a cool guy and the cool guy would like her and then she'd not only be best friends with Cass, she'd have a boyfriend too and her whole life would be perfect.

Fat chance of that, she thought.

But it was worth a try. She decided to choose the pale blue velvet dress.

"How's this?" she asked Cass.

"Looking great, Abs. We better get going or we'll be late for the bus. I'd like to skip this whole thing, but at least it means getting out of here."

Cass hadn't been excited about any dance, not the whole time she'd been friends with her. It didn't make sense because Abby knew Cass didn't have a boyfriend in Minneapolis. One time she had asked her why she was always so reluctant to go to dances.

"Boarding school boys are boring," Cass had replied. "Teenage boys in boarding school are silly too. They think they're great, but they act like ten-year-olds."

The best song on the bus ride had been "I Say a Little Prayer."

"And who exactly does Aretha think will be listening to that prayer?" Zoey had asked after it finished. "I'm praying that I won't be matched up with a zombie, but I'm not sure God or whomever we're praying to would really care about my overriding concern tonight. At least I fervently hope he, she, or it wouldn't."

As the boys and girls stood facing each other in line, Abby noticed him. He had his arm in a sling, and she liked the amused but not arrogant expression on his face. Plus he was cute. He had shortish dark hair and bright blue eyes. Strangely, though, what drew her most to him was his shoulders. She'd never thought of shoulders as being attractive before, and maybe it was the sling that gave them some extra dimension, but whatever it was, she found herself constantly looking at him and hoping against hope that their names would be called together.

When, miraculously, they were, she tried not to look as excited as she felt.

"I'm Jimmy," he said when he walked up to her.

"I'm Abby."

"Do you think we have anything in common, Abby? Do you like Cream? *Laugh-In*? Sports?"

"Sports. I love sports. Especially basketball."

"Tell me you're a Celtics fan. Any other team and I'm walking away right now."

"Are you kidding? I was at Bob Cousy Day. I cried when he cried."

"Jesus. Far-out. I would have killed to be there. I want to hear everything about it. Don't leave out one single detail."

Talking with him was easy, dancing with him was easy, even though on the slow dances his broken arm—from a football tackle—made getting close a little difficult. He was smart, he was funny, and she was beyond happy.

At one point, during "Sunshine Superman," she looked to her left and saw Cass dancing with her date. He had a bad case of acne and was about as uncoordinated a dancer as she'd ever seen.

Then, when Jimmy and she went to the table at the far end of the hall to get a glass of nonalcoholic punch, Cass was beside her.

"I can't wait for this to end," she whispered. "He hasn't said a word."

Probably because he can't believe his luck, Abby thought. *He probably thinks if he says something he'll break the spell and you will disappear.*

"How are you doing?"

"Really good," she whispered back, then turned to Jimmy. "Jimmy, this is my friend Cassidy. She's my roommate."

And then she held her breath and waited for him to take one look at Cass and forget all about her.

"Hi, Cassidy," he said. Nothing about his expression changed. "How's it going? Who are you paired up with?"

"I think his name is Tim."

"Tim Coulter?"

"Yeah, that's it."

"Nice guy."

"I guess."

"We're going to take our punch and go somewhere we can hear ourselves talk. Nice to meet you, Cassidy." Putting his cup in the hand of his right broken arm, he grabbed Abby's hand with his left and led her out of the hall. "We're allowed to get some air out here as long as we don't wander off into the bushes."

"Good idea." She paused, then dived in. "Cassidy's beautiful, isn't she?"

"Yes. She looks like she's much older than everyone, though. Is she your age?"

"A month older, that's all."

"Huh. Anyway, I was thinking. Maybe we could go to a Celtics game sometime. Where do you live? Can you get to Boston?"

She'd had crushes on boys, she'd had that one kiss at a party, but she'd never been asked on a date or come close to doing the kinds of things most of the girls at school talked about. Not only wasn't she a Star, her experience with the opposite sex was pretty much limited to her brothers and their friends and the sports they all played together.

"I'm sure I can get to Boston," she said, inwardly repeating the mantra: *Act like Cassidy.* "I live in Connecticut."

"So do I. Anyway, I'll write you. And we can arrange something during the Christmas holiday."

Act like Cassidy.

"That sounds pretty good."

"I'll settle for pretty good," he said, smiling.

Back on the bus she did her best to remember every single detail. His sweater had smelled of autumn leaves even though it was December. His cast was crowded with signatures and drawings and exclamation marks. He'd asked her on a date. He'd said he'd write to her. He hadn't stared at Cass the way 99.999 percent of all people alive stared at Cass.

"So—" Zoey's voice rang out. "Did any God answer any prayers for anyone tonight?"

Sitting beside her, Cass nudged Abby with her elbow and whispered, "Seems to me like your Protestant God did. You landed a looker, you little devil. Is the tomboy thing over now? Shit, Abs, you could be a Star soon."

"Everyone—" Cass half rose from her seat. "I have an announcement."

Grabbing her arm, Abby pulled her back down. "Don't! I'll kill you!"

"OK, Abs. I was only teasing."

"It's not funny."

"You're right." She put her arm around her shoulder and gave it a squeeze. "It's a big deal. I know. Sorry."

Now, if only the Vietnam War would end, the world would be perfect.

Chapter 20

Cassidy

Cassidy was sitting in the Senior Room when Angel came in, walked over to the bulletin board, pulled out a pen, and put a star beside her name.

"Wow!" she said. "When did that happen?"

"Last weekend. I'm giving it a five." Angel turned and grinned.

Angel's real name was Martha, but she had long blond hair and pale blue eyes and played the harp. So obviously she was nicknamed Angel.

"Who's the lucky guy? Has to be Kenny, right?"

Angel and Kenny were childhood sweethearts, so she wasn't surprised when Angel nodded.

"Do you want to talk about it?"

"Not right now. I'm having a harp lesson in a few minutes."

"OK. But was it really a five?"

"It really was."

"Far-out."

Angel left, and Connie Hopkins and Harriet Gedling came

into the Senior Room, walked straight over to the bulletin board, scanned the List.

"The Angel has fallen! Shit!" Harriet exclaimed.

"And a five!" Connie chipped in. "She better get her ass in here so we can get all the juicy details."

I won't be able to see Jeb on Christmas, but we can still talk on the phone when we get the chance, and the next time I see him I'll be able to give him his Christmas present: a Swiss Army knife.

When he opened it he'd laugh, she was sure. What would he get for her? It didn't matter. What mattered was that Christmas was coming and then it would be New Year's and it would be 1970, which meant it would be the year she graduated from Stonybridge and he graduated from Yale and they could tell everyone about their relationship. And be together. No more sneaky phone calls, no more letters she had to hide. When she went back to Minneapolis for the Christmas break, she'd go to a place that could make holes in his watch strap so she could wear it. In 1970 she'd be able to walk around everywhere wearing Jeb's watch.

Angel was happy, but in the year 1970, Cassidy knew that she was going to be the happiest girl in the world.

Chapter 21

2018
APRIL 20

Someone told me once that it's a sign of good psychological health to have a nightmare. It means you can cope with those memories from the unconscious instead of leaving them buried. "In other words," I remember replying, "it's scarier not to have nightmares than to have them."

"Exactly" had been his response.

Bullshit, I didn't say.

A nightmare was a nightmare, and nightmares were scary. The one I had a few days after I'd accepted her Friend request and sent her a message was scary, definitely.

I was handcuffed to a radiator. The key to the handcuffs was just beyond my grasp on the floor of a strange room. I had no idea where I was, but I knew if I didn't get that key and unlock myself, I'd die.

Each time I reached for the key, the key moved further away. I was crying, weeping. Terrified.

When I woke up, I felt the relief that always came when you discovered it was all just a dream. You were home, in your bed. Alive and unthreatened. Not a pair of handcuffs in sight.

What was that all about? Handcuffs? Why handcuffs? Why was I tied up?

The nightmare lingered with me during the day, as some dreams do.

That night my husband was going out to a political dinner. He put on a suit, then picked out a tie.

"How about this?" he asked, holding it out to me.

A blue-and-white-striped man's tie.

Oh my God.

A blue-and-white-striped man's tie.

How had I forgotten? In all these years, why hadn't I once thought about it?

Friendship Weekend.

That was the nightmare.

After he left for his dinner, I went downstairs and sat down. I didn't turn on the TV or pick up a book. I sat on the sofa and did it yet again. Threw myself back into that world, the world that had been buried deep in my mental graveyard.

Nineteen seventy had begun with a vengeance. January was one of those memorable New England months of misery, the cold intense and unrelenting. Our classrooms were brutally frigid, and even when we played basketball in the gym we didn't come close to breaking a sweat. We shivered and piled on extra blue sweaters, ran across the quad as quickly as we could to get back to our rooms, and huddled under blankets hibernating as we settled down to the drudgery of preparing for those all-important SATs. Because of the cold there were far fewer trips into town, so the nonsmokers, bored and restless, found themselves in the Senior Room passively inhaling on an epic scale. No one dared crack a window open.

The snow, when it came, wasn't welcomed the way it was before Christmas. We tramped through it, our heads down, our shoes sodden, feeling more penned in and cut off. The hallways were covered in slippery sludge that disconcertingly resembled the slimy stews served up at lunch and dinner.

Stonybridge was a frozen hive of anxious, exasperated worker bees desperate for escape, with nothing coming up on the calendar except the most bizarre school ritual of all.

Friendship Weekend.

Who had thought of it in the first place? No one knew. Doubtless a particularly sadistic headmistress. Yet no subsequent headmistress had called a halt to it: it was as firmly a part of school tradition as the May Day maypole dance.

In a way, Friendship Weekend was similar to the May Day maypole dance the seniors always performed. But instead of holding on to ribbons and winding them around a maypole, we tied ourselves to each other.

On the third weekend in January every year the senior class gathered for Assembly on Friday morning and watched and waited as names were pulled out of a hat—two at a time. Whomever you were paired with was then your "Friend" for the Saturday and Sunday. A friend you couldn't escape because you were literally tied together. With a man's tie.

We were already tied. That was what made this tradition so loathed by the students. It was a physical manifestation of a psychological state of being we had never encountered before we went to Stonybridge and would never encounter again. Yes, we had grown up in families, but even families had time off from each other. Siblings went to school, spent time with different people during the day, but we were always with each other. At school, at sports, at mealtimes. There was no respite. You couldn't run to your room, slam the door, and be alone—you had a roommate.

No one was leaving for work in the morning because no one was leaving.

We spent nine months a year for four years seeing the same people every single day, every single moment of those days. They weren't family members or friends we had chosen or partners we'd made a conscious choice to share our lives with.

Our only power was whom, out of the random group of girls we'd been thrown into, we chose to hang out with.

Friendship Weekend took even that away from us.

On the third Friday morning of January we'd find out with whom we'd be tied up, and on Saturday morning Miss Adams would tie each pair's wrists together, thus bonding us for the entire weekend. The only times we could untie ourselves were to go to the bathroom and to bed at night.

To make us feel even more infantile, teachers took shifts over the weekend, patrolling the corridors and the sports fields, popping into rooms to make sure no one was untying those ties and cheating.

If the senior class had an odd number of students, some poor girls were tied in a threesome.

Inevitably every year there were fights and tears. Even if the best of friends were luckily twinned, they'd often find themselves, by the end of Friendship Weekend, not speaking.

Maybe that taught us something about friendship and boundaries, but none of us sitting in the gym that Friday morning in mid-January were interested in learning any lessons.

All we wanted was not to get stuck with someone we didn't like or someone whose habits drove us crazy. So we sat in the gym, cold and irritable, waiting for our names to be called out in pairs and the ludicrous tradition to begin.

I hadn't thought of Friendship Weekend for forty-eight years. I'd repressed it all.

Perhaps my handcuff nightmare really did mean I could cope with those Stonybridge memories now, I told myself.

Yeah, right.

Bullshit.

Chapter 22

1970
JANUARY 16

Abby

Idiotic stupid fucking Friendship Weekend.

Abby sat in the freezing gym crossing her legs tightly, closing her eyes, desperately praying not to be paired with Karen, who, she was sure, was doing the same. When her name came out of the hat first, followed by Mary Greene's, she uncrossed her fingers and opened her eyes. She liked Mary; she could cope with Mary. Two days tied together would be bearable, maybe even fun. As the names kept being read out, it seemed no pairing would be particularly tricky. Until it came to Zoey Spalding's name, which was immediately followed by Cassidy Thomas's.

Heads swiveled: everyone was trying to find Zoey and Cass in their seats, trying to see the expressions on their faces. There was a collective sound of gossipy whispering.

"Quiet!" Miss Adams said. "We haven't finished. I want your full attention. Now." She reached into the hat. "Karen Mullens." She reached again. "Becky Powell."

When all the names had been called, they filed out of the gym and she found Cass in the courtyard.

"Will you be all right being tied to Zoey?"

"Sure, Abs. I don't have a problem with Zoey. If she has a problem with me, that's her bad luck. Hey, Zo—" she called out. Zoey was about five feet away. "You're cool with being tied to me for a while, aren't you?"

"I'm fine."

Karen was standing beside Zoey.

It was easy to tell she wasn't fine.

Chapter 23

Karen

Her first class after Assembly was biology and she should have been concentrating, but she couldn't. Because things couldn't have been worse. Well, maybe they could have if she'd been paired off with Abby, but this was the next-worse outcome to Friendship Weekend.

"You're cool with being tied to me for a while, aren't you?"—she could still hear the smirk in Cassidy's voice. As if she wanted this outcome, wanted to get Zoey in her thrall again.

It was a stupid, ridiculous tradition. But then everything was beginning to feel like a stupid tradition, even Christmas. Normally she enjoyed decorating the tree and opening presents and hanging out at home. But this year? It had been horrible.

She missed Zoey. There was no one she could talk to. When she did try to talk, her family made things worse. "It's all well and good to talk about Vietnam or this new friend of yours, Zoey, but what about college, Karen? You haven't said a word about college. Where are you going to apply to? What are your plans?" her father asked as they sat around the dining room table on Christmas Eve.

"Don't you know? She's a lesbian now, Dad," her brother, Ed, said, laughing. "I bet you're going to apply to Smith or Wellesley, Karen, aren't you? You'll be happy at one of those all-girl places. With all the other lesbians."

"That's not funny, Ed." Her mother glared at him.

"It's true, though, isn't it? She never stops talking about Zoey what's-her-name. 'Zoey says this about the war.' 'Zoey says this about some idiot poet.' As if we're all supposed to care. Karen and Zoey sitting in a tree . . . k-i-s-s-i-n-g . . ."

"Shut up, you fucking idiot."

"Karen. Don't talk like that. It's rude. What's gotten into you?"

"He's the rude one."

"Both of you, stop it right now," her father commanded. "Your mother's right. That's no way to talk. I'm saying that to both of you. Behave yourselves or leave the table."

She stayed sitting, but she remained silent as Ed told stories about his basketball games and all the normal things he did at school and all his normal friends. All the unimportant, bourgeois shit.

What had happened? She used to feel uncomfortable, wondering why she was the only ugly one in the family, but now she felt so much more than that. As if she had never belonged here and never would. No one at the table was actually seeing her. She was invisible to them, and they didn't even know that because they had no idea who she was and she didn't have any idea who she was either—except when she was with Zoey.

The more Ed talked, the more she ate, until her mother barked: "Karen, really. That's enough, don't you think? You can't be that hungry. No one is."

"Well, I am." She heaped some more mashed potatoes on her plate. "I'm starving."

That was Christmas in a nutshell: her brother and she arguing, her parents trying to stop them, her choking, enveloping misery, all interspersed with phone calls to Zoey, plus tons of trips on her own to buy cigarettes and candy so she could smoke and eat on the sly.

She wished that she'd spent Christmas Day the way she'd spent Thanksgiving: in a diner in Manhattan with Zoey.

And now, just as she was feeling good again after two weeks back at Stonybridge with Zoey, Miss Adams reached into that fucking hat and pulled out Cassidy's name after Zoey's.

Tomorrow morning they'll be tied together for two whole days. It isn't fair. We should be the ones tied together. Why? Why did it have to be Cassidy Thomas?

The bell rang, signaling the end of biology class. She stood up to leave, but Mr. Doherty motioned to her. "Karen, can you stay here for a minute? There's something I'd like to discuss with you."

"OK."

After everyone had filed out, Mr. Doherty pointed at a chair in the front row of the class.

"Sit down for a second, please."

"Have I done something wrong?"

"No. Nothing wrong. But I have noticed that your grades are slipping. And you don't seem to be paying attention in class. What was I talking about before the bell rang?"

"Photosynthesis?"

"That's not a very good guess, Karen. We covered photosynthesis in October. Listen—" He sat down on the edge of his desk. "You can afford to slip a little, and I know January is a difficult month at the best of times. Post-Christmas blues. The weather. But you need to remember the SATs are coming up and colleges are going to look closely at your school records. You've been doing so well, it would be a shame not to keep that up. I know you could get into one of the Seven Sisters if you want to, Karen." He smiled. "And you have such an interesting and productive future in front of you."

"OK. Can I go now?"

"Karen? What's wrong?"

"Nothing." She shook her head, but she could feel tears forming and didn't know how to stop them. "It's this Friendship Weekend. I hate it."

"I see."

"No other school has anything as dumb as this."

"No, no other school has it. But they probably have other equally odd rituals. And I'm sure one day you'll look back at this weekend with fondness."

"I don't think so."

"Perhaps not. My advice would be to use the time to do some studying along with your partner. No one can get upset if they sit side by side reading books, now, can they?"

"I guess not." She had to get out of there before she really started to cry. "I'll study harder. I promise. Can I go now?"

"Of course."

She bolted for the door.

Chapter 24

Zoey

A lot of girls must have complained to their parents about the frigid temperatures because now the heating had been cranked up in their rooms at night and it was stifling. She'd thrown off her blanket and was about to go open a window when Karen said: "They've put up the heat, but it's still cold in here, isn't it?"

"Are you kidding? It's like an oven."

No sound for a second, then:

"Yeah, actually, you're right. It is."

Stop it! she wanted to yell. *Enough already.*

Since they'd gotten back from Christmas vacation, Karen had agreed with every single thing she said and tagged after her like a desperate shadow. It was too much.

And since they'd come back to their rooms after dinner, Karen had been saying negative things about Cass nonstop. "I can't believe you have to be tied with *her*," she'd moaned. "It will be awful. How will you stand it?"

And: "She's so arrogant, you know. Everyone thinks she's friendly, but she feels superior to all of us. And she's dumb."

No, you're the dumb one right now, Zoey thought. *You are being so boringly obvious and jealous. You're like a wood tick that's trying to burrow its way into my skin and stay there. Those ticks whose heads stay in even when you pinch their blood-bloated bodies off you.*

Over Christmas vacation, Karen had phoned her every day. After the first week Zoey had asked her mother to lie and say she was out most days.

When it got to the point where she was asking her mother for help, well, that was really saying something.

Miss Adams may have pulled Cassidy's name out of the hat, but Karen was really the one Zoey was tied to, and not just for this absurd weekend.

She'd gotten herself into this mess, she knew, the minute she had asked Karen to room with her. It had been fine for a while, but there was a limit. Karen had begun to copy her every move: talking about the war with the exact same phrases she used, taking an interest in poetry when she'd had none before. Using the same vocabulary. "Inane," Karen would say. "That's a good word," and then she'd use it—all the time. She'd even started to buy and wear the same type of clothes on the weekends they weren't in their uniforms.

"So, you're into black now, are you, Karen? You want to be a beatnik too?" she'd asked at one point.

"Your mother was so mean about that over Thanksgiving. She has no idea who you are, does she? She doesn't see you. It's as if you're invisible. She's really blind."

Wait a minute. I'm allowed to criticize my mother. You aren't.

What was it with people that once they began to annoy you, they kept on annoying you until every single thing they said got on your nerves? At first all this devotion was pleasing in its weird way. Now it was creepy. One afternoon Karen had turned to her and said: "You know what would be groovy? If we were forever roommates."

Overwhelmingly, skin-crawlingly creepy.

If Karen knew the truth, she'd go berserk.

Because the prospect of being tied up with Cass for the weekend was a huge relief.

Cass may have ditched her for Abby, but she wasn't some freaky copycat. In the days when they'd been best friends, Cass gave her shit and laughed at her. Which was part of the reason Zoey had liked her so much.

"Should I open the window?" Karen asked.

"No, leave it."

"But if you're too hot—"

"Just leave it, OK?"

"OK. But tell me if you get too hot and I'll open it."

The beat goes on, Zoey thought, closing her eyes. *And on and on and on . . .*

Chapter 25

JANUARY 17

Abby

They'd done it. It was Saturday morning and they'd gone to the gym, listened as Miss Adams spoke, then gone up to her in pairs and waited for her to tie each tie around their wrists.

"I expect good behavior from all of you. Friendship is the bedrock of a happy life. With female friends you will always find comfort and support. That's what this weekend is about. Treasuring female friendships." After the ceremony was finished and they were standing together in the gym, Mary Greene recited the speech Miss Adams had given at the end word for word. "Can you believe it? I mean, if that's the case, if it's all about female friendship, why use *men's* ties?"

Abby liked Mary a lot. They sat beside each other in math class and passed funny notes. Both of them were athletic and were on the basketball, softball, and field hockey teams together.

Sharp-featured with straight brown hair down to her shoulders, Mary had a natural self-confidence. Sometimes Abby wondered what she was thinking, because she was quieter than most of the girls. When she first heard Mary laugh, Abby was surprised because it was a deep, throaty, joyous laugh, a contagious one. Mary kept to herself most of the time, but it felt as if there was always a part of her that was waiting to laugh that laugh.

"You're right, it is pretty hypocritical wearing men's ties, isn't it? At least this one is blue and white, not like the ugly orange and brown one Angel and Connie got. Anyway, what are we supposed to do now?"

They were still in the gym, standing there tied like the Two Stooges.

"Let's go over to the sports fields," Mary suggested. "It's sunny. Maybe we should be outside for a while since we're going to be cooped up for so long."

"Good idea."

Most of the Lenox winter inhabitants had seen this strange sight of tied-up girls before. They did get a few quizzical looks, though, as they made their way to the sports fields.

When they got there, they wandered around for a few minutes, trying to keep in step with each other. Miss Lee was stationed on the edge of the field, watching, making sure they didn't untie themselves.

"This is ridiculous." Abby shook her head. "It's like some kids' game. A three-legged race except we're walking and it's cold and I'm already bored."

"I'm boring you already, Abs? Why? Because I'm not Cassidy?"

"No." She stopped, forcing Mary to stop too. "No, of course not. It's being tied up that's boring. Not you."

"Sure. Anyway, look at the snow on the mountains: It's so pretty, isn't it?"

"Mary—why did you say that?"

"Don't you think it's pretty?"

"You know what I mean. About me being bored. About Cass."

Mary tried to walk ahead, but Abby wouldn't budge.

"Forget it. Let's go back and do some studying."

"No. Cass and I are friends. What's wrong with that?"

"Nothing. Nothing at all. Unless you happen to be Karen."

Mary swung around so she was facing her. They were standing in the middle of the field hockey field, their breaths visible in the cold.

"Right. I wasn't going to say anything, but I can't not. Have you seen what's happened to Karen, Abs? Have you even bothered to notice?"

"Karen's friends with Zoey now. She seems happy to me."

"Well, then go ahead and think that if it makes you feel better. Don't pay any attention to the way Karen worships Zoey, how she copies her all the time, how she hangs around her like a, I don't know, like a dog on a leash or something. Don't notice that her grades are slipping. That I'm now number two in the class instead of her. She doesn't laugh anymore. She used to laugh a lot. She used to make me laugh. And you know, you used to make me laugh too. But you've changed, Abby. I used to think you were someone who cared."

"Wait a minute. What are you saying? That I'm not allowed to be friends with Cass?"

"You're not allowed to not care about Karen."

"I do care."

"Sure." Mary looked up at the sky. "Sure you do. Everyone cares. That's why that awful List is up there on the bulletin board. Because we all care so much about each other's feelings. It's gross. It's wrong. You shouldn't have let it happen."

"It wasn't my idea."

"No, it was Zoey's, I know. But you're president of the class—you should have torn it down. We used to be a cool class. Now we're . . . I don't know. No one has any scruples anymore."

"Scruples?"

"Yes."

"Jesus, you're taking everything so seriously. And you're being such a prude. Who made you the moral authority anyway?"

"No one." She shook her head. "Let's go back now. It's too cold here."

They walked back to school in silence as Abby fumed.

Was she a criminal because she'd found a new friend? Was she supposed to have ripped the List off the bulletin board to show how many scruples she had? Everyone would have laughed at her.

Mary giving her a lecture like that was wrong. Who was she to judge, and what did she know about anything?

Why had Abby thought she liked Mary in the first place? She was judgmental and self-righteous.

"So what are we going to do next?" Mary finally broke the silence when they arrived back at the campus.

"Study. I have English to do."

"Fine. We'll go to my room first, pick up my math book, then go to your room to pick up your English, then to the study hall—OK?"

"Fine."

It wasn't easy to sit side by side, flipping pages of their books while their hands were bound, but they managed.

All the while her brain was whirling with the injustice of Mary's remarks. What was wrong with finding a new friend? Did she have to keep tabs on Karen for the rest of her life because they'd been friends for a while? If Karen wanted to hang out with Zoey and act like her dog, as Mary had put it, that was her choice. Karen was practically college age. She wasn't a little baby.

And tear down the List? That was a joke. If she'd made a big deal about it, Zoey would have done something even more outrageous, and everyone would have been on her side.

Mary was jealous, that was it. Jealous of her friendship with Cass.

Unable to read a word, she stared at the pages of *Emma*, the book they were reading for class, and made herself think of Jimmy. In a couple of weeks, over the February break, she'd be seeing him again.

In a couple of weeks she might be a Star.

Chapter 26

Zoey

Cass came out of the bathroom, dutifully retied the yellow-and-blue polka-dot tie to their wrists.

"You smell like vomit."

"That's because I threw up, Zo. That's what you smell like when you throw up. Especially when there's no toothbrush in the bathroom."

"Then we better go back to your room so you can brush your teeth. It's heinous. Did you eat something bad at breakfast?"

"I was feeling sick all night. I had some coffee. It must have made it worse."

"You look awful."

"Thanks a bunch. I'm sick. It happens when you're sick."

"Oh, great. Now *I'm* going to get sick."

"Hey, you already look awful. So don't worry about it."

"Thanks a bunch to you too." Zoey laughed.

Finally, she thought. A normal conversation. Cass giving her shit again.

After they'd gone to Cass's room and she had brushed her teeth, Zoey suggested that they go to the Senior Room.

"I'm still not feeling that great. Let's sit here for a while."

"OK."

Cass sat down on her bed, so Zoey had to sit down too.

"The Un Girl—sorry, Abby, is still a maniac about basketball, isn't she?" she asked, looking at the poster of the Celtics player on the wall.

"Yeah. But she's got a boyfriend now. She met him at the Choate dance. He's pretty cute, actually. Jimmy. They went out a few times over Christmas."

"So she has a crush on him?"

"They're into each other. How about Karen? Does she have a crush on anyone?"

On me, she thought but wouldn't say. Because she could tell from her tone of voice that Cass wouldn't say anything negative about Abby. So she wasn't going to say anything negative about Karen either.

"No. Karen's really smart, you know. Too smart to have a puerile crush on a puerile boy."

"Oh Christ." Cass sighed. "Are you going to give your speech about all the girls getting married and giving up their lives for stupid men?"

"Yes. Are you still going to refuse to talk about Vietnam?"

"Yes."

"How can you not be political?"

"I don't know, Zo. How can you think we can do anything about it sitting here on my bed talking?"

"So what should we talk about? How fabulous the Un Girl is?"

"Let's stop arguing. I'm not in the mood for this."

"You're not in the mood for anything. What the fuck are we supposed to do? I know: go to the Senior Room so I can have a cigarette."

"Do you want me to throw up again?"

"Oh, come on, Cass. You mean I can't smoke while I'm tied to you? All weekend?"

"Until I feel better. I have to lie down now."

"Which means I have to lie down next to you. There's no fucking room on this bed."

"You can sit by my side while I lie down, OK? Tell me a story or something."

"You're kidding." Zoey snorted.

"No, please. Tell me a story. Any story."

The way Cass asked made Zoey look at her closely and realize that her face was scarily pale; she'd never seen her look anything but stunningly beautiful with or without makeup, at any time of day, but now she looked washed-out, as if she had the kind of killer hangover her own mother sometimes had.

She really was sick.

"OK. A story. I can't think of one." Her eyes went to the bookshelf, scanning titles. "Listen, I'm going to untie us for one second while I go get a book. Trust one of the faculty to come check on us just while I'm doing it, but I'm going to take the chance."

She undid the knot of the tie, went and grabbed *The Scarlet Letter*, raced back, and tied up the tie again.

"Whew. We did it. You want to know who I have a crush on? Nathaniel Hawthorne. I love *The Scarlet Letter* especially. So here we go. I'm reading the beginning to you. Ready?"

"Thanks, Zo," Cass said quietly. "A weird choice. But thanks."

Chapter 27

Karen

Where is she? Where's Zoey? Where have she and Cassidy gone?

Karen had dragged Becky Powell with her to town, to the sports fields, to the study hall, to the Senior Room, but there was no sign of them. They had to be in Cass and Abby's room, but what were they doing there for so long? It was almost lunch, so they had to have been sitting there together for three hours. Talking about what?

Cassidy didn't discuss politics; she didn't know anything about poetry. What could Zoey have in common with her now?

"Karen, can we please sit down somewhere for a second?" Becky begged. "We could use this time to do some studying instead of going around aimlessly."

"I need a cigarette," she stated. "Let's go back to the Senior Room."

Zoey would have to be there at some point. She couldn't survive much longer without a Marlboro.

"All right."

Becky Powell was the mouse of the class. She tried hard at everything, she was eager to please, and she was tiny. Only five two with long red hair she wore in a ponytail.

Cassidy, whenever she passed Becky in the hall, would pat her on the head and tug her ponytail, saying: "Give me good luck, Beck." Karen wished Becky would slap Cassidy, but it never happened. Instead Becky always giggled and looked thrilled.

The big surprise had been when Becky had returned from Christmas vacation and put a star beside her name on the List followed by a 4. There'd been a larger-than-normal group of girls there when she'd done it.

"Rebecca Powell, you little devil!" Cassidy had laughed. "Who's the lucky guy?"

"Someone I know from home. He's really cute."

"How tall is he?" Connie Hopkins asked.

"Um . . . six foot four."

"Six foot four? With tiny little *you*? Ouch. That must have hurt." Zoey made a face. "But welcome to the heavens, Becky. You're a Star. We'll have to grill you about it soon."

"So when are *you* going to lose it, Karen?" Zoey had then asked—in front of everyone.

"When Robert Redford shows up at my door," she'd answered. Her response had gotten a laugh, but that comment of Zoey's stung. So many girls were Stars, and now even mousy little Becky was one.

At least Abby was still a virgin, but word had it she had a boyfriend too, so who knew when she'd walk in and put a star beside her name? Probably soon.

Meanwhile Karen would be left on the sidelines.

Maybe that was what Zoey and Cass were talking about up in Cass's room. Their sexual experiences. They were probably swapping stories. And Cassidy was saying: *God, even Becky is a Star now. What's wrong with Karen, Zo? Why can't she get a guy? Too fat? Too ugly?*

She hadn't thought when she'd helped Zoey start the List in the first place that it would backfire on her this way.

As she and Becky shuffled into the Senior Room together, Karen swore under her breath. Zoey and Cassidy weren't there.

"There she is, the dark horse!" Connie exclaimed when she saw

Becky. "Come on, sit down. We need more details, Becky. Did it last all night? Where were you? In someone's house or outside? Or were you in your room or his room with parents downstairs? That would be a real trip."

"And six foot four? Jesus Christ, Becky," Angel, who was tied to Connie, chimed in.

"What's his name?" Connie pressed. "Where does he go to school?"

"I don't feel like talking about it now," Becky said.

"Come on. We're bored. We're sitting here tied together and there's nothing else to talk about. He must have big feet—so what exactly did he do, and does he have a big—"

"Shut up, Connie. It's none of your business."

Becky standing up to Connie surprised Karen. Normally Becky didn't stand up to anyone.

"Actually, it is our business, Becky. You didn't have to put the star up. If you put the star up, you should *have* to talk about it. That's the rule."

"Can we go now?" Becky turned to Karen. "I need to study. Can we go to study hall now?"

"OK."

"I can't believe you're not going to tell us." Connie rolled her eyes. "But one of these days we'll get all the gruesome—oh, sorry, amazing and wonderful—details out of you. Even if we have to tie you up and torture you to get them."

"Connie, come off it," Karen protested.

"It was a joke." Connie shrugged. "We're not going to tie her up. We're going to hold her at gunpoint."

"Very funny."

Becky and Karen shuffled out of the Senior Room and headed to the study hall.

"I should never have put that star up," Becky muttered.

"Don't worry, they'll leave you alone at some point."

"No, they won't." She stopped, forcing Karen to stop. Tears were sliding down her cheeks.

"Becky, are you OK?"

"No," she said, gulping. Karen could see her chest heaving.

"Wait a second. Come in here."

There was a large sitting room where parents or special visitors waited by the side of the front door. No one was there, so Karen pulled Becky in there with her and they sat down on one of the sofas. A nice sofa, not like the ratty ones in the Senior Room.

"You don't have to tell them anything, Becky. Like you said, it's your business, not theirs."

"They keep asking. And it's the rule." She raised her free left hand, tried to wipe away her tears. "You know, all the time now, when I walk through the halls, someone will shout, 'Ouch!' I'm so stupid."

"No, you aren't. Honestly, you don't have to worry. Connie wouldn't actually force you to say anything. She was joking back there."

"You don't understand. The whole thing is a joke." She dragged her hand down her face. "I'm not a Star. I just pretended to be."

"Oh."

She'd thought once in a while of doing the same thing herself, but she worried how she would handle being interrogated, guessing she'd be like Becky right now: miserable and scared.

"It's not OK, Karen. I swore on the life of my unborn child. I lied on the life of my unborn child. It's a disaster. Why'd I have to make that up? I got carried away. I'm not used to getting attention from people like Zoey. It made me, you know . . . feel like I was part of something."

Where is Zoey? What are she and Cassidy doing together?

The lunch bell rang out, startling them both.

"Listen, Becky. Swearing on the life of your unborn child was a way to get people to tell the truth, that's all. And someone else will become a Star soon and they'll move on to her. You don't need to worry so much."

"That's what you think," Becky moaned. "Promise you won't tell any-one."

"Of course I won't. We've got to go to lunch now, come on." Karen stood up, pulling Becky with her.

Zoey and Cassidy *had* to be at lunch.

She'd see Zoey in a minute. And Zoey would give her a reassuring look, she knew. A look saying: *Cassidy's not like you, Karen. I'd forgotten how inane and boring she is.*

"Come *on!*" She pulled Becky harder.

Chapter 28

Thomas Doherty

Friendship Weekend had always struck him as an odd tradition, but he supposed there was some purpose in it. Being tied together for two days was nothing in comparison to being married to someone for years; since most of these girls would find a husband and settle down, it was probably good practice.

Yet he'd seen some fierce arguments break out on these weekends. He didn't like patrolling the school looking for miscreants either. Miss Adams should trust them not to cheat and untie themselves.

A school like Stonybridge should have an honor code. That was part of the maturing process. Put trust in the girls and they would appreciate and repay that.

Lunches and dinners on Friendship Weekend were the worst. Because it was difficult for the seniors to eat with one hand, the school served up insipid finger sandwiches that were either soggy or impossibly dry. He dreaded seeing what would be on the platters on the tables.

He had only two pairs of seniors at his table for lunch: Martha—or, as everyone called her now, Angel—Connie, Karen, and Becky. They were perfectly nice girls; in fact, Martha, when she played the harp, definitely deserved her nickname. They all seemed to be getting along fine. As far as he could tell, no major ruckus had broken out between any of the yoked couples as yet, although little Becky seemed unusually downcast.

Miss Adams swanned from table to table, checking on the seniors, asking how everyone was getting along. Wearing a long purple silk scarf, a white silk blouse, and a black tailored suit, she struck him as looking even more European than usual. He hadn't seen that scarf before. She'd probably bought it in Venice, which was where she'd gone for Christmas vacation. Every Christmas and every summer she visited some European city and came back raving about the art, the food, the people.

He wouldn't have minded seeing Venice or Paris or London. If he'd had a decent salary, he'd have been on a plane in a shot. Veronica could afford it because headmistresses were paid a lot more than humble teachers. For what? he wondered. Liaising with parents? He could have done that. Why had he never pushed himself?

Because he wanted to work at an all girls' school, and parents expected a headmistress at an all girls' school. They didn't mind spinsters with silk scarves who allowed teenage girls to smoke whenever they wanted to. But a man? Much less a bachelor? That was impossible.

There were times when he despaired of the choices he'd made. He was alone, after all. In a job that wasn't financially rewarding. He had saved enough so that when he retired he might finally get to go to some of the places Veronica had been.

What did it add up to, though? Here he was, eating a disgusting ham sandwich, avoiding looking at Janet Lee, who was sitting at the neighboring table. The girls were chattering away about nothing. The walls of the dining room were painted an ugly brown; the ceiling was full of cracks.

Was he the only one in this school who had a desire to see it flourish? Even the dining room windows were smeared, not that there was any joy to be had from looking outside. The sun had fled, replaced by menacing clouds. More snow? More sludge? More nothing?

There was a beauty in renunciation.

Wasn't there?

Where was that beauty?

Then, as if drawn magnetically, his gaze shifted and he caught sight of Cassidy across the dining room. Her face was framed by her long hair. Just as he decided she looked like a Madonna, a Madonna Veronica wouldn't have found in all the paintings in Venice, he felt her eyes meet his and he could sense her sadness. She gave him a small nod. As if she were saying: *I know. I understand.*

He nodded back.

Chapter 29

Cassidy

"I don't know if I can take being tied to Mary for another day," Abby said. She was lying on her bed, her elbow crossed over her eyes. "The only good thing about this whole Friendship Weekend business is not having to stay tied when we have to go to the bathroom and when we go to bed. That would be a total bummer. Anyway, how's it going with Zoey?"

"Zo's OK. I was feeling sick this morning so we hung out here until lunch and then I was better so we went to the Senior Room. What's wrong with Mary? I thought you liked her."

"She gave me a lecture about Karen. And the List. She thinks we don't have any scruples. After she lectured me we went to the study hall and stayed there all morning and all afternoon after lunch. We didn't talk. I think she hates me."

"Why would she hate you?"

"Because of the List. Even though I didn't start it, I'm supposed to get rid of it. And because of Karen. Because Karen is now copying Zoey and, you know, getting worse grades. She thinks that's my fault because of us becoming friends."

"That's a bummer." Cassidy closed her eyes. All she wanted was to sleep. And forget.

"Yeah, it is a bummer. *You* don't think it's my fault, do you? That Karen is getting bad grades because of me?"

"No. But Karen *is* copying Zo. She's right about that."

"But that's not my fault."

"Jesus, I didn't say it was, Abs. I'm really tired. Can you turn off the light? I need to sleep."

"Are you all right?"

"Yeah, I'm fine. I'm just tired. And I'm kind of fed up with all this stuff."

"What stuff?"

"All this who's-friends-with-who stuff." She sighed. "Everyone thinks it's so important. As if we were having romances with each other. We're a bunch of girls stuck in the same place for a few years. It's not real life. It's not that important."

"You mean it's not like the war?"

"Fuck the war."

"Cass? Is something wrong?"

I need to get out of this school. Away from Abby, away from everyone.

"No. Everything is hunky-dory."

Chapter 30

JANUARY 18

Zoey

It was the exact same routine. After breakfast, Cass said she felt sick and went to the bathroom again. So Zoey waited outside the bathroom down the corridor from the dining room until Cass came out, wiping her mouth.

While she had waited, a thought had hit her. Hard.

"You seemed fine yesterday afternoon. You said you were better. But you're obviously not."

"It must be some forty-eight-hour bug."

"Right. OK. We should go back to your room so you can brush your teeth again."

As they walked back across the quad to Cass and Abby's room they didn't speak, but that same thought hit her again.

Harder.

When they got to the room and she stood at the sink beside Cass, who was brushing her teeth, Zoey felt the flip of a switch: the moment when a thought turned into a certainty.

"Jesus Christ, Cass. How pregnant are you?"

They were staring at each other's reflections in the mirror above the sink.

"What the fuck are you talking about?"

"It's Jeb Madison's, isn't it? Shit."

"Zoey, I'm not—"

"You think I don't know you, Cass? You think you can bullshit me? Give me a break. Forty-eight-hour bugs don't get better suddenly. And then worse again in the morning. Have you told Jeb yet? Have you told Abby? Christ—what are you going to do?"

They were still staring at each other in the mirror. Cass looked away first.

"What are you going to do, Cassidy?"

Cass threw the toothbrush in the sink, started frantically to untie the tie binding their wrists.

"I need to get out of this place. Now."

"No—" Zoey grabbed her hand. "You need to sit down and talk to me about this. You can't run away. That won't work. You need to let me help you figure this out. Come on—" She dragged her over to the bed. "No one is coming in here, no one can hear."

"What if one of the teachers comes in?"

"They'll only come in to check we're still tied. They won't be eavesdropping outside the door. Besides, we can hear them coming down the hall. We'll keep the door open, OK? And we'll whisper."

"Shit. This stupid Friendship Weekend. Shit."

Zoey could hear the fear and panic in Cass's voice.

"Did you think you could get away with it? Jesus, Cass. Someone would have figured it out soon. You're lucky it's me who did first."

"Lucky?" She snorted. "I'm lucky? I'm seventeen years old and I'm pregnant and I'm stuck in this school and Jeb . . . oh God, Jeb . . ."

"Have you told him?"

She shook her head.

"Have you told Abby?"

"Are you kidding? Abby doesn't even know Jeb and I are together."

"And she hasn't noticed anything?"

"No." Cass hung her head.

"OK." Zoey's brain was whirling, trying to put facts in place. "So no one knows. Except me."

"Wait a minute. How did *you* know—about me and Jeb, I mean?"

"Shh. Keep your voice down. I overheard you talking on the phone to him a while ago. And I was pissed off at you for . . . Look, it doesn't matter anymore. It's irrelevant. The point is, you need to make a plan."

"I have to tell Jeb. But I'm scared to. He wants to be with me, he loves me, but—"

"But a baby? At his age? With his family?"

"What *do* you mean?" Cass's head snapped up. "'With his family'? What does that mean?"

"Listen—" She reached out, put her free arm around Cass's shoulder. "I know the Madisons. I mean, I know those types of people. You don't know them. I'm sure they're friendly to you every time you go there, but don't believe for one second they want a teenage girl like you to be the mother of their grandchild. And what's Jeb going to do? How's he going to support you and a baby?"

"I don't know. He wants to write books, be an author. But he doesn't want to take money from his father."

"So he isn't qualified to do anything, right? What's he majoring in? It has to be English. That's not a qualification that gets you anywhere. It's not like he can go be a lawyer or doctor or something. If he doesn't get some shitty job pumping gas, he'll have to ask his father for money. And if he is pumping gas or gets some other shitty job and comes home every night to a screaming baby, how's he going to be an author?"

"I don't know. Zo—you don't understand—we love each other."

"Oh Christ."

Lost for words, she looked up, noticed the *West Side Story* album cover taped on the wall.

"Is that it?" She pointed at it. "Is that what you're thinking? That you're Maria and Tony in *West Side Story* and love will conquer all? Don't you remember the end of that movie? It wasn't exactly happy, was it? Uh-oh, I can hear footsteps. Someone's coming. Shhh."

"Is everything all right in here?" Miss Rutgers, the nurse, arrived at the doorway.

"Fine, Miss Rutgers." Zoey raised their arms. "See—still tied. We're talking about colleges. Is that all right?"

"That's a good topic of discussion. I'll leave you to it. Are you all right, Cassidy? You look a little pale."

"I'm fine, thank you."

"She needs some sun, maybe a vacation in Florida, Miss Rutgers. You're responsible for our health. Do you want to pay for her trip?"

"Always the joker, Zoey. I'll come check again later."

"Of course you will, Miss Rutgers. Bring the plane tickets to Florida while you're at it. Pretty please."

She left, and Cassidy hung her head again.

"It doesn't have to end badly. Jeb and I could have a happy ending. I know we could."

"Maybe. But not with a baby. Not now. Jeb would end up resenting you. You know that's true. He'd end up blaming you for ruining his life."

"So what am I supposed to do?"

"Don't tell him. Don't tell anyone else. That's the important thing, You've got to keep anyone from knowing while I figure out how to arrange things."

"What *do* you mean?"

"I mean an abortion, Cass. We get a week off in February. I'll figure out how you can get an abortion then, and then no one has to know. Not Jeb, not anyone."

"You want me to kill Jeb's and my baby? No. Don't tell me I have to do that. I can't do that. I'm a Catholic. And I love him. He loves me. No."

Jeb Madison had screwed Cass and obviously not used protection. And now Cassidy was bearing the weight of his mistake and having to make a choice she didn't want to make and shouldn't have had to make. It was a mess, and Zoey felt so angry she wished she could go to Yale right then and confront him and tell him what a pampered, entitled, selfish little boy he was.

It no longer mattered that Cass had suddenly switched to being best friends with Abby or any of that teenage angst she'd felt, not when it was pitted against the reality of this pregnancy. This wasn't about Stonybridge anymore—it was about the rest of Cass's life.

"Listen." She undid the tie, knelt down so she was in front of Cassidy, and grabbed both her knees. "Listen carefully. You don't have a choice. If you go ahead with this, your future is compromised. Right now this isn't a person inside you, OK? It's a bunch of cells. That's it. Got it? A bunch of cells. When you have an abortion, you can live your normal life and if you end up with Jeb, that's cool and you can have other children. I never figured you'd end up married to some Yale guy, but if that's what you want, OK. Nothing changes—that's my point. But if you go ahead and have it, every single thing changes. Forever. Your father will freak out, Jeb's parents will freak out, and Jeb will freak out. Is that really what you want?"

"I want to be with him. We love each other—doesn't that count? I have to tell him."

Jesus—what is it with girls and romantic dreams? Why do they all fall for the myth?

"Sure. And then? Think about it. He decides he has to do the 'right' thing and stand by you, even though it's the last thing he wants right now. And like I said, he either begs his father for money or he ends up driving a cab or something and he comes home to you and every time he's quiet, you can bet he's thinking: 'Wait a second, I was going to be a great writer. Why's this baby screaming? Why does that dirty diaper smell so rank? Why can't I get some fucking sleep?' Do you want him to suffer for this?"

"Why do you care so much about Jeb?"

"I don't give a fuck about the guy. I've never met him. I care about you. Do you want to suffer for this? You're my friend."

"But I haven't been your friend."

"So what? That was temporary. We're friends. I care about you. And I'll fix this for you, I promise."

She tied their hands back together and lifted them. "It's Friend-ship Weekend, remember? We're inextricably intertwined."

Chapter 31

Karen

Something had happened, she could tell. They were different at lunch. There was something going on between them, something shared. She could see it in Zoey's eyes and Cassidy's eyes too. She wished she could rip off the goddamn tie, leave Becky, and get closer to them somehow, because right now she was two tables away from them and she couldn't hear what they were saying to each other. All she could do was keep looking over and noticing.

Becky had wanted to avoid the Senior Room all morning, so they'd gone to the study hall, and although there was plenty of work Karen knew she had to do, she hadn't been able to concentrate.

Cassidy and Zoey. Zoey and Cassidy . . .

When the lunch bell rang, she'd dragged Becky behind her as she went as quickly as possible to the dining room. And then she watched.

It wasn't that they were talking that much. It was something else that she couldn't put a finger on. They weren't laughing either. They looked almost subdued, actually. But they looked comfortable with each other. That was it: they looked as if they shared something. It hadn't been that way the day before. Something had changed.

"Karen."

Mr. Doherty's voice startled her.

"Yes, Mr. Doherty?"

He wouldn't lecture her about her grades dropping in front of the others, would he?

"I was hoping you'd join in on the conversation. We were all discussing patterns of migration. Isn't it amazing that birds can fly so far, can fly across continents?"

"Yes, it is."

"The plover, for example . . ."

She kept her eyes focused on him as he spoke, but her mind was racing elsewhere. Six more hours of being tied to Becky—she had to cope with that before she could be alone with Zoey again.

Zoey—who had gone to bed the night before without really saying anything except that Cass had been sick but thank God had felt better in the afternoon so Zoey could finally smoke.

So nothing momentous had happened on Saturday. But today was different. She could see it. She could tell.

Karen reached out and grabbed another sandwich from the plate sitting in the middle of the table. She'd eaten a bunch of sandwiches already, but she was still hungry. It was a different type of hunger, though. An ache inside her, an unidentifiable yearning the sandwiches couldn't really quell.

It was a feeling she was experiencing more frequently, one that only subsided when she was alone with Zoey.

"Albatrosses are the largest species of flying birds. They circle the earth—unbelievable, isn't it? And they take years to find a mate. In fact, they do ritualized types of dances to attract their mate over a period of years. But once they've mated, they stay mated for life."

"Dances?" Becky asked.

"I'll find a film of them," Mr. Doherty replied. "And show it in class so you can see."

"They probably do the twist," Karen offered up, but no one laughed.

Everyone would have laughed if Zoey had said it.

Once again she looked over, just in time to catch Zoey putting her hand on Cassidy's shoulder; then, as if she could sense Karen's glare, Zoey pulled it away.

The ache in her stomach turned into a ball of knotted fury.

Chapter 32

Cassidy

She wished she could pull off the tie, run to her room, pack a bag, and get the hell out of Stonybridge. Catch a bus or just put out her thumb and start hitching. But with her luck some Charles Manson type would pull over and pick her up. Besides, she had no idea where she wanted to go.

Should I go to New Haven? Find Jeb and tell him?

The problem with everything Zoey had said was that it made sense. The last thing Jeb needed now was a baby. How could he support a child without taking money from his family? He might be able to, but Zoey was right: If he had a full-time job, how would he be able to write his novel with a baby needing attention all the time? What if he did end up resenting her?

Because it was her fault. She had been the one who had begged him to go ahead when they were in the parking lot that Thanksgiving Day. He'd pulled out, but not soon enough; she knew it as soon as she was late because she was never late. Yet some desperate part of her still hoped it couldn't be true. Until her period was overdue and she had started throwing up in the mornings.

Of all the people to be tied to, she had ended up with Zoey, the one who was smart enough to figure it out.

Was that a good thing? She glanced over at Zoey, who had put her hand on her shoulder, then quickly taken it away.

Was it a good thing because Zoey was right? Because Zoey was the only girl in the school who could figure out how to get an abortion?

She tried to picture telling Jeb, and all she could imagine was the look of fear in his eyes. The same look she'd had herself when Zoey and she had been standing in front of the mirror.

She was scared shitless. Jeb would be scared shitless.

And he'd resent her. He'd try not to, but he would. Wouldn't he? Everything Zoey had said made sense.

Except it was her baby. Hers and Jeb's—and it was conceived in love.

But it would bring unhappiness.

The Madisons *would* freak out. She'd come into their house, accepted so much of their hospitality. They'd been a family to her. Jesus. What would they think of her? How much would they hate her?

Mr. Madison would loathe her. Mrs. Madison would think she was a lying tramp. And Abby? She'd end up siding with her family. It was probably the one thing that would bring them all together. They'd stop arguing about the war and spend their time saying what a deceitful, gold-digging slut Cassidy Thomas was.

She would end up cutting Jeb off from his family. Both of them would be outcasts, and she hadn't even begun to think about what her own father would say. After spending all his and the family's money to send her to Stonybridge to make sure she turned out well, she'd end up a teenage mother.

I've done a great job, haven't I, Dad? Made you so, so proud of me.

Everyone was getting up—lunch was over. Which was lucky because she knew that any minute now she'd burst into tears.

She wasn't a practicing Catholic, but she believed in God. Killing a baby was a mortal sin. Could she go off somewhere and have it without anyone knowing? How would she explain disappearing for months? Jeb would ask questions, her father would too. If she told her father she knew he'd make Jeb take responsibility. And even if she managed to keep it a secret from both of them, what would she do when it was born? Give it up for adoption?

She'd spend the rest of her life wondering what had happened to her child; where he or she was, what he or she was doing. What if her baby's adoptive parents turned out to be horrible people who were cruel to it?

"It's a bunch of cells," Zoey had said. If she didn't start thinking about it as if it were a bunch of cells, she might ruin Jeb's life and go crazy herself. Every time she asked herself these questions about the future, all she could see was potential disaster.

"Let's go to the sports fields," she whispered to Zoey. "I need some air, and we need to talk more in private."

Chapter 33

<u>Abby</u>

"This is ridiculous," Mary said as they were leaving the dining room after lunch that Sunday. "We only have a few hours left tied to each other and we've barely spoken since yesterday morning. I'm sorry if I offended you, but I feel bad for Karen, that's all. I remember what good friends you two were. I was only trying to make you remember too."

"I do remember. But things change."

"OK, I get that. The thing is I'm worried about her. I caught the way she was looking at Zoey all through lunch. It was kind of scary."

"She likes Zoey—there's nothing wrong with that."

"All right." Mary shrugged. "I'll drop it. Let's forget about it and go back to being friends ourselves. This no-talking thing is bullshit."

"It is bullshit. But, hey, so far we seem to have been the only ones who have argued during Friendship Weekend. That's a first."

"Amazing." She laughed that great laugh of hers. "So tell me about this boyfriend of yours. What's his name?"

"Jimmy."

"Do you love him?"

"I don't know. Maybe. I guess."

She and Jimmy had seen each other four times during the Christmas vacation, and each time she'd liked him even more. They both loved basketball and cheered wildly together at the Celtics game. He was funny and smart and cute and a great, amazing kisser. On their third date he took her ice-skating, and she watched as he glided around, like a dancer on the ice. When he skated up to her, stopped on a dime, took off his wool cap, and smiled, she thought she must be in love.

They wrote to each other every day, and she couldn't wait to run to the mailboxes and get his letter. Even his handwriting was sexy. The rest of her world might have seemed at war with all the arguments Jeb, Peter, and her father had had over Christmas, but with Jimmy she was at peace. An excited, expectant, happy peace. February break was coming up, and she'd see him again then.

She didn't know when she'd lose her virginity, but she did know it would be with him. The List didn't bother her anymore. It was seen only by the senior class, so it wasn't as if the whole school or teachers knew. The fact that it was their class's secret was kind of fun. Especially now that she anticipated being one of the Stars on it.

Over February break? That soon?

Why not?

As she and Mary walked into the Senior Room together, she glanced over at the List on the bulletin board. It couldn't be that scary if so many girls had done it. But would it be Jimmy's first time too? Would he have expectations? Be disappointed at her lack of experience?

Sitting in the Senior Room, they talked about colleges. Mary wanted to go to the University of Chicago, while Abby was hoping for Vassar or Smith.

At 6:30 p.m. all the seniors duly trooped to the gym for their "untying."

"I hope you have all learned from this," Miss Adams stated. "And

I want to congratulate the Class of 1970. There have been no tears, no tantrums. You've all behaved impeccably, and I'm sure the value of female friendship is not lost on you. You will take it with you as you proceed in life, and believe me, it will be an important part of that life. Now you can go back to normal, but never forget, friendship is an unbreakable bond."

They all cheered themselves as they untied the ties and threw them up in the air.

"One of these days they'll call a halt to this," Mary commented as they filed out together. "Shit, I thought you wanted to stab me yesterday, you looked so pissed off."

"Sorry."

"It's cool, Abs. Let's go back to the Senior Room."

When they walked in, Abby saw that Cass, Zoey, Karen, Connie, Angel, Becky, and a few other girls were already there.

"Freedom," Connie announced, holding up her hands and waving them in the air. "The ties that bind have been unbound."

"About fucking time," Angel replied. "No offense, Connie."

"Hey, you're the one who smells," Connie countered, and everyone laughed.

Except Karen, who was sitting on the floor, her legs crossed, puffing away madly.

"I'm going back up to our room," she stated between puffs. "Zoey? Are you coming now?"

"No, not yet."

Karen, who had half risen, sat back down heavily.

"So what movie is your father working on now, Zoey? And who's in it? And when are we going to meet some groovy actors?" Connie asked.

"He's doing something with Dustin Hoffman. And I've arranged it so Dustin Hoffman is coming here to speak to us all."

"You're kidding! Far-out!" Angel squealed.

"Groovy! When?" Connie asked.

"Soon."

"You never told me that," Karen said, her eyes fixed on Zoey.

"Because it's a joke," Cassidy said. "Come on, guys, you should know when Zoey's joking by now."

Zoey shrugged, held up her hands. "I couldn't resist. I wanted to see that starstruck look on all your faces."

"Bummer." Connie shook her head. "That's such a bummer. I was already thinking about what to wear and what to say to him."

"I knew you were joking, Zoey. I was playing along." Karen put out her cigarette in an already overflowing ashtray on the floor beside her, lit another. "Of course I knew you were joking. You knew I knew you were joking, didn't you, Zoey?"

Abby saw Mary glance at her with a knowing look, one that made her wish they'd never come in to this scene. It was impossible not to see how tense Karen was. Did Mary think that the weird way Karen was being now was her fault too? God, she wished Karen would laugh or say something normal.

Zoey didn't respond to Karen, didn't even look in her direction, and addressed her next words to Connie.

"So were you going to lose your virginity to Dustin? Become a Star with a star? That would have been something."

"I'm not Mrs. Robinson," Connie replied. "No, I'll wait for someone more special than him."

"Like who?"

"Richard Chamberlain. I've always loved *Dr. Kildare*."

"Jesus, Connie." Zoey shook her head. "You're going to have a long wait. He's a homosexual."

"He can't be."

"He is. A lot of actors are and don't say because it will ruin their careers."

"You're kidding again," Connie said in a pleading tone. "Please tell me you're kidding."

"Of course she's kidding. See, I know when Zoey's kidding." Karen glared at Cassidy.

"No, Karen. You *don't* know when I'm kidding." Zoey sounded furious, and she still wouldn't look at Karen. "Because I wasn't kidding. Richard Chamberlain *is* a homosexual."

"Zoey knows everything," Cass stated, and exchanged a glance with Zoey that Abby couldn't interpret.

"You're wrong. Zoey doesn't know everything, Cassidy." Karen's tone was venomous. "And neither do you. You're wrong. You think you know Zoey, but you don't. Zoey doesn't know everything. There are things Zoey doesn't know."

"What don't I know?" Zoey finally looked at Karen. "What don't I know, Karen? Tell me something I don't know."

It was a crazily strange conversation, a bizarre showdown, that felt like it should have been part of a script in an off-off-Broadway play. Not only was Karen furious, but Abby was taken aback by how angry Zoey had suddenly become as well.

"Go on, Karen. Tell me something I don't know."

"You don't know . . ."

They were all staring at Karen, waiting. "You don't know . . ."

"Stop stalling, Karen. Enlighten me as to the nature of my lack of knowledge."

"You don't know that Becky isn't a Star, that she lied about it."

"Wait a minute!" Connie exclaimed, turning to Becky, who had been sitting mutely in one of the chairs. "You lied? What the fuck, Becky?"

Becky bit her lip but didn't speak.

"Yes, she told me. Yesterday. She lied. Right, Becky? You might as well tell them. You lied. So you're wrong about that, Cassidy. Zoey doesn't know everything. And neither do you."

There was a second of silence, then Becky shot up from her chair and ran out of the room.

"Jesus—why did you do that, Karen?" Cassidy sounded like a parent about to say "I'm disappointed in you" to a young child.

"Why the hell shouldn't I? It's the truth. It would have come out sooner or later."

"Really?"

"Yes, really."

Cass just shook her head.

"Wow. That's pathetic to make it up like that," Angel said with a sigh. "Really pathetic."

"Shit. So there's no six-foot-four guy? She invented the whole thing?" Connie asked.

"Yes. So see, Zoey—you didn't know that. Which means you were wrong, Cassidy. Zoey doesn't know everything. Admit it—you were wrong. You don't know everything about Zoey."

Cass was now looking at Karen with a bewildered expression.

"What the hell is going on here?" she asked. "I don't get it."

"You're always right, aren't you? You're perfect. But not now. You're wrong, Cassidy. You're—"

"Karen—" Mary tried to interrupt.

"Shut up, Mary." Karen ground out her cigarette, stood up, approached Cass, stood in front of her, her hands on her hips. "Cassidy Thomas. It's always Cassidy Thomas. You get away with shit none of the rest of us can. Because what? Because you happened to have been born beautiful. Well, fuck that because you didn't earn it. You got fucking lucky and now you think you own the world and everyone in this school should bow down at your fucking feet. Not me,

OK? I'm never going to bow down to you. Get that through your stupid little brain."

"I never asked you to bow down to me." Cass's voice was calm. Which clearly enraged Karen further.

"'I never asked, I never asked . . .'" Karen's whole body was shaking as she mimicked Cass. "Of course you didn't ask. Because you don't ask, you assume. I'm fucking sick of the sight of you. You're a stupid fucking asshole."

With that, she stormed out of the room, leaving the rest of them mute. Until Zoey said:

"So, do you guys think maybe Karen doesn't like Cass very much?"

Chapter 34

Zoey

Everyone else had left the Senior Room, but she stayed on, smoking. There was no point in going up to their room and telling Karen what a fool she'd made of herself. In fact, the last person she wanted to see right then was Karen. She'd be sitting there waiting to defend herself, ranting on about Cassidy. That was a whole world of irritation Zoey didn't want to cope with. Besides, she didn't have the time. She had half an hour before dinner, and she needed every minute of it on her own to focus and think.

When she was a kid, she remembered other kids throwing something at someone and saying: "Think fast." Meaning: think fast and catch this or it will hit you. Now she had to think fast because otherwise Cass would get hit—hard.

As they'd walked around the sports fields after lunch, she had repeated about a million times that this was just a bunch of cells, not a baby. Not even close. And then she'd assured Cass that she could find someone qualified who could do an abortion. But that was a big bluff she'd used to make Cass feel better.

At least Cass had come to her senses and figured out that she had to have an abortion—that was a starting point. But how to find someone who'd give her one? Someone not in a back alley who wasn't a professional? Racetrack might know someone, but odds were he'd know someone even shadier than he was. And then they might botch the job . . .

No. Not Racetrack. He was out of the running.

She couldn't ask her mother or any of her mother's friends. Definitely not anyone at Stonybridge. Which left her, she suddenly realized, with only one possibility, and as soon as she thought of it, it made complete sense. Her father.

He had to know someone, or at least know someone who knew someone. He moved in those circles. Actresses must get pregnant and need to have abortions. Actors must get girls pregnant all the time and need to get them abortions. And movie stars wouldn't have to go to back-alley places. They'd find someone decent.

It wasn't as if she were asking him to find someone to do it to her. He couldn't suddenly get on his high horse and say: *That's my grandchild you're talking about.* He wasn't the type to get on a high horse anyway. How could he be when he had such a young girlfriend?

She hadn't asked him for anything for a long time. He owed her this.

Zoey stubbed out her cigarette and stood up. She'd sneak down to the phone late that night when no one could overhear her and call him then.

He'd have to fix it so Cass could have the abortion during their week break in February. And wherever it took place, she'd go too.

Because she and Cass were in this together, all the way.

Chapter 35

FEBRUARY 7

Thomas Doherty

How many times had he been to Old Sturbridge Village? He didn't want to try to count them. It was one of the trusted destinations on the school excursion list, and every year he'd troop there with one of the classes, seeing yet again a "rural Northeastern town of the 1850s" in all its historic dimensions, complete with "townsfolk" dressed in mid-nineteenth-century garb.

The first time he'd gone had been relatively interesting. By the third, he'd wanted to rip the white bonnet off one of the women bending over her lace sewing. It was too cute for words and too boring for them too. This particular Saturday, however, he didn't mind as much as he normally did because he was with a group of seniors, one of whom was Cassidy.

They were as disinterested as he was, it was clear. Most of them had already been there too, so there was a lot of eye-rolling and not-so-muffled laughter as they trudged around the town, taking in the meetinghouse, the school, the country store.

It didn't help either that it was such a bleak day. Gray and drab and cold: the dregs of winter. As they'd traveled there on the bus, he'd looked out the window and had a sudden urge to scream:

Get me off this bus. And then he thought how shocked all the girls would be. Mr. Doherty doing something crazy. And that made him even more depressed.

"Do we really have to watch ye olde village blacksmith doing his thing with horseshoes?" Connie asked as they reached Sturbridge Village. "Can't we just skip it, get back on the bus, go to Pittsfield and do some shopping, and see twentieth-century people in twentieth-century outfits?"

"I'm afraid not, Constance."

"Bummer."

"I like the horse-drawn stagecoach," Angel announced. "Let's go look at that."

"The bank is the first stop on our tour," he replied.

He'd dispensed with the services of a guide. He knew the village by heart and had the patter down pat as well. Although he was tempted to tell the soldiers in Revolutionary War army uniforms that they were the wrong century and should go to Concord, Massachusetts, and join some historical site there.

"What are those hats called again?" Abby asked. "You know, the ones the men are wearing."

"Stovepipe hats."

"They make the men look taller," Angel said. "I don't think there were any six-foot-four guys in those days. Too bad, Becky, right? No tall guys."

Little Becky Powell was staring down at the ground. She'd been quiet throughout the bus trip.

"Of course you could always invent one, Becky," Connie said with a snigger.

"Fuck off, Connie," Becky spat out.

"Becky!" He was shocked, and even more shocked when Becky then strode straight up to Karen Mullens and shouted:

"I hate you! I hate you! You've ruined my life. I hate you!"

Then she raced off in the direction of the general store, her red ponytail bobbing crazily.

"Stay here, all of you," he barked, and ran after Becky.

When he caught up to her, she was leaning against the wall of the store, sobbing.

"Is there anything I can do for thee?" One of the men in a white stovepipe hat who had been in the doorway of the store approached them.

"No. No, thank you. I can take care of this," he said. "It's a school problem. Not yours."

"Thou art sure?" The "villager" was looking at Becky, who nodded and feebly waved him away. Thankfully he disappeared back into the store.

"Becky. What happened back there? I don't understand. Are you all right?"

"No. I hate Stonybridge. I want to leave. I want to go home." She was struggling to get the words out.

"But why? What's happened? What did Connie and Karen do to make you use language like that? It's not like you."

"Nothing. They didn't do anything."

"Becky, really. This can't be nothing. If you tell me, I can help."

"I can't tell you." She kept shaking her head, making him think of one of those fake puppy dogs in the back window of cars.

"Mr. D., let me talk to Becky." Cassidy was suddenly at his side. "Please, leave it to me. This has to do with girls', you know, girls' things. I promise you, you can't help. We'll be back in a few minutes. I swear."

"All right." He may have sounded dubious, but he was relieved. If it was a "girl problem," she was right, he couldn't help. And clearly Becky didn't want to talk to him about it.

The whole incident was worrying, he thought as he returned to the others outside the bank. Becky lashing out was so uncharacteristic, and at Karen Mullens too.

Karen hadn't heeded his warning. Her work for class was getting worse and worse, her participation in it close to zero. Her total disinterest made him wonder whether he should talk to Veronica about her.

What a shambles the day was turning out to be. Still, he trusted in Cassidy's ability to deal with Becky and smooth over the situation.

He'd have to speed up this expedition, get it over with as quickly as possible. Every time one of the "villagers" said "thee" or "thou," the girls would laugh. They weren't learning anything.

The only students who were ever interested in Old Sturbridge Village were the freshmen, and even they grew tired of it after about twenty minutes. He'd tried to persuade Veronica to organize class outings to Boston or Manhattan or even Washington, D.C., for a weekend. She of all people should want them to go to a good museum, for example. She always pleaded money as an excuse, but she should have worked harder to get it.

"Is Becky all right?" Angel asked when he returned to the group of girls milling around outside of the bank.

"I'm sure she'll be fine. Go in the bank now. I'll be with you in a second. Karen, you wait a minute. I need to speak to you."

As he walked over to her, he thought how surly she looked, and how unkempt.

"I don't know what that was all about, Karen. But it's time you started working in class again. Your attitude lately has been alarming. If this goes on, I'll need to speak to Miss Adams."

She bit her lip, shifted from foot to foot. Her black hair, which had always been relatively neat and shoulder length, was now longer and clearly uncombed.

"Are you listening to me, Karen?"

"Yes, Mr. Doherty. But this is all"—she waved her hand to take in the village—"so inane. School is inane. People are so inane. I didn't mean to upset Becky. It's not my fault."

"Karen. I know you're intelligent, but you're not intelligent enough to think of yourself as above others or above education. No one is."

"Cassidy went to talk to Becky, didn't she?"

"Yes. Cassidy very kindly offered to help."

"It's all a joke." She shook her head. "An inane joke. I give up."

"Karen—"

"I'm going into the bank now, Mr. Doherty, and I'm going to learn something, all right? I'll learn yet again about how they all bartered. Then *thee* won't have to complain about me and *thee* won't have to blame me for everything. The way everyone blames me for everything."

Turning her back on him, she walked off to the bank.

He was definitely going to have to talk to Veronica about her.

Chapter 36

Karen

Zoey hadn't come on the expedition to Old Sturbridge Village. She'd been excused because she had bad cramps and Karen had thought of using that excuse herself, but when she'd suggested it, Zoey had said, "I need some time by myself, Karen. I really do feel lousy. Go."

So she'd gone and Becky had made that scene and Mr. Doherty had blown up at her and Cassidy had ridden to Becky's rescue, of course, like some fucking white knight on a charger. They'd come back together, walked into the stupid bank together.

Becky then proceeded to stay by Cassidy's side the rest of the time and even sit beside her on the bus back to school. Abby gave up her usual sitting-beside-Cassidy seat because of course Abby wanted to rub it in too, show Karen what a terrible person she had been for divulging Becky's secret.

Everyone was against her. Ever since she'd told people that Becky had lied, she'd been treated as if she were the one who had done something outrageous. What was the point of the List if you could lie and get away with it? Why was it so wrong to have told the truth? They acted as if she'd turned Becky in to the police and landed her in jail.

Karen sat on her own at the back of the bus and counted the minutes until they got back and she could see Zoey again.

Because there had to be a way to get things back to normal, to how it had been with Zoey.

She knew she had been annoying, but she found it so hard to stop herself. All she wanted was to please Zoey. Was that so bad? She guessed so because Zoey was drawing away from her and not sharing things anymore and acting as if they'd never been as close as they actually had been. So she had to figure out a way to make it the way it had been again.

Zoey hadn't invited her to New York for the February break yet, but she would, Karen knew. Zoey needed her there: an ally against her mother, a friend to talk to and walk the streets with. They'd go back to the same diner they'd gone to at Thanksgiving and sit and smoke and talk. Talk about important, interesting things. Only this time Karen had been working hard to find out more about poetry and politics. Her grades might have slipped, but she could talk about the subjects Zoey was interested in now. She'd be able to contribute; they could talk nonstop for days.

Her fears had subsided after the misery of Friendship Weekend. Whatever had happened between Zoey and Cassidy, Zoey wasn't spending more time with Cassidy. Whatever had transpired between them had been temporary. So it was just a case now of figuring out how to tune in to Zoey's vibe again. Which would be easy in New York. That was all they needed: time away from Stonybridge—together.

"How are you feeling?" she asked when she finally got back to their room. Zoey was sitting at her desk. She might even have been studying.

"Not great. But better."

"You didn't miss anything at Old Sturbridge Village. It was so inane. It has no relevance to what's happening today."

"Would you stop saying 'inane'?"

"Why? I thought . . . OK, right. Anyway, what are you reading?" Karen flopped down on her bed.

It has to get better. It just has to.

"Our English book. *Emma.*"

"Tedious. See, I didn't say 'inane.'" She laughed, expecting Zoey to laugh with her.

Instead, Zoey sighed and said: "No, actually. It's good."

"I'm surprised you like it."

"Karen." Zoey looked over at her, heaved another sigh. "You can't predict everything about me. We're not a married couple, you know."

These days Zoey sighed a lot. It was all going wrong. Again.

Nothing she said worked anymore.

"OK, I'll shut up. I won't say another word."

"Now you sound like a two-year-old."

Should she ask her what she was doing for the February break? She didn't dare, not right now. Zoey had had a bad day with her cramps. The best strategy was to wait until Zoey felt better. Maybe tomorrow.

But that night she wasn't able to sleep. She kept going over and over what she might have done wrong, how she could have said things better or been funnier or . . . or anything, anything at all.

She'd stopped trying to get good grades because good grades were for the make-believe girls. She didn't make an effort to look better or wear makeup; she didn't talk about boys. At least with Abby she'd known what had happened to change things: Cassidy. There hadn't been anything she was able to do about that. But with Zoey there wasn't any reason. It didn't make any sense.

As her brain was racing, she heard Zoey getting out of bed and assumed she was going to the bathroom. But the bathroom on their floor was right next door to their room while Zoey's footsteps were going in the opposite direction down the hallway toward the stairs.

Where could she be going at 1:00 in the morning? Karen didn't think for long; she got up and followed her, heading for the stairs herself.

Halfway down she heard: "I want to make a collect call, please."

She stopped and stood still.

"To David Spalding. It's his daughter."

Calling her father at 1:00 in the morning? Why? Was she in some kind of trouble? Was that the reason she'd been so difficult lately? Karen held her breath, waited.

"Dad—hi . . . yeah, I know it's late, but I figured you'd be up. Did you manage to . . . ? Is everything . . . Canada? Really? . . . I know, I know . . . No, but I can remember, OK? . . . OK. Got it. Can you fix flights for us? Her last name is Thomas. As in Thomas the boy's name. And her first is Cassidy. C-a-s-s-i-d-y. And can you get a room for us in a hotel or motel or something? Thanks, Dad, I . . ."

Hearing the word "thanks," Karen knew the call might be over soon, so she crept back up the stairs, then ran to their room and climbed into bed.

Two minutes later she heard Zoey return and climb into hers.

Zoey and Cassidy were going to Canada together. Over the February break, obviously. Zoey's father was probably doing some film there.

Karen curled up and smothered her face with a pillow. If she kept the pillow over her face long enough, maybe she'd stop breathing and this misery would stop too.

So there *was* a reason after all. The same reason as always.

Cassidy Thomas.

Chapter 37

Cassidy

She'd never been a liar before. When she got into trouble, she admitted to whatever she'd done and took any punishment from her father. When he grounded her for a week, she stayed home and suffered without complaining. She didn't try to weasel out of anything. Up until now, she'd thought she'd had principles. Maybe not amazing ones, but still— some. Lying didn't come naturally to her. But it was beginning to.

She was lying to Jeb, to her father, to Abby: the three people she was closest to. There were good reasons for doing so, she understood that. But it still felt shitty. Everything did.

The reputation she had for being streetwise was based more on the fact that she was practical than anything else. She'd had to work in the summers, and she'd had to figure out a lot of things by herself because her mother wasn't around. The other girls could daydream the whole time. She couldn't, except about her life with Jeb.

That daydreaming hadn't turned out so well. If she'd been streetwise, she wouldn't have had sex with him without a condom. Now she was paying the price for being like the others and letting herself live in a fantasy world.

Zoey had made her think practically again. She'd been the one who set up the abortion and worked it all out. They'd be going to Canada next week and getting it done there, where there was a real doctor who could do it safely.

Her morning sickness hadn't been too hard to hide; after breakfast they had ten minutes before classes started. She'd found a bathroom near the music room no one ever used and went there to throw up. The only lucky thing about her pregnancy was the fact that the sickness was only in the morning. She could deal with being tired occasionally.

Abby didn't suspect anything. No one did. She and Zoey had steered clear of each other so no one would wonder anything. Anyway, all the gossip recently had been about Karen ratting out Becky and Becky lying.

Little did poor Becky know that her lie was nothing compared to all the lies Cass had had to tell. Like pretending to Jeb that she had to go home to Minneapolis for the February break and pretending to her father that she was going to the Madisons'. Zoey had told her she could call Jeb and her father from their hotel room when she had to, just not collect.

What would have happened if Zoey hadn't figured out she was pregnant? If she'd been paired with someone less smart on the Friendship Weekend? If Zoey's father hadn't offered to pay? Would she have told Jeb the truth? But if she had, where would she be now?

She could hear someone playing "Born to Be Wild" on their stereo.

She'd always felt older than the rest of them. Now she felt like she was a hundred. They were playing records and thinking

about dances and boys and February break, and she was thinking about an abortion.

The only way to get through it all was to blank it out. She'd
managed to do that pretty well with her mother. Any time she
missed her with a terrible longing, she'd wipe it all out, as if
she were erasing some math equation on a blackboard. Except for times with Jeb and when she went and talked to Mr. D.,
she never mentioned her mother. She never cried. She wiped
it out.

She had to go with Zoey to Canada and get it done and forget about it.

No crying, no what-ifs.

Just wipe everything out.

Chapter 38

FEBRUARY BREAK

Abby

Abby had lied to her parents, telling them that she was visiting Karen for the day midway through the February break.

"That's nice," her mother said. "You haven't been seeing much of her lately, have you? I always liked her."

It was a risk, she knew. Her mother had Karen's parents' phone number and might call them if something important happened and she'd be found out, but she was assuming that nothing important would happen, and she'd be home by 9:00 p.m. anyway, so she should get away with it.

Jimmy had a friend from school, Paul, whose parents were away, so the plan was to go to Paul's and stay there for the afternoon. Paul told Jimmy he'd go out and wouldn't come home until about 6:00 so that they could have time alone.

It was all planned out. The town where Paul and Jimmy lived was only a half hour bus ride away. The whole ride there all she could think was: *I'm going to be a Star.*

The biggest thing in her life so far was about to happen. Her nerves felt like they were all exploding.

Was she supposed to have bought sexy underwear? She hadn't.

She was wearing a normal white bra and underpants. And on top of that, normal jeans and a black turtleneck sweater and a blue peacoat. She didn't look or feel sexy, but how could she have dressed like a seductress when she was supposedly going to see Karen? And anyway, she knew she would never get the right seductress look.

The trip seemed to take forever. She kept wondering what she'd feel like afterward. A woman? What was that supposed to feel like?

She pictured herself going back to Stonybridge the next Sunday, walking into the Senior Room, and putting a star beside her name. Who would be there when she did? Would they cheer? Cross-examine her? What would Cass say? Would everything in her world change?

When she finally got off the bus, Jimmy was there to meet her. They were both nervous and shy and awkward with each other.

"This is . . ." He didn't finish the sentence. He had borrowed his parents' car—a Mercedes—and all the windows were open even though it was freezing outside. Which was fine by her, because she was starting to sweat and then starting to panic because she was sweating.

"How far away are we?" she asked.

"About ten minutes." He turned on the car radio and "Brown Eyed Girl" came on.

She loved that song, but right then she hated it because she had blue eyes, so she wasn't that girl behind the stadium worth singing about.

She was a tomboy. What she really wanted was to get out of the car at Paul's house and find a basketball net and shoot a few hoops. Or throw a football. She knew how to do those things. She didn't have any idea how to have sex for the first time.

It was a brick house with a yard out front, on a typical suburban street. Paul had left the door unlocked for them, but she felt like a

thief when they went in. It was immaculate and full of family photographs, and the kitchen had a monster fridge and a round white
Formica table with three orange swivel chairs placed around it. She
sat in one while Jimmy got two glasses out of a cupboard and filled
them with water.

"If you don't want to do this," he said as he placed a glass in front
of her, "it's OK."

"No. I do. I mean, you know, yes, I do want to do it."

"Then"—he reached out his hand to her—"let's go upstairs."

"With the water?"

Dumb question. What a dumb, dumb question.

"I guess," he answered. "Maybe not. I don't know."

They both stared at the glasses of water.

"Let's leave the water," he finally said.

She took his hand.

They'd had a lot of make-out sessions, but none of them had been
like this. It had always felt natural with Jimmy. But they were creeping up the stairs together and she could feel his hand shaking. Or
maybe it was hers shaking.

"This is Paul's room on the right," he said when they reached the
landing. She followed him inside. It was painted purple and black
and looked as out of place in that house as a room could be. Like an
opium den. He had black sheets on the bed too. She wondered if he'd
bought them himself. And what Jimmy and he had in common. Did
they come up here and smoke dope?

"This is really . . ."

"Far-out, I know." Jimmy smiled. "Paul's a trip."

"Right."

Now they were both staring at the bed.

"Come here," he said, and pulled her to him and kissed her. For
the first time that day she felt normal. In the middle of the kiss, he

pulled her down gently to the bed and they began to do what they'd always done—make out with a vengeance.

After a couple of minutes he pulled off her sweater, then his gray one. And unzipped her jeans. Then every piece of her clothing was off.

This is it, she thought. She watched him as he got a rubber out of his pocket, then took off his own jeans, then got the rubber out of its wrapping.

She turned her face away as he tried to put it on. She didn't know how long it was supposed to take him, but she knew it was taking too long because he was swearing.

And then he stopped swearing and climbed on top of her. And started kissing her again.

She felt him enter her: it wasn't as painful as she'd feared. Just weird. She felt him move a little, up and down, inside her. And then he made a noise and then he wasn't inside her anymore.

"Are you OK?" he asked.

She was too confused to answer.

"Was that all right, Abby? I mean, I know that was . . . but you know it's my first time too and . . ."

It's over?

That was it?

"It's fine. I'm fine," she mumbled.

"Are you sure?"

She nodded.

"Next time, I mean . . ."

"OK."

She turned her face away again as he dealt with the used condom. What was supposed to happen next?

"Right, well—" He was sitting beside her on the bed. "Paul might come back early. Maybe we better get going."

"Right." She sat up. "I'll get my clothes on."

Would she have to do that again? Could they go back to just making out? But how could she ask him to go backward?

As she was dressing, she snuck a look and saw he was smiling. He wasn't a virgin anymore—she could tell he was thinking that. And she should have been smiling and thinking that too.

Instead all she felt was disappointment.

"You're not disappointed, are you, Abby?"

"No. No, that was great."

Should she go over to him, kiss him, lie some more?

Was something wrong with her? Was that why it had been so . . . so . . . flat?

Was it her fault?

Did she have to add "Unsexy" to the list of her Uns?

She'd have to talk to Cass. Cass could fix any problem.

Chapter 39

Cassidy

It wasn't until they arrived in Montreal that wiping everything out of her brain became impossible.

Zoey's father had set it all up. He'd arranged for a taxi to pick them up at the Montreal airport and take them to a hotel.

"He's got us a room for three nights," Zoey had told her on the plane.

They'd stayed in Zoey's mother's house in New York for the first couple of days of vacation, then Zoey told her mother a version of the truth: "Dad suggested we go meet him in Canada. He's got some work there or something. He thought it might be fun."

"Well, will wonders never cease? Your father making an effort? That's a first."

Luckily Mrs. Spalding had left it at that.

"Anyway," Zoey told Cassidy, "we get to the hotel around eleven and then he's coming to pick us up around noon and we'll go with you to the place—it's in the suburbs somewhere—and then he and I will go out for a little while . . . then we pick you up and take you back to the hotel and you and I hang out there for the next few nights and then fly back to New York in the morning."

"He's coming with us to the place?"

"Yeah. I guess he wants to make sure it looks OK. It should be. There's a good doctor in Canada who does these things. But not for people like you—I mean, teenagers. So it's kind of an offshoot of his regular place, if you know what I mean."

Cassidy wasn't sure she did understand, but what difference did it make? All that mattered was it wasn't in some back alley and it wasn't being done by some quack.

The hotel Zoey's father had arranged for them turned out to be the Ritz-Carlton. She'd never stayed in an expensive hotel before. If she hadn't been so nervous, she probably would have had a blast. She might have ordered tons of food from room service or maybe she would have sat in the lobby watching all the rich people come in and out. Instead she sat on the bed, staring out the window, trying not to think. Zoey had turned on the TV and was sitting beside her, commenting on how silly the show was every two seconds.

An hour—that was how long they had to wait, but it felt like forever. It had begun to rain, tiny little drops running down the windowpane. And then what? Landing splattered on the sidewalk below. Dead? Was there such a thing as a dead raindrop? Or did it not count because it was only a bunch of cells?

What was Jeb doing now? Yale didn't have this week off. Was he in some class listening to some professor talk about some book? Probably. He wouldn't be staring out the window; he'd be paying attention and taking notes. He'd be happy to be there with all those other smart people.

She shouldn't be angry about that. All this . . . it was making her feel things she shouldn't.

She had to stop thinking.

"This soap opera is so ridiculous it's almost funny," Zoey commented. "Look—that guy there is in love with his wife's sister, and the sister is in love with her own brother except it really isn't her brother. At least I think that's what's happening."

Cassidy pulled Jeb's watch out of her pocket and looked at it. "It will tell *our* time," he had said.

What was he doing now?

Stuffing the watch back inside her pocket, she sighed, grabbed one of Zoey's Marlboros, and lit it.

"It's weird you've never met my father before." Zoey lit one too. "Be prepared. He looks about seventeen years old."

"You've told me that a thousand times. And I've seen that photograph."

"Yeah, but I bet you'll still be surprised."

I don't give a fuck what he looks like, she thought. *I want to get this over with.*

"I wonder what you'll think when you meet him. He's different, you know? A hippie. The complete opposite of my mother, the WASP witch. She's such a shitty parent, she hates kids, she should never have had . . ."

Zoey left the "me" hanging, catching herself in time. But not enough in time.

Are you serious? Do you really wish she'd had an abortion— that she had once sat like I'm sitting now, waiting to get rid of you?

But that was what happened, she knew. People said and did the wrong things when they were nervous. She'd lost count of the number of insensitive things people had said when her mother died.

If you don't know what to say, don't say anything. She'd wanted to scream it then, and she wanted to scream it at Zoey now.

But she had to remember that Zoey was helping her.

She shouldn't be angry.

She couldn't be.

"What are you and your father going to do while I'm . . . you know?"

"I'm not sure."

"But you'll be there when I get out, right? Promise me? I need to get out of that place as quickly as possible when it's over, OK? I need you to be there for me."

"I'll be there. I promise."

"Thanks."

Cassidy inhaled as deeply as she could, then pulled out Jeb's watch again and held it tightly.

Chapter 40

Zoey

Zoey kept her eyes on her father when she introduced Cass to him. She saw him step back a little, startled. He hadn't expected this beauty, and she'd bet a lot of money that he was imagining exactly how the camera would react to her face. But he got his act together quickly, shook Cass's hand, and guided them through the lobby to the car waiting outside.

There was a chauffeur sitting in the driver's seat, so he took the passenger one while she and Cass both climbed into the back. *At least he hasn't brought Shelley,* she thought. That was a big bonus.

"So how's that school treating you?" He turned around in his seat so he was facing them. "Is it a prison? Do the girls spend their nights secretly digging tunnels for an escape route?"

"Yeah, and then we ride motorcycles over barbed wire fences."

"Cool catch, Zoey. You know the book that *The Great Escape* was based on was written by an Australian guy. He was in the camp, but he was too claustrophobic to take part in the escape. Crazy. Great, great film."

Make a reference to another film, she wanted to say. *Then I can answer you and you can say "cool catch" again.*

"Thank you for doing this, Mr. Spalding," Cass said quietly.

"It's all right, Cassidy. You needed help and I could get it for you. And I'm David."

"I'll pay you back, I promise. I'm used to working, and I'll do whatever I have to to pay you back as soon as possible."

"I'm sure you will. Don't worry about it."

"Thanks. Really. Thanks very much."

"You're welcome."

Cass's voice had been shaky. She turned her head and stared out the car window. Was she crying?

Cass would keep her promise to pay her father back, Zoey knew. Cass wasn't someone who'd go back on a promise.

Zoey looked at her father. He was wearing bell-bottom jeans and a white turtleneck sweater. He didn't have any beads around his neck, but he could still be a teenager, someone who'd be standing in line waiting to be paired up at one of their school dances.

He'd made promises he hadn't kept. She wondered if he remembered any of them.

"I'll take you to Rome when you're eighteen," he'd told her one morning when he had walked to school with her. She must have been about ten years old. "Eighteen is a good age to go to Rome. There's a restaurant there I went to when I was a teenager. If it's still there, I'll take you to that."

"Your mother is a hopeless driver. So when you first start to learn to drive, I'll give you lessons. We'll drive out here, to Long Island, how about that? It will be easier on the roads here than in Manhattan."

She'd been eleven when he'd said that. He and her mother had brought her with them to some friend's house in Sag Harbor. After lunch, he'd taken her out onto the beach and built really terrible sand castles. They'd both laughed at how bad they were.

"I can't build a sand castle worth a damn, but I can drive like the wind. I will be a masterful driving instructor."

He'd given her that crappy scarf for her eighteenth birthday.

He'd never mentioned driving lessons again.

Still—for once he'd delivered. He'd gone out of his way to do all this: it was amazing enough that he'd set it all up and was paying for it, but the fact that he'd actually come himself was incredible. And this would be the most time she'd spent with him in ages.

"Speaking of escapes, if I were younger and eligible for the draft, I'd probably run away here to Canada," he stated. "People have to keep coming up with schemes to avoid it. I know some who are starving themselves so they'll be underweight, others who are getting psychiatrists to write letters saying that they're queer. It's ludicrous, this war. No, it's obscene."

"Nixon's obscene. LBJ was obscene. They're all obscene."

"Not all of them, Zoey. McCarthy was a hero. And even though I wasn't a big fan of Bobby Kennedy's, if he hadn't been assassinated, he would have stopped this insanity. What do you think, Cassidy?"

"What?" She turned away from the window.

"What do you think about the war?"

"I don't."

"You don't what?"

"I don't think about it. Sorry."

"You're not interested in politics?"

"No."

"It's not your bag?"

"It's not my bag."

"That's a funny expression, isn't it?" Zoey cut in. "I wonder where it came from."

"I have no idea." Her father turned back around then. "How far away are we?" he asked the driver.

"About twenty-five minutes."

"Excuse me, girls, but I have a script to read." Leaning over, he picked up a sheaf of papers from beneath his feet.

He had dismissed them in a way that was sadly familiar to her. Cassidy had no interest in politics, so he had no desire to talk to her—Zoey could understand that—but what he hadn't done was turn to his daughter and continue the conversation.

For a few seconds she'd been almost happy.

What would it be like after they dropped Cass off? Would they sit not speaking while he continued to read scripts?

What was Cass feeling now?

And what was it like to love someone who loved you back?

Chapter 41

Karen

No Doz. Pills that worked. You took them and they kept you awake, but more importantly they kept you from feeling hungry. And you could get them from any drugstore. Easily. Why hadn't she thought of them before? The day after she'd come home for the February break she'd gone to the drugstore to buy some Tampax and there were two college-age guys in front of her. One had a packet of No Doz, and after he paid for it, he turned to his friend and said: "These little magic pills will keep us up and running and we won't even have to spend money on pizza because we won't want to eat."

Bingo.

Two birds killed with a supply of white pills. She'd lose weight and she'd catch up on the studying she hadn't done. Even though she didn't want to be one of the make-believe girls, she didn't want to go to some shitty junior college either.

No Doz. Amazing. Her mother didn't get on her case anymore because she wasn't eating much, and at night, after she'd studied, she'd stay up and think about what she would do when she got back to Stonybridge.

Most importantly, she'd decided that she had to play it cool. Why hadn't she thought of that before? If she stopped trying so hard to please Zoey, Zoey would start to think again. She'd wonder why Karen was being remote and standoffish. She'd miss her.

Zoey and Cassidy might have had their fun in Canada, but when they got back, Abby would be around and Karen would have put a lot of money on the fact that Cassidy wasn't going to abandon Abby for Zoey. Not at school. Maybe for a trip to Canada to watch some movie being made or something, but not back at school. Cassidy wouldn't give up those summer weeks on Long Island. No chance. She was a manipulative bitch and a user. She'd want to hang out with Abby and her family.

Jeb. A lot of her fantasies in the past had centered around him.

By the summer, with enough No Doz, she'd look like Twiggy. Jeb would come to the graduation and he'd see her and he'd be stunned. *Is that Karen Mullens?* he'd ask. *Wow. What happened?* And he'd come up to her and give her a hug and say, *Hi, Karen. How are you? I've missed having you around.*

The great part was that she wouldn't care. Jeb was an inane prepster with no soul. He didn't feature in her dreams of the future anymore.

But it would still be a buzz to see how his opinion of her changed.

The point was, her whole world was going to change. When you were thin, everything was different. People looked at you differently. They didn't stare and think: fat. They stared and thought: Twiggy. Cool. Hip. Amazing.

Zoey would be proud of her.

It would be a good idea to go to different drugstores and stockpile No Doz just in case the woman at the local drugstore started asking questions.

She'd ace her SATs, get 800s, and then decide which college she actually wanted to go to. Maybe Oberlin. That was a cool place. Zoey would love it there. It would be perfect. They could keep rooming together. They'd spend all their time together and have a blast and decide what they'd do next together when they got out of college.

No Doz.

Bingo.

Chapter 42

Cassidy

It looked like a small office building from the outside, not a place where they would abort babies. That was reassuring, she guessed. Women wouldn't be scared if they were going into a clean building, the type of building where normally men would sit in white shirts, adding up sales figures.

When they got out of the car and went in, they were directed to the third floor. She wanted to walk up the stairs, not take the elevator. It would take longer to walk. And she probably wouldn't see anyone else. On the elevator there might be other people, staring.

So they walked up. She was behind Zoey and her father, counting the steps. If she concentrated on counting, she wouldn't have to think.

Block it out. You're walking up some stairs. That's all.

Normal, everyday stairs.

There was a sign on the door to the left that read "Clinic" on it. They walked through the door, into a waiting room. Which could have been any waiting room. A dentist's or a waiting room for people who were going to have their eyes tested.

"I'll take care of this," Zoey's father said. "You two sit down."

He went over to the reception desk while she and Zoey sat down on two of the chairs. There were bowls of flowers on the table in front of them. It took her a second to realize they were fake.

No one else besides the middle-aged receptionist was in the room. There were no pictures on the beige-colored walls. She watched as Zoey's father spoke to the receptionist, saw the woman glance over at her, then focus her attention back on him.

"Are you OK?" Zoey asked.

She nodded.

She was OK. She was sitting in a chair. That was all she was doing. Sitting in a normal chair. In a normal waiting room.

She and Jeb were in the car on Thanksgiving morning. She remembered it so clearly, the way he'd kissed the back of her neck, how tightly he'd hugged her.

She put her hands on her stomach, then took them off.

A bunch of cells.

Zoey's father came up to them.

"You're all set. A nurse is going to come in a second and take you with her and it will be about four hours because you have to have time to rest afterward."

She nodded again.

"We'll come back and pick you up around five."

"Thanks."

She was staring at the fake flowers. Her heart felt as lifeless as they were.

A woman wearing white slacks and a white blouse was standing in front of her.

"You can come with me now," she said.

Zoey gave her a quick pat on the shoulder, got up. Started to move away.

"We'll be back soon," Zoey said. "I'll be waiting for you when you come out."

No. No. Please don't go. Please don't leave me. But she said it only to herself. She closed her eyes. Then she opened them and stood up too.

Chapter 43

Zoey

"So, we're going back to the city now and visiting a friend of mine in his apartment. You're cool with that, right?" her father had said as soon as they got back into the car.

"Sure." She'd nodded, thinking at least he wouldn't abandon her back in the hotel room and go read his scripts by himself.

The apartment turned out to be a penthouse with floor-to-ceiling glass windows that led out to a terrace and overlooked the city. If it hadn't been raining, she guessed everyone would be sitting out there. Instead they were lounging around the huge living room, splayed on sofas and the floor. One long-legged blond girl was sitting in a hanging basket kind of chair.

The "friend" had a lot of other friends there. It was a party, obviously. Which was pretty strange considering it was a weekday afternoon, but then her father's friends didn't keep the same hours most people did. They were all, she figured, in their twenties or thirties. Most of the girls/women were wearing peasant blouses and jeans; some were in miniskirts with turtleneck tops. The boys/men all had long hair and wore jeans.

The minute she'd entered the apartment, a wall of smoke had hit her. It could have been the Senior Room except for the furniture, the view, and the fact that it was marijuana smoke.

"Kyle—" Her father had led her over to one of the guys who looked to be in his thirties. He was sitting on a sofa, a joint in his hand, his arm around a girl who looked a little like Buffy Sainte-Marie. Kyle had a ponytail and could have been Racetrack if he weren't so clearly rich. "This is my daughter, Zoey."

"Groovy." He gave her a peace sign. "Welcome to my humble abode."

"It doesn't look so humble to me," she'd replied. He'd laughed, and so had her father.

"Take a seat." Kyle waved. "Anywhere. David, we can talk later, yeah?"

"Sure."

"Hey, David," a male voice called out. "Come sit here with us."

Again, she let her father lead her, this time across the room to a man who was sitting on the floor. Unlike most of the men, who were wearing paisley shirts, he had on a red-and-black-checked lumberjack top. His pale blond hair was surprisingly short, and his eyes looked capricious.

"Move over," Lumberjack said to the girl to his right. She did, and Zoey and her father both sat down on the floor.

"Jesus. Great to see you here, David. I mean, nobody ever comes to Canada. This is a trip. Who's the chick?"

"This is my daughter, Zoey. Zoey, this is Larry. Larry's an actor. A damn good one."

"Gosh, a compliment. I'm blushing," he said, staring at her. He actually was blushing, but he looked more amused than embarrassed. "Wow. I can tell already. You're a feisty one, aren't you?" He had watched her as she sat down.

"So I've been told."

"What are you going to do when you grow up?"

"Not live in Canada."

"A feisty one indeed. I think I'm in love." He switched his gaze to her father. "Is she allowed to smoke, man? I mean pot?"

"I'm not sure about that."

"I've smoked pot before," she stated. "Plenty of times. I'm eighteen now, Dad."

"What can I say? There are no rules for this parenting gig anymore." He shrugged.

"OK, then." Lumberjack pulled a joint out of his pocket. "Let's get high. Or in my case, higher."

It was strange sharing a joint with her father, but she wasn't going to back away from it. Still, she didn't watch him as he inhaled, and she kept her eyes averted from his when she inhaled too. Lumberjack kept glancing from one to the other, smiling.

"Must be the season of the witch."

Lumberjack was singing along to the song unselfconsciously. She couldn't figure him out. Was he trying to do an unscripted audition for her father, or was this just him?

"Zoey—" her father said after exhaling a puff. "You're not going to tell your mother about this, right?"

"Of course not."

"Good."

When they'd finished the joint, Lumberjack stood up, held out his hand to her.

"Come on, let's get something to eat. And don't worry, man. I'll take good care of her."

"You better." Her father tilted his head to the side, rubbed his chin. "I haven't."

Lumberjack laughed.

Her father laughed.

She started to laugh.

The three of them stayed laughing for a long, long time.

Chapter 44

Cassidy

She woke up in a windowless room. The walls were painted white; there were no pictures or mirrors. She was dressed in a blue type of gown. Her head felt heavy. Her body felt numb.

It took her only one second to remember.

The same woman who had taken her out of the waiting room was sitting in a chair beside her.

"So. You're awake. That's good."

Is it? she wanted to ask, but she didn't. From the moment she'd followed this woman out of the waiting room to the back, she hadn't said one word. She'd done everything she'd been told to do without speaking.

"You've had some very special treatment today, young lady. I hope you've learned something."

She stared up at the ceiling.

"I'll take your blood pressure and temperature now, and if that's all right, you can go. Your clothes are over there—" She pointed to a chair in the corner. "The waiting room is two doors down on the left. You need to see a doctor in a couple of weeks to make sure you're all right. There's a piece of paper on top of your clothes that has some advice for how to cope with the next few days. And some painkillers. Needless to say, I hope never to see you again."

You sound so angry. Why are you working here? Why did you take this job?

"Right. Your blood pressure is fine. So is your temperature. You can get dressed and get out."

The bitch left.

The ceiling was white, but there was a patch of what looked like mold in the corner.

Why weren't there any windows?

Why hadn't they fixed that patch?

How long could she stay lying here before the bitch came back?

She sat up. Swung her legs over the table. Looked over at her clothes.

After today she'd never put them on again.

Dressed, and with the piece of paper in her hand, she walked back toward the waiting room.

Don't think about it. Zoey and her father will be there and we'll be back at the hotel soon and I won't ever think about it again.

But if it was only a bunch of cells, why do I feel so lost?

And why am I crying?

The receptionist was still at her desk.

The waiting room was empty.

Chapter 45

Zoey

The party had begun in the morning and was going to keep going all day. That was what Lumberjack had told her as they sat side by side on the kitchen counter sharing a bowl of ice cream.

"It's Kyle's birthday, and he thinks celebrating in the night doesn't do justice to it, you know? He wanted the whole day."

"Makes sense." She nodded. "Who is Kyle anyway?"

"Never met the guy. He's a friend of a friend."

"He knows a lot of people."

The doorbell kept ringing, and more and more people came in while others stumbled out. All of the females, she'd noticed, looked like singers. There were a lot of Joan Baezes and Joni Mitchells. There were no Mama Casses but one semi–Janis Joplin fuzzy-haired woman who was slouched in a corner and was clearly spaced-out on more than pot.

Maybe a lot of them were on stronger drugs. It was hard to tell.

"Yeah." Lumberjack nodded. "Kyle does know tons of people. He has a ton of money too. I'd call him a capitalist pig, but he seems to like sharing it, so I'll give him a break."

"Have you read *Das Kapital?*"

"Yeah, but I can't remember, how does it end?"

He was funny and different. She liked hanging out with him. They'd been shooting the breeze for a while now, talking about Vietnam, obviously, but also about his childhood growing up on Prince Edward Island, how remote it was, how he missed it but didn't miss it at the same time. And she'd been telling him about the poets she loved.

All pretty heavy, yet somehow they'd managed to keep it light and she was liking every minute of it.

And she found herself thinking how ironic it was that she was the one who had started the List and she wasn't a Star. Of course she put one beside her name with a 4 rating, knowing no one was going to ask her for any details. They wouldn't have dared.

Not now, of course, not with her father there, but maybe someday she'd see Lumberjack again and maybe then . . .

One of the look-alike folk singers had come into the kitchen handing out glasses, followed by another pouring champagne into them.

She wasn't going to say no to that either.

It might not have been Rome or her actual birthday, but her father was treating her like a real adult, and for once in her life she was having fun.

"Hey, the rain has stopped. Do you want to go out on the terrace for a while?" Lumberjack asked.

"Sure," she replied.

They made their way back through the living room, where she saw her father having what looked like a serious conversation with Kyle, and out onto the terrace. A few of the other partygoers were out there too, smoking away.

There wasn't a pinpoint moment when she turned from slightly tipsy and high to drunk and hugely stoned. It must have been a gradual process. At some point she realized she had to sit down to stop her head from reeling and somehow ended up on Lumberjack's lap.

He was braiding her hair, and then suddenly he was standing up and she was standing up, supported by him, and they were back in the living room and some guy carried a cake into the middle of the room and people sang "Happy Birthday" and Kyle gave some speech that made people laugh and the room was fading in and out of her vision and she was seeing yellow spots instead of furniture and she decided she hated lava lamps, that they should be banned, and then she closed her eyes.

The next time she opened them, she was on a bed. Her father was sitting beside her.

"What happened?" Raising her head, she looked around the room. It was white, but there were sentences painted in black ink everywhere, trailing across the walls. She could make out "To thine own self be true."

"You passed out."

"Are they all Shakespeare quotes?"

"What?"

"All these—" She waved her hand at the walls.

"You need to get up. We should leave."

"No, wait." She sat up. "Wait a minute. How long have I been asleep? What time is it?"

"Seven."

"Seven . . . seven p.m.?"

"Yes. Shit, I guess I should have been keeping a closer eye on you." He sighed, pushed his hand through his hair. "Sorry. I got caught up with Kyle."

"Seven? But . . . wait a minute . . . Cassidy . . . oh fuck. Cass . . ."

"Don't worry. I sent the driver to pick her up. He was an hour or so late, but I checked and she's back in your room at the Ritz now. She's fine."

"No. Jesus, no. We've got to go. Now."

"That's what I just said." He laughed. "Wake up, Zo."

"I can't believe it. Shit."

The second she got up, she felt her head throbbing so badly it was as if someone had whacked it with a hammer.

"Oh Christ." She rubbed her forehead.

"That's what champagne in the afternoon will do to you."

"Where's Lumber— I mean Larry?"

"He deposited you on the bed and told me he'd been a perfect gentleman and that you should sleep it off for a while. Then he left. You know, I might just give him a part in my next film."

Was it all an audition? For my father's benefit?

Why am I even asking myself that when . . . ?

"I've got to get back to Cass."

"Sure." He began to walk to the door. She followed him.

"Groovy party, right?" he said over his shoulder. "I bet you never forget today."

Chapter 46

Cassidy

Zoey burst into the room coming up with every apology in the book. There was this crazy party her father had taken her to. She'd been stoned, she'd been drunk, she'd passed out. She'd had no idea what time it was. It was her father's fault for not waking her up before. But it was the first time her father had taken her to something like that and she wanted to be an adult and . . . and . . . and . . .

"Forget it," she cut in. "I don't want to hear about it."

"Are you OK? How was it? How are you feeling?"

Zoey was sitting at the bottom of the bed.

If she'd had the energy, Cassidy would have kicked her, sent her flying across the room. That might have shut her up.

"I don't want to talk about it."

"I didn't mean to leave you there. I was going—"

"I mean it. I'm not talking about it. Not now, not ever."

"But—"

"No buts, Zoey. You weren't there when I came out? Big deal. It's over. All I want to do is sleep and watch TV. Then get on the plane and go back to New York and then back to school. That's it. I'm not talking about it, OK? Got it?"

"OK."

Zoey looked frightened. It wasn't a normal Zoey look.

Cassidy didn't give a fuck.

She'd sat in that waiting room for an hour and a half. Crying the whole time.

She curled up in a ball and turned her face to the wall.

PART THREE

Chapter 47

2018
APRIL 24

It had been twelve days since I'd accepted her request and messaged her, so I was slightly surprised when I heard the ping, looked at my Messenger app, and saw her reply.

"So great to hear from you. Sorry it has taken me a while to get back to you, but life has been hectic here. I'm fine and everything is going well, but you must have a really exciting life in London. Do you travel all the time? Are you going anywhere exotic soon? I'm jealous xx."

I messaged straight back:

"Life is going well for me too, but I'm not going anywhere for a couple of months at least so you don't have to be jealous! What are you up to these days? Feeling old like I am?"

A few seconds and then a ping. Her words whizzed across the Atlantic.

"I'm feeling the way I think we all feel—twenty in our heads, a hundred and twenty in our bodies. So glad you're not going anywhere soon. Believe it or not, I'm coming to London at the beginning of May. I'd love to see you. It's been way too long. Are you free any time between May 2 and May 6? I really hope so. xxx."

What?

I stared at the message, reread it. She was coming to London?

Had she trapped me? It felt like it. I couldn't reply saying I wasn't going to be here when I'd just said I was.

Being friends on Facebook was one thing; meeting in person was another.

I took a sip of the glass of wine beside me.

Maybe I was being silly. What if, when she came, we did a little harmless reminiscing? We could laugh about Miss Chase's tweeds and cane, Miss Adams's scarves.

She must have been waiting for my reply.

"Fantastic," I typed. "You'll have to send me your flight details. I can pick you up."

I paused. Should I invite her to stay? No, that would have been too much.

"It will be so terrific to see you again xxx."

I finished typing, then hesitated, unsure whether to press Send.

Maybe I could make something else up. A visit to one of my children in the country. Was it clear from my Facebook page that all my children lived in London too? I doubted that, but—

Another ping.

"Hi—are you still there? It would be mind-blowing to see you in person. Mega groovy. Far-freaking-out! I'm wondering whether I should book a hair appointment and a mani-pedi before I come. I may be old, but I want to look my best for my classmate. We're all still teenagers at heart, right? How sad is that? xxx."

Laughing, I pressed Send.

What was I worrying about?

Forty-eight years had passed.

We were in a different century.

Chapter 48

1970
MARCH

Janet Lee

She stopped her car a ways down the driveway. She didn't want to be seen, not yet. She had to collect herself first. Not comb her hair or put on lipstick, but collect her thoughts. She didn't want to go in unprepared. When she'd left the school, she'd been full of purpose. Now she wasn't so sure this was a good idea. She needed time to think things through again.

It had been interesting to notice how much of a different atmosphere there was at Stonybridge now that the College Board time had arrived. The girls looked worried and nervous—for once. That was one of the things she couldn't understand about the school. Everyone was so casual. Yes, the girls went to classes and the teachers taught them, but aside from Tom, none of those teachers seemed to care, and neither did the girls. Even the athletic ones didn't really care about sports. They always lost the games they played against other schools.

Nothing she had said had made any impact. Almost from the moment she'd arrived, she'd felt tired and helpless and wished she'd never taken the job.

The only reason she had chosen Stonybridge in the first place was the location. She loved Lenox, the mountains, the whole ambience of a small New England town. She'd been at a day school in Philadelphia before, and when a job had come up that allowed her to get out of the city, she had taken it.

She should have known from the beginning, when Veronica Adams interviewed her, that this wasn't the place for her. The scent of Veronica's perfume had made her want to gag, and the way she waved her hands around in the air was disconcerting. The word was "fey." She had come across it in a book a few weeks after meeting Veronica, looked it up, and thought: *That's Veronica Adams in a nutshell: fey.* But she'd put aside all her worries because of Lenox.

Well, as it turned out, a pretty little New England town didn't save you from a school that allowed the students to get away with murder, to stroll in and out of town unsupervised, to smoke cigarettes brazenly in that ridiculous room of theirs, to act as if nothing actually counted. Even the rules that were there were blatantly disregarded. There was a skirt length for the uniform, for instance. But no, the girls went around with uniform skirts that were miniskirts. Did anyone pull them aside and tell them this wasn't allowed? Of course not. There was no discipline. The older female teachers had obviously lost whatever zeal they'd once had and kowtowed to a bunch of teenagers. It was depressing.

For a while, in the fall term, she'd thought that at least one person was on her wavelength—Tom. But as time went on, she saw that he had also capitulated. Which was even more depressing. He was someone who cared, she could tell, and yet he'd let the senior class run rings around him too.

The whole thing looked more and more like a shambles.

So she'd finally given up hope and applied to other schools for a job. The fact that she'd spent only one year at Stonybridge wouldn't look great on her résumé, but she could explain that in any interview. So far two schools—one in Vermont, one in Connecticut—had shown interest.

Leaving Lenox would be sad in a way, but staying on would be miserable. More miserable than she could ever have imagined.

Which was why she was here in her car.

From the moment she'd walked into Stonybridge, she'd been stereotyped by everyone, teachers and students alike. She was the Spinster Sports Teacher. Not as old as the other female teachers, but a dyed-in-the-wool spinster nonetheless, one who had made advances to Tom Doherty and been rebuffed, the poor fool. Poor, poor Janet.

There were days she wanted to shout out, *No, it's not like that*, when she walked into the faculty lounge, but no one would believe her—least of all Tom—and she'd end up looking even more foolish. So she didn't. She let them think what they wanted to think.

And now it was March and spring was coming and soon the term would be over and she'd be gone. The object of ridicule among the students and other teachers would disappear, and they could all laugh about someone else for a change.

Tom wouldn't have to avoid her anymore; the students wouldn't whisper, "Is she a dyke? No, wait, she has a crush on Mr. Doherty, she can't be, but she looks like one." Veronica Adams wouldn't make it so clear every time she saw her that she was badly dressed. While at the same time not even bothering to look truly disapproving because really, how else would a female sports teacher dress but badly?

Female sports teachers were the lowest of the low. Worse than janitors, she decided. An outcast species, if ever there was one.

She was sick to death of being alone and shunned and avoided. What she was about to do wouldn't change anything, she knew. But at least there would be someone who had some idea of who she really was.

It was time to stand up for herself.

She restarted the car, drove all the way up to the front door, got out, and knocked.

When he answered the door, he took a step back in surprise and, she could see, horror. *Aha*, he must have thought, *she's come to beard me in my den. How can I get her out of here as quickly as possible?*

"Janet," he said. "This is a surprise. I didn't know you were coming." He was dressed in blue corduroy trousers, a white shirt, and a pale green sweater.

"That might be because I didn't tell you I was. But don't worry, I won't stay long. There's no need to think of some excuse to get rid of me immediately."

"I wasn't—"

"Yes, you were. Can I come in and sit down, please?"

"Of course. Please." He ushered her inside. "Take a seat. Can I get you something? Tea? Coffee?"

"How about a shot of whiskey? No, don't look so panicked again, Tom. I wasn't being serious. And I don't want anything to drink. I've come here to say something. After which I'll leave."

"Oh." He looked so confounded she almost took pity on him.

"Sit down. Really. This won't take long."

She watched as he sat down, then made sure she straightened up, sitting with the best posture possible. This wasn't a time to slouch.

"Tom, I want to make something clear. I was never interested in you romantically and never would be. Not that I'm a lesbian—

and believe me, I know people think I am, but I'm not. The funny thing is I share the same story as so many of the other female teachers here. I was engaged, and my fiancé was killed too. Not in any war, and God knows anyway whether those other fiancés existed, but who am I to ask? The point is, I actually had one. He died in a motorcycle crash.

"And I know I'm not a beautiful woman, not by any means, but I was actually loved, wildly loved, by a man who rode motorcycles. Can you believe it?"

"Janet—"

"Let me finish. He was a phys ed teacher too. Or sports teacher—whatever you want to call us. That's what we were, and that's what I am. Funny—when he was alive, I never felt I had to apologize for my job. Anyway, I have worked at various schools, but I have never experienced what I have at Stonybridge. I have never been treated like such dirt."

"Janet, please—" He half rose from his chair. She waved him back down.

"I was lonely when I came here, Tom. I didn't know anyone. For some crazy reason I thought you and I might be friends, that we shared some of the same values. I thought you realized that these girls need some discipline, some guidance and boundaries. I thought you were civilized. So, yes, I made an effort to see you. And I even called you on Thanksgiving because I was *really* lonely then. I'm not even going to get into my whole family situation. That's not the point.

"The point is you humiliated me. How could you assume I was after you for more than friendship? Really, Tom? Do you think I'm that naive?"

"I don't know what to say, Janet. I'm sorry if I hurt your feelings. I never intended to."

"What *did* you intend? If you'd bothered to talk to me for more than one minute instead of running away like a scared rabbit, you'd know I had no desire to rip your clothes off and screw you on the carpet."

"Janet!"

"Oh, give me a break. I'm not supposed to talk about sex, is that it? No one can mention sex in front of you? The quote confirmed bachelor unquote?"

"What is that supposed to mean?" He stood up. "I've apologized. What else can I do? Obviously it's too late for me to make it up to you now."

"You bet it is." She snorted.

"I don't like your tone. It's unbecoming. I think you should leave now."

"Unbecoming? That's rich." She stood up as well. They were facing each other. What had been supposed to make her feel better had only enraged her further. "I'm more than happy to leave. But one more thing, Tom: Stop pretending. Stop looking at Cassidy Thomas as if you are attracted to her. You're not and never will be. So stop pretending. Stop pretending you're something you're not."

Chapter 49

Abby

When the time came to put down her pencil, she did and took a deep breath. The SATs hadn't been a piece of cake, but they hadn't been awful either. She guessed that she'd done reasonably well, hopefully well enough to get into Vassar, which was her first choice of college.

Looking around at the other girls, Abby could feel the collective air of relief. It was over. They could go back to normal.

Miss Chase was picking up all the papers. Everyone could celebrate soon. A few more months and they'd be out of there and Stonybridge would be behind them. Even the weather was promising—a nice spring day.

But then she caught sight of Karen's sweaty face and wild eyes and her heart sank. What was going on with her? She'd lost a lot of weight, and she looked really sick. As much as Abby still resented Karen for calling her the Un Girl, she still cared about her. Mary had been wrong. You could care about someone and not know what to do to help. Karen had skipped a lot of the first morning classes recently and told Miss Rutgers, the nurse, that she had some bug.

Maybe, maybe not.

Had Karen screwed up her SATs?

Shit. If Karen doesn't get into a good college, will Mary think that's my fault?

As she stood and filed out of the room with the others, she saw Karen surreptitiously reach into her waistband, pull something out, and pop it in her mouth.

So she was taking some pill—maybe for the bug she had?

Maybe not.

If she's turned into an addict, is that my fault too?

Why doesn't Mary blame Zoey instead of me? Zoey is probably supplying the pills, whatever they are.

It's not my fault.

Cass, who was a few girls ahead of her in the line out, didn't seem in great shape either. She had been really quiet since the February break. She would have said something if there was anything really wrong, though. She was probably just worried about the SATs.

As she stepped out of the building into the sunlight, Abby began to sing, "We're out of the woods, we're out of the dark, we're into the light."

She stopped, remembering.

She and Karen had put on a silly skit back in freshman year based on *The Wizard of Oz.*

That night they'd had a pillow fight in their room and gone to bed exhausted from laughing so much.

Shit.

It's not my fault. It's not my fault. It's not my fault.

Chapter 50

Karen

Total concentration. She'd raced through the SATs, filling in bubbles. Writing. Doing it all so easily, her mind whirling away, her brain in fifth gear. Eight hundreds. No problem. No Doz.

The pounds were dropping off her. She could almost hear them thudding onto the ground. Gone. Oh—and there was another one dropping. Gone too.

Everything in her plan was working out. When she got back to Stonybridge after the February break, she'd been unbelievably cool. She hadn't asked Zoey how her week had been. Or even mentioned Cassidy's name. She wasn't going to fall into that trap. Besides, Zoey wasn't hanging around with Cass. However great their trip together to Canada had been, it hadn't rekindled their close friendship. Cassidy was back buddying around with Abby.

She knew Zoey was waiting for her to be the way she had been, but if she had been the way she'd always been, she would have fallen into the trap and Zoey would have sighed and rolled her eyes.

Everything was working. Zoey kept looking at her curiously. As if she couldn't understand the New Karen.

No way was she going to show Zoey all the poems she'd written to her over the February break. Not yet. She had to wait for the right time. Meanwhile, she watched. Taking everything inside her and keeping it close.

The way Zoey moved. How she'd put on her uniform, half the time getting her sweater the wrong way around. Or leaving a shoelace undone.

No one else saw how Zoey would cover her mouth with her hand when she yawned, then take it away and smile. As if she'd had fun yawning.

It wasn't Cassidy Thomas who was beautiful; it was Zoey Spalding.

Why was she the only one who saw that?

Maybe that was good, though. She was the only one who understood Zoey, the only one who really saw her.

And one day soon Zoey would wake up and be so happy to be so perfectly loved.

Chapter 51

Thomas Doherty

There were times when he thought that he and Cassidy had what some people might call a psychic bond, and this was one of them. Something had drawn him to go to the music room, and when he walked in, there she was, sitting in front of the piano, looking uncharacteristically disconsolate.

"Mr. D." She looked up at him. "Hi."

"We haven't met here for a while, have we, Cassidy?"

"No. How did you know I was here?"

"I didn't. Can I sit down?"

"Of course."

He took his usual seat beside her on the piano bench.

"How were the SATs?"

"OK, I guess."

"You were looking a little sad. Are you worried about them?"

"No. Not really."

"Are you worried about something else, Cassidy?"

She looked up at the ceiling as if she wanted to ask it a question. Then she lowered her eyes and looked straight into his.

"You know how you always say 'Beauty is truth, truth is beauty'? What does that mean exactly?"

"I'm not sure I can pin it down. It's a line from a poem by John Keats. In my opinion it's about the importance of truth. How truth enriches the soul."

"And everyone has a soul?"

"I would hope so."

"Even a bunch of . . ."

"A bunch of what?"

Now she looked down at the floor.

"Even a raindrop?"

"I'm not sure about that." He smiled. "I suppose a Buddhist might say a raindrop has a soul, but it's hard to imagine a raindrop having a soul."

"Right. OK."

"Why so philosophical, Cassidy?"

She shrugged, still studying the floor.

"You know, I've noticed you haven't been your usual ebullient self in class."

"You sound like Zoey. What does that word mean?"

"Upbeat. Full of the joys of spring. It *is* spring now, you know. SATs are over. You'll be graduating soon. There's a lot to be happy about."

When she didn't respond, he said, "Tell me—what's wrong? Look at me, Cassidy. You know you can talk to me."

"I guess . . . I don't know . . ." She didn't lift her gaze. "It's just that the truth isn't always beautiful. That's what I think. And sometimes . . . I don't know . . . I'm scared that you do things sometimes, things that aren't truthful—or beautiful—and they never go away. You want them to go away, but they don't."

"I think I know what you mean."

Janet Lee. He *had* behaved badly. The way she'd confronted him, what she'd said, had been uncalled for and ugly, but that didn't change the fact that he wished now he'd acted differently toward her.

"But time passes, Cassidy. Someone—actually he was a priest I knew when I was younger—he said something I've always remembered. He said that everything is redeemable. No matter what you've done or how bad you think you've been, it's redeemable. You can make up for it."

He could tell she was struggling with whatever thoughts she was having. He waited. When she finally looked up at him, he sensed her mood may have shifted.

"A real priest? And you really believe that?"

"Yes, a real priest. He was a Jesuit in fact, so that means he was a real, *real* priest, and I really believe that."

"That everything is redeemable? Really?"

"Yes." He nodded.

"Thank you." She exhaled, and her shoulders dropped. What had made her so worried that she now looked as though he'd rescued her from a firing squad?

"Cassidy, I—"

"No, really. Thank you, Mr. D."

"You're not going to tell me what's upsetting you, are you?"

"No. But you've made it better. And I better"—she stood up, grabbed her book bag—"get going now." She started toward the door, then turned around. "You're special," she said. "A really special man. I love you, Mr. D. In the right way."

And then she left.

Chapter 52

Zoey

Karen was driving her completely crazy. It wasn't like it was before. She wasn't copying everything Zoey did or hanging on her every word, but she kept looking at her. Which sounded ridiculous, she knew. People looked at each other all the time. They shared a room. Of course Karen would look at her. It was the *way* she looked, though. Expectantly. As if she were waiting. But for what? And it wasn't only expectant. It was *knowing*. Those brown eyes of hers were saying: *I know you better than you know yourself. And I'm waiting.*

But for what?

Some kind of announcement?

Yes, Karen, I am the Second Coming, and I have arrived to save the world, and you are my disciple. Together we will rescue all humanity.

Jesus Christ. It was chronic.

Not only that, Karen was popping pills like someone out of *Valley of the Dolls*. During the day she was wired; at night she'd sleep so soundly there was no point even attempting to wake her up for classes. Zoey had tried a couple of times, but it was as if she were trying to rouse a sleeping polar bear.

Of course she wasn't going to tell Miss Adams or anyone what was going on. Although there were times she'd been tempted, if only to get Karen out of the room. But telling on people wasn't her bag.

Her bag . . . That conversation with her father when they were driving Cass to that place . . . Cass. Who hadn't forgiven her for not showing up at the clinic that afternoon. Cass, who had never been outright angry at her but who was acting like she didn't exist. No, not that exactly. Acting like she knew her vaguely.

Well, Cass knows me well enough to count on the fact I'll never tell on her either. I'd never go into the Senior Room and say, "Hey, guys, guess what? Karen's an addict, and by the way Cassidy had an abortion in Canada."

So yes, she'd made a mistake and left Cassidy in the lurch that afternoon, but she was still trustworthy.

Crossing off another day on her calendar, she thought: *Only a little while longer. As of June 6, I'll never have to see Karen staring at me again.*

Chapter 53

Abby

There were a dozen or so girls in the Senior Room when she went up to the noticeboard.

"Uh-oh, drumroll . . ." Connie said. "I think Abby's about to join the crew."

"Look, look, she's blushing." Angel laughed. "She's definitely a Star. Wow, Abby! I think this deserves a round of applause."

They'd started clapping.

"Ah, but how's she going to rate it? Remember, Abby. No cheating. This is the life of your unborn child we're talking about. You can't pull a Becky and cheat."

Becky wasn't there. Becky rarely came into the Senior Room.

The pen was in her hand. She drew a star beside her name.

Could she lie?

That was why she had waited a month before putting the star up. The rating part. If she hadn't been superstitious, she would have marched in after February break, given herself a star and a 5. The problem was that she did kind of believe in stupid things like lucky charms and curses. What if she lied and something bad did happen to her first child?

The wise move would have been not to put the star up in the first place, but being able to put the star beside her name was the only good thing about the whole experience.

Zoey had threatened them in order to make them tell the truth, Abby knew. It was Zoey's way to have power over them. Only there *was* something witchlike about her. It was too easy to picture Zoey leaning over a cauldron, stirring and chanting. And actually getting something bad to happen.

Fuck it. I can't take the chance.

She wrote the number 1.

"Oh shit." Connie was behind her looking over her shoulder. "Sorry, Abby. Was it a total bummer?"

Cass *had* fixed all her problems. As soon as Abby came back to school after the February break, she rushed to their room and confided in her.

Cass shook her head and said, "Think of the first time you took a basketball shot. It was probably a long way from going in the net. You play enough and you improve. Don't sweat it, Abs." Then she'd frowned. "You were careful, right? You guys were careful?"

"Of course."

Weirdly, Cass had then stood up and left the room without saying where she was going. When she returned, she put a Richie Havens album on the stereo, lay down, and said, "I'm really tired. Do you mind if we don't talk about you and Jimmy and stuff now? I want to listen to this."

"OK. Are you all right? Sorry, I haven't asked about how it was at home. How's your father? Was Minneapolis really cold?"

"It was freezing. Can we not talk? Like I said, I'm really tired."

"OK."

They'd never talked about her and Jimmy since then either. Which didn't matter, not really, because Cass had solved the problem already with the basketball-shot analogy.

"It wasn't a total bummer," she told Connie. "We just need to practice, that's all."

"Oh, practice? Is that what you call it?" Connie smirked. "Are you going to practice with him or by yourself?"

"This is all horrible. You're all so immature." Mary Greene, who had been sitting quietly on one of the sofas, stood up. "You really think it's an accomplishment to get some guy into your pants. Really? An accomplishment? As if he isn't dying to get into any girl's pants? I feel complicit just being here."

She strode out of the room.

"Mary gets on her high horse," Connie commented. "I think we should call her Virgin Mary. Maybe she's a dyke."

"Maybe her fiancé died in the war," someone said.

Not Zoey. Zoey wasn't there. But it got the laugh Zoey would have gotten if she'd said it.

Abby didn't join in on the laughter. Not at first.

Chapter 54

APRIL

Karen

She'd read enough poetry by now to know that April was the cruelest month. It hadn't been for her, not to begin with anyway. Once the SATs were over, she could have stopped the No Doz, but she couldn't, not really. She needed to lose more weight.

That was cool, though, because she knew how to handle the No Doz, she was used to it and she liked the buzz and no one had given her any shit for skipping morning classes, but then again she'd run out of the Valium she'd stolen from her mother's bathroom cabinet, so she wasn't sleeping so late anymore in the mornings and she'd managed to wake up in time for a whole week, so why *would* they give her shit anymore, and because she was waking up on time she was living on a lot less sleep, but so what? Who needed sleep?

She was sitting in the Senior Room, right in the seat she'd been sitting in when she and Zoey had started talking that first day in September. She sat in it as often as she could, feeling the feeling, remembering. She'd hated that first cigarette. Now she chain-smoked when she could and she loved every puff.

Connie and Angel and Abby and Debby and Zoey and Cassidy were all there so it was pretty crowded but that was cool and anyway Cassidy and Abby's friendship didn't bother her anymore. The only person who counted was Zoey.

Debby was over by the noticeboard studying the List.

"Wow," she said. "Almost all of us are Stars now."

"Who's left?" Angel asked. "Besides Virgin Mary, I mean."

People laughed. They always laughed when someone called Mary Virgin Mary.

"Karen, Christ, you're a virgin too. You can stop laughing now," Zoey barked.

"Yeah, Karen, when are you going to lose it?" Debby turned away from the noticeboard. "Or are you holding on to it too? Waiting for true love?"

"Get off her back."

It was Cassidy defending her. She didn't want Cassidy Thomas defending her. Never, ever.

"I'll be a Star soon," she said. "You'll see."

"Really?" Zoey sounded surprised. "I mean, Karen. That's unlikely, isn't it? I, for one, would be genuinely astounded."

Is that what you want? For me to be a Star? You are my star. You are all the stars in the universe.

"So listen, guys. I've been thinking." Cassidy stood up. "Why don't we astound everyone and change the whole 'vote one of the teachers May Queen' tradition? Why don't we vote for Mr. D. and make him May *King?* We can start telling everyone now so when we vote next week it will be no contest. Miss Adams will have to go along with it because it's a democratic election, right?"

You're all the stars in my galaxy, Zoey. If you want me to astound you, I will.

No one was looking. They were all talking about Mr. D. She reached into her pocket and hunted for that little white pill.

Chapter 55

Cassidy

Had she liked going to these dances once upon a time? She knew she had, but she couldn't remember that feeling of excitement, getting dressed and ready to go and meet boys and listen to music. It was different, at least. Getting out of Stonybridge and going on a bus ride and getting matched up. The anticipation was fun.

But now, as she heard her name being called and she walked toward some boy and he walked to her, she felt sick. Why wasn't it Jeb walking toward her?

She hadn't seen him since before Canada. They'd talked, sure, but they hadn't been able to meet. He'd had to do stuff at Yale on the weekends, and she'd had to study for the SATs.

Maybe that was better. Because she had to feel better soon, and she had to be like her old self, the Cassidy he knew and loved.

Every time she talked to him, she felt the lie. It was there, always.

At first she'd been worried that Abby and maybe even some of the other girls would notice that she wasn't behaving the way she normally did. What was that word Mr. D. had used?

Bull-something? She didn't want to joke around or talk about the usual shit, so she kept quiet. But she kept wondering what she'd say when someone asked her what was wrong.

Except nobody ever did ask her. Not even Abby.

It didn't take her long to figure out why not. All they cared about was her being Cassidy. As long as she looked the way she looked, no problem. So what would happen to her popularity if she got in an accident and her face was scarred? Or if she gained a ton of weight? How would they feel about her then?

Sometimes she thought that the only one who cared about her as a person was Mr. D.

When the bus pulled up and they all got off and went and got matched with boys, all she could think was: *Why isn't this Jeb? I have to spend the night dancing with some schmuck who isn't Jeb.*

It turned out he was a schmuck. A little boy who thought he was a grown-up and tried to pull her too close whenever a slow dance started. She wanted to kick him in the balls. Instead, she asked him if there was any place she could go and have a cigarette, knowing there must be one and he'd tell her because he wanted to impress her and be cool.

They snuck out the side door of the gym and he took her hand to lead her around the back of the football field. If holding his hand was the price she had to pay for a cigarette, she'd pay it. If he tried anything else, she really would kick him in the balls.

"Hey."

Zoey and her "date" suddenly appeared beside them.

"Fancy meeting you here, Cass."

"I need a cigarette."

"So do I." She nodded her head toward her date, then whispered in Cass's ear: "He's a moron. They're all morons in this school. I think it's even worse than Stonybridge."

The guy was about six inches shorter than Zoey. Something had gone really wrong on the height-matchup plan. Cassidy almost laughed, but the thing of it was she didn't ever get to the point where she actually laughed anymore. That had to change too, she knew. Before she saw Jeb again she'd have to be able to laugh.

There was a shed out by the football field—at a boys' school there was always a shed—and they always went there to smoke. So the four of them stood, lighting up and puffing, leaning against the back wall of the shed.

Jeb would have given her his jacket to keep her from being cold, but the Schmuck wasn't Jeb.

Zoey was staring up at the sky.

"It's a full moon. Where are the werewolves when we need them? I bet you don't know that people suspected of being werewolves were put on trial in Switzerland the way people suspected of being witches were put on trial in Salem. But my question is: What makes someone suspect someone of being a werewolf? I mean, is it only being hairy? How hairy do they have to be?"

The two boys exchanged "Who is this crazy person?" looks. Cass came even closer to laughing. If she hadn't been so alone and lost and empty and miserable when Zoey broke her promise that day, maybe she would have actually laughed.

"In my opinion, werewolves are—" Zoey stopped and turned. They all did because the back of the shed faced some woods and someone was coming out of the woods toward them.

"Jesus. Karen," Zoey said just as Cass recognized her too.

Karen was stumbling toward them, weaving from side to side.

"Fuck," the Schmuck said. "What the hell is she—"

"I see you!" Karen yelled. "Zoey! You're smoking. Give me a cigarette. I need a cigarette."

"Karen—" Zoey started toward her.

"I'm a Star! I'm a Star! Give the Star a cigarette!"

Her hair was a mess; her dress, a hot pink velvet one, was a mess.

"I told you I'd be a Star! Where's . . ." She looked behind her. "What's-his-name. He'll tell you. I'm not making it up."

A boy appeared. His shirt was hanging out. He had a silver flask in his hand. He tossed it back into the woods.

"Tell them—whatever your name is—Tom? Is it Tom? No, Tim? Ted? Tommy? Teddy? Timmy? Fred? What's-your-name. Tell them I'm a Star."

Cassidy saw it all. His quick smug smile. And then his look of fear.

"We've got to get out of here. Now."

He was saying it to the other boys.

And then they ran. All three of the boys took off.

The little rats, Cass thought. *Little rat cowards.*

"I'm astounding!" Karen collapsed onto the ground and sat there with a crazy smile on her face. "Give me a cigarette."

"Here." Zoey sat down beside her, lit a cigarette, and handed it to Karen, who missed putting it in her mouth the first two times she tried.

Zoey looked up at Cass. "What are we going to do? She's drunk as a skunk."

"We have to cover for her somehow."

"How?"

"I'm astounding." The cigarette dropped out of Karen's hand. Cass stepped on it.

"OK, OK, you're astounding." Zoey put her arm around Karen's shoulder. "But you need to shut up for a second while we think."

"I'm a Star. I'm astounding."

Looking at Karen, Cass felt sick. What had the sex been like in those woods? Had she actually wanted to do it? Had that rat been careful? Jesus. Why had she ever thought before that sex wasn't a big deal? It was the hugest deal of all. It could hurt you in ways you never imagined.

"What are we going to do, Cass?" Zoey stared up at her. "She reeks of booze. She'll get kicked out. It's not like she's my best friend or anything even close, but I don't want her to get kicked out. Fuck . . . wait . . . let me think . . . OK, Miss Gambee is chaperoning tonight and she's not as bad as some of the others, but at some point she'll notice we're gone. So you should go back to the dance.

"While you're gone, I'll get Karen to stand up and walk around, try to walk it off. If Miss Gambee starts asking where Karen and I are, if she starts to look like she's looking around for us, head her off at the pass and tell her Karen was feeling sick and went out for some air."

"Head her off at the pass? Jesus, Zo, you sound like John Wayne. Anyway, then what? Miss Gambee will smell her. She smells like a bottle of scotch. How do we cover for her on the bus?"

Karen threw up. All over herself. It was so disgusting Cass almost threw up too.

"Well, now she smells of vomit so that takes care of that. Come on, let's get her up. Then you go." Zoey stood up, and together they took an arm each and hoisted Karen off the ground, but she sagged between them. And vomited again.

Karen wanted to be a Star badly enough to lose it to some
punk in the woods? So she could be what? One of the gang?

The lyrics barged their way into Cass's head: "When you're
a Jet, you're a Jet all the way. From your first cigarette to your
last dying day."

Chapter 56

2018

We were never going to send our children to boarding school even though it's more common in England and I know quite a few people who have. For starters, my husband is a Labour MP. Having a child at what they call a public school here would be against the Labour ethos. I didn't want to send our kids away either, and not just because of the horrible Stonybridge legacy.

Because:

You send your child away to boarding school.

Who do you get back?

The headmistress or headmaster and teachers have a duty of care, but how far does that go?

And how can you know they're not abusing it?

Even if they're not abusing it, how much do they truly care?

You've abrogated your responsibility, put it into the hands of others. You hope for the best, but you have no idea of what's going on day after day.

You can't see if your child is depressed; you're not there to ask her or him how their day went.

It's a lottery. Sometimes it works well and children prosper in that environment. These days there is a lot more interaction with parents and staff: parents can see their children more often, talk to them whenever they want to; but these days there are still scandals in boarding schools. Rapes, sexual harassment, drugs, alcohol, bullying—all possible in day schools as well, but with one difference. In a boarding school there's no parent on the scene.

A girl can get drunk, lose her virginity in a horrific way.

She can go home after a dance and be taken care of by her peers, not her parents. Her peers whose aim is to keep her from getting kicked out, not to counsel her. The peers who might know she's popping pills too but aren't about to tell on her.

There can be teachers and fellow students, a headmaster or headmistress, all these people who can try to take care of her.

But what if there's not one single person there who loves her?

Chapter 57

1970
APRIL

Karen

She was lying down across the back seats, her head on Zoey's lap. And Zoey was stroking her, running her hand down her hair, saying: "Shh. It's going to be all right, Karen. Shhh . . ."

And a couple of times in between the "shhs," Zoey said, "That fucking asshole, what a bastard," and the stroke of her hand would get heavier, but then she'd say "shh" again and her hand was light again and Karen kept her eyes closed and felt every second of every touch.

Then she felt Zoey's breath in her ear, a warm, soft breath smelling of old cigarette smoke, and she heard Zoey's whisper: "Everyone's getting back on the bus now. Keep quiet. Keep your eyes closed. When we get back to school, put your arm around me and groan. Like your stomach is killing you. Don't say a word until we get to the room."

She remembered telling Miss Rutgers that Zoey was sick that day of the afghan coat, how Zoey had cried when she found out the coat wasn't hers.

Zoey had never cried in front of anyone else, Karen was sure of it. Zoey would never stroke anyone else's hair.

Nothing else mattered. That boy in the woods didn't matter. It had all been so ugly and awful and it hurt and she hated it, but none of that mattered.

She'd passed a test. And now she was in a haze of hair-stroking and Zoey and love.

Chapter 58

Thomas Doherty

Veronica's office had a surprisingly small desk. Of course it was antique. Doubtless French. It looked dainty and old and ridiculously out of place. How could she work at it? Was it there to impress future parents? Would any of them really decide to send their daughter to Stonybridge because the headmistress had a bijou desk?

She was wearing a beige suit with a white blouse and a dark brown scarf. Brown didn't suit her, which was off-putting because normally everything she wore suited her.

Still, he was resolved to talk to her, regardless of what she was or wasn't wearing.

"What can I help you with today, Tom?" she asked, her pale blue eyes looking uninterested. Bored, even. It was time she retired.

"I'm worried about Karen Mullens. She's been skipping a lot of morning classes. And now she comes to them but her mind isn't engaged. It's as if she were somewhere else. She keeps looking out the window and smiling to herself. Daydreaming, I suppose."

"Yes, I heard about her skipping classes. But I also know she's not skipping anymore. And she took the SATs."

"Yes, she did take them. However, that's not the point. Something is clearly wrong with her. The way she's acting is unhealthy."

"Unhealthy, Tom?" Her eyes narrowed. And he could see the beginnings of a smile. "Daydreaming is unhealthy? That would mean all our students are sick, wouldn't it?"

"There are different types of daydreaming, Veronica."

"Really? How interesting. Has someone done a study of daydreaming? I'll have to read that. Whatever the case, good or bad daydreaming, the school year is almost over. Exactly what would you like me to do?"

"Talk to her. See what you think. Perhaps she'd consider getting some help. Some counseling."

There was one heavy, round glass paperweight on the desk. Picking it up, Veronica peered at it as if it were a crystal ball, then put it back down.

"Is that really necessary? She's a bright girl, she's taken her exams, I'm sure she'll get into a good college."

"Jesus, Veronica." He slapped his hand on her desk. "She's a student. I think she's in trouble. Don't you care anymore?"

"Tom." She leaned back, folded her arms across her chest. "You're overreacting. Calm down. Of course I care. And I will talk to Nurse Rutgers about Karen if you're so anxious about her. There's no need to get so worked up."

Whenever Veronica went into her patronizing mode, he found himself wanting to scream.

"Fine," he stated, and stood up, preparing to leave. She waved him back down.

"Actually, I'm glad you came to see me. There's something I want to talk to you about. Although I *do* still care, Tom, I should tell you I have decided to retire. In fact, this will be my last year.

I've been at Stonybridge long enough. People to see." She smiled. "Places to go."

"Veronica, I—"

"Obviously I informed the board about my decision a while ago, and they have now found my replacement."

She was staring at him, clearly waiting for this announcement to make an impact. Which it did. A new headmistress? From where? What would she be like? A variation on Veronica or someone entirely different? But if so, how different?

And was that part of the reason the school had been going to seed? The fish stinks from the head down. This head was clearly more than halfway out the door and had been for a long time.

"I can see you're surprised and wondering who will replace me." Picking up the paperweight again, she passed it from one hand to the other. "It's funny, isn't it? The Class of 1970 just voted you May Queen, oh, sorry, May *King*—a deviation from tradition. I'm sure they thought they were being very progressive. But not as progressive as the board of trustees. As of next September, Stonybridge will have a headmaster. A man will be in charge of an all girls' boarding school. The times certainly are changing."

"A man?"

"Kenneth Yates is his name. He's currently deputy head at St. Stephen's."

"A man? That's . . . that's ridiculous. This is a girls' school."

"Well, you teach here, Tom, and you're a man. Apparently Kenneth is quite progressive too."

"What does that mean?"

"I'm not really sure." She laughed. "But it's not my business anymore. Oh dear, you look shocked." She leaned forward, put her elbows on her desk. "And also very upset. Did you think, if they were going to hire a man, that they might choose you?"

He saw it then, her utter disdain of him. Why hadn't he seen it before? They'd had run-ins—over the Senior Room, for one—but he'd always thought they got along reasonably well. He wasn't prepared for the venomous joy she was taking in his discomfort.

"No, Veronica. I didn't think they would choose me. But I never expected they'd choose a man. I assume this man is married?"

"Kenneth. Yes. He and his wife have two children. A boy and a girl."

"I see."

"Oh dear. You really are upset, aren't you? I'm sure you'll get over it with time. You have the whole summer. Now—" She stood up, adjusted her scarf. "I will certainly talk to Nurse Rutgers about Karen. Don't worry. You worry too much."

"Jane Rutgers is a drunk, Veronica. I don't think she can help anyone, least of all herself. She's a hopeless nurse. You should have fired her years ago."

He stood as well, started walking to the door.

"Oh, Tom," she called out. "Apparently Kenneth is going to be more progressive than any of us could imagine. *Très avant-garde.* He's planning to hire a few younger male teachers. That will be nice for you, won't it?"

Chapter 59

Becky Powell

It had been raining forever, and the quad was one big mess of mud and it was impossible to know who started it, who threw the first handful of mud, but then the whole thing was like a chain reaction, everyone hurling mud at each other.

They'd all gotten out of their last class and were heading for the gym to change for sports but then the mud fight started and for some reason it was only the seniors doing it—all the other younger girls were standing around watching.

And for one minute Becky forgot the awful feeling of shame she had about lying, how everyone knew she'd lied about being a Star and would never forget it.

Angel was beside her, that long blond hair smeared with mud, and she was yelling and laughing and bending down to get a handful of mud and flinging it at Connie, whose blue shirt was now brown and who screamed and bent down herself and picked up a handful of mud and threw it at Debby.

It's like a molecular chain reaction, Becky thought as she watched one girl after another get splattered, then splatter someone else.

Laughing and screaming, they chased each other around the

quad, looking like NFL players on a muddy field. She dived into the center, picked up a wet mass of sludge, and smeared it on Abby's back.

"Becky!" Abby yelled. "Watch it—I'll get you!" and she felt absolutely, completely normal again as Abby tore after her.

But then she saw Karen pick up a handful of mud and cover Zoey's shirt with it and Zoey was retaliating, leaning down to pick up more mud, but she slipped and fell and then Karen fell on top of Zoey and it looked like she was trying to kiss her.

She was definitely trying to kiss her, because Zoey screamed, "Get off!" so loudly that everyone stopped fighting and stared. It was as if someone had yelled, *Freeze!* because they were all standing there like statues staring at the same thing: Karen on top of Zoey in the mud. Pinning her down. Trying to kiss her.

They were writhing in the mud, and Zoey kept moving her head from side to side, trying to avoid Karen's mouth landing on hers. But she couldn't keep avoiding it and Karen had her mouth locked on to Zoey's.

Cassidy had said people would forget about her List lie, but Becky hadn't really believed her because she still remembered the name of the girl in her old school who had wet her pants in third grade—Susan Halley—and probably everyone had told Susan Halley too that people would forget. Which she told Cass, but then Cass said: "Listen, someone will do something else, Beck. It will probably be a lot more embarrassing than what you did, so don't worry, everyone will start talking about that."

How could anyone do something more embarrassing? She didn't really believe that either, not for a minute.

But now she did.

What everyone stood watching was awful. And unforgettable. And really, really gross.

Chapter 60

Abby

It was horrible to watch. Zoey finally managed to push Karen off her, yelling: "Get away from me, you fucking psycho!" while Karen lay beside her in the mud, suddenly motionless, like a splattered corpse.

No one moved, no one said a word, until Mary walked over to them, offered her hand to Zoey, pulled her up, and said something to her no one could hear. Then Mary turned to the rest of them.

"Go to the gym and get cleaned up everyone. And you"—she pointed to the girls from the lower classes who were standing gawping—"get to the gym too. Now. I mean it."

They all followed her order and headed for the gym.

"Christ." Abby caught up to Cass in the changing room. "That was awful."

"It was bad. Was Karen ever like that with you?"

"Like that? You mean . . . no, no. Never."

"At least none of the teachers were there."

"But they'll find out. You know they will."

"And then what will happen?"

"I have no idea."

They began to take off their uniforms. Normally girls would talk to each other and joke around in the changing room, but no one spoke or even cast a glance at anyone else. It felt like naked female bodies were suddenly dangerous.

"What are we supposed to do? Go to sports like nothing has happened?" Connie finally broke the silence as she stood in front of her locker.

"I guess," Angel replied. "I mean, what else can we do?"

"We have to shower the mud off first," Cass said, which was what they all proceeded to do. After which they went back to their lockers, towels wrapped extra tightly around themselves, and changed into their gym clothes.

Abby could feel it: as soon as they'd put on shorts and gym shirts, there was a collective sense of relief.

Then Zoey stepped away from her locker, put her hands on her hips.

"Someone has to switch with me. I can't room with her. OK? Get it? I'm not sharing a room with her anymore. Anybody else. Who wants to switch?"

Silence.

"I mean it. You saw what she did. That's assault. This morning she showed me fucking love poems she'd written to me. I didn't tell her to fuck off then like I should have. I was polite, right? I just put them in my desk drawer. And then look what she does. She fucking *assaults* me. I'm not rooming with her. I don't want her anywhere near me ever again."

Chapter 61

Karen

Miss Adams had moved her into the infirmary. Zoey had made a formal complaint, and Miss Adams had tried to get someone to switch rooms, but no one would, so they'd put her in the infirmary. Like a sick person. Like a variation of Mr. Rochester's wife hidden up in the attic. Stuck in this room with white walls and strip lighting.

They were all walking around whispering.

Karen's nuts. She kissed Zoey. She has to be nuts. Bonkers. Crazy.

Karen was crazy because she fell in love.

They were sane.

They fell in love too, but with the right people. With inane boys. Which meant they were sane.

Which meant they had the right to whisper about her and stick her in the infirmary. And ignore her.

Karen's a leper.

It started the first time after the Mud Fight Day when she got up enough courage to go into the Senior Room. She was sitting in one of the old chairs, smoking. Zoey, Cassidy, Abby, and Angel were there, along with a few others. Zoey was talking about the yearbook. She had taken the senior class photos for it.

Karen asked her when she could see hers.

Zoey didn't reply. Or even look in her direction. She kept talking to Angel, saying she had shot all the photos in black-and-white. Karen asked again when she could see hers. Zoey kept on talking to Angel.

Karen then asked Debby if she knew who was going to speak at their graduation. Debby stole a look at Zoey, then stayed silent.

"Debby—" *Really? Is this really happening?* "Didn't you hear me? I asked you if you—"

"So, Debby," Zoey said, cutting in. "What are your plans for summer vacation? Horse riding? Shell collecting? Exotic dancing?"

Everyone laughed.

Karen lit a cigarette from the butt of the one she was about to put out, then asked:

"Angel, do *you* know who's speaking at our graduation?"

Of course Angel looked over at Zoey. Of course Angel didn't respond either.

Yes, this was really happening. No one was speaking to her. Zoey had fixed that. They were all going to ignore her.

Because she had fallen in love with a girl.

Zoey.

Zoey, who was supposed to be better than this. Zoey, who thought the whole marriage thing was ludicrous. Zoey, who believed in poetry and Sylvia Plath and being *different*.

Except she isn't different. She's the same as all of them.

They were all talking about the upcoming summer vacation. It was as if the whole senior year hadn't happened and she was listening to these idiots talking about stupid shit the way she hadn't wanted to listen that first night in September to the talk of how they'd spent their summers. That first time she'd walked into the Senior Room to avoid Abby and Cass and seen Zoey.

It was as if none of what happened then had actually happened. As if Zoey hadn't asked her to room with her. Gone with her to Racetrack's.

Cried about that coat. Invited her to New York. Talked with her for hours and hours in the diner. Stroked her hair on the bus.

It was all wiped out. All of it. Canceled. Obliterated.

"Have you decided which colleges you're applying to, Karen?"

It took her a second to register that Cass was interrupting the others' conversation to ask her that question.

"Karen? Do you know what college you want to go to?"

Enraged, she turned on her.

"Right. Of course. Cassidy Thomas. The amazing Cassidy Thomas. I know what you're doing. You think if you talk to me, then everyone will talk to me and you can show how powerful you are. You never stop, do you? Fuck that."

She stubbed out the cigarette and left the room.

After that, no one except Mary Greene and teachers spoke to her. Not in the Senior Room, not in class, not at meals, not at sports.

They'd ostracized her. *Ostracize.* A Zoey word. Well, Zoey had proved that she was one of the make-believe girls she claimed to despise.

When Abby had ditched her for Cassidy, Karen had sulked and suffered silently.

This was different.

There had to be a way to get revenge. On all of them. But especially Abby. If Abby had been a real friend, none of this would have happened. Cassidy too of course. She needed someone to knock her down from her Miss Perfect ledge. Abby and Cassidy and Zoey. They'd all turned her into a leper, but the Leper wasn't going to go gently into the night. The Leper was going to rage.

Chapter 62

Cassidy

Everything was redeemable: that was what Mr. D. had said, and she was beginning to believe it. Not that she was happy exactly, or had forgotten, but she found herself smiling more, and when she talked to Jeb on the phone, she wasn't tempted to blurt out, *We had a baby. I killed it*, the way she had been tempted to so many times before.

Maybe it helped that the weather was getting better. They were going out to the softball field now during sports time instead of staying in the gym, and she actually enjoyed herself then, standing in the outfield, watching everyone run around and yell and scream and miss easy catches and strike out.

Only one and a half months left to go and they'd be out of Stonybridge and Jeb would graduate from Yale and he'd tell his parents they were seeing each other so they wouldn't have to sneak around and she could be honest with Abby again.

And maybe she'd get into the University of Connecticut, in which case life would be a whole lot easier.

So things were definitely getting better.

"Hey—" Zoey came into the room without knocking. "We have time before dinner. Where's Abby?"

"I'm not sure. I think in the study hall."

"I was hoping you could come check out your yearbook photo. See if it meets with your approval."

Zoey taking on the job of doing the yearbook pictures would have surprised everyone—she wasn't exactly full of school spirit—but no one else offered and she ended up saying, "OK, I'll do it then if none of the rest of you idiots know how to work a camera. I hate to think what you'd come up with."

"I'll come now if you want."

"OK, cool."

The photography lab was beside the music room on the second floor of the classroom building. They didn't talk as they walked there, until they were climbing the steps and Zoey said:

"You know, I liked taking the pictures. I didn't think I would, but I did."

"That's good." Cass thought of Mr. D. as they passed the music room. He'd been really pleased, she could tell, when he was told they'd voted him May King.

She'd keep in touch with him after she graduated. She'd introduce him to Jeb. And they'd invite him to their wedding. In Paris? In Venice? It didn't matter at all where it was. The only thing that mattered was that it happened.

"So here they all are."

Zoey led her to one of the trestle tables where a bunch of photographs lay.

"I think taking them in black-and-white is more stylish."

"Wow!"

They were great pictures, all of them. As she bent over and

looked at each one, she marveled at how Zoey had captured the spirit of every girl. But when she saw her own, she picked it up, surprised.

"That's weird. I mean, I look different. I've never seen a photo of me like this. It makes me look . . . intelligent."

"You *are* intelligent."

"I don't think anyone would ever use that word to describe me."

"I would. Listen, Cass, I know we're not supposed to talk about it, but you were really intelligent to have the abortion. That was—"

"I'm going to pay your father back, you know. Every cent. I'll get a job this summer and save my money and—"

"I know. I know, OK? What I was saying is that you're smart. You're not just a pretty face, Cass. You shouldn't put yourself down."

"I was stupid to get pregnant in the first place."

"That's Jeb's stupidity, not yours. And I can't say it enough times: I'm really sorry. I'm so sorry for leaving you like that."

"Forget it. I have."

And she had—almost.

"Does Abby—see, I'm being good and using her name now—anyway, does Abby still not know about you and Jeb?"

"Not yet. We're going to tell everyone this summer." She replaced the picture of herself and looked at the others again. "Jesus. Karen looks happy in this."

"I took it a while ago. Before . . . you know."

"I feel sorry for her."

"Really? I don't. That fucking mud fight? And you should have read the mawkish shitty love poems she wrote to me. They were nauseating. Anyway, she'll be fine when she gets

out of here and goes to some all girls' college. She'll find someone else to go crazy over. Besides, she hates you, Cass—with
a vengeance."

"I know. But still—this whole silent treatment, I think you
should drop it. Give her a break. It must be terrible staying on
her own in the infirmary."

"I don't care what it's like. You're not the one she practically
raped in the mud fight, you don't know what it was like living
with her every day. It was torture. Anyway, we'll be rid of her
soon. Come on, we should get going now."

"Wait—let me look at these for a few more minutes. They're
really good. Do you ever use that special camera your father
gave you? The one in your room?"

"No."

"You should."

"I will. You know, it's funny. I've always said going to college was for the make-believe girls, but I've decided there's
one college I'd really like to go to. It's ironic because Karen
was the one who told me about it. Oberlin. When I had to
go see Miss Hanley for the college advice thing, I mentioned
Oberlin, and she knew girls who had gone there, and the way
she described it—it sounds perfect for me. I'm hoping I didn't
screw the SATs up because I'd really like to go there. I'm even
excited about it."

"No shit."

"I know, doesn't sound like me, does it?"

"People change. And that can be a good thing. Listen, Zo—
don't worry. I mean about Canada. We all screw up sometimes. I know that more than anybody. And getting your dad
to arrange it and pay and everything—you really did help me.
You didn't have to do any of it."

"So"—Zoey smiled—"I guess that means we're friends again."

"As long as you keep saying I'm intelligent."

"Don't count on it, Cassidy Thomas. Especially if you end up living in the suburbs."

They laughed.

And she thought: *Maybe everything really is redeemable. Maybe Mr. D. is right.*

Chapter 63

2018

It is May 1. May Day. Which means she'll be arriving tomorrow. I have her flight details. I'm going to pick her up at Heathrow late tomorrow morning and drive her to her hotel in Notting Hill.

May 1. I hadn't clocked it until I saw May 1 on my calendar today.

Was this a coincidence?

Or could she have planned the date a long time ago? To coincide so neatly with history?

"Paranoia strikes deep / Into your life it will creep."

Buffalo Springfield.

Great lyrics.

I'm being paranoid.

Aren't I?

May 1, 1970. We looked so innocent. Standing in a perfect circle at 9:00 a.m., wearing bright, not-too-short spring cotton dresses, we could have been young milkmaids from a Thomas Hardy novel, ready to perform at a local village fete before skipping back to our respective farms. White cotton ribbons splayed out from the maypole in the center of the circle, the ends waiting at our feet.

The music began, we each picked up our ribbon. The annual Stonybridge Senior Class May Day Maypole Dance commenced.

We circled, holding the ribbons down, holding the ribbons up, going under and over each other as the ribbons interlaced and drew in until they were tightly knotted, covering what had been a bare wooden pole in a coating of white cotton. Like a branchless, snow-bedecked Christmas tree standing on its own in the middle of a field in the wrong season.

What was strange was that we hadn't colluded. No one had discussed what to wear or whether to try, for once, to be appropriate. The choice came naturally, as if there were a belief lurking in every single one of us: we could be young and sweet. We could wear skirts that weren't too short, follow the rules we were supposed to follow, do what was expected of us, and even enjoy doing it.

Miraculously, no one made a mistake. Zoey—who during practice the day before had stopped in the middle, taken the ribbon she was holding, wrapped it around her neck, and choked out, "You've got to be kidding!" And then, in a voice pitched at the exact volume to be heard by us but not the watchful few faculty members attending the dress rehearsal: "Fuck this!"—even Zoey had decided to behave. She was wearing a flowered print dress that almost reached her knees. Her long dark hair was in a ponytail. She looked clean.

The music was the type that you hear in Shakespearean plays, pastoral; flutes and lutes hearkening back to ye olden days. At the end, when it stopped and we had returned to our original places in the circle, we were more surprised than anyone that we'd managed to get it all right. We looked around at each other in bewilderment. I'm not sure who was the one who yelled, "Farout!" but someone did and we all burst out laughing, such infectious laughter that the teachers joined in too.

The senior class had always voted for a May Queen: a female faculty member who would wear a special May Day red robe and preside over the dance. Cass had suggested we change that tradition and vote for Mr. Doherty, so we all did. We were looking forward to seeing a man bedecked in red velvet.

But Mr. Doherty was the only one not in attendance. He hadn't shown up, and no one had been able to get in touch with him. Just before we began, we switched our choice to Miss Gambee, the math teacher.

It was a warm, sunny, perfect spring morning. The sun lit up the field behind Miss Adams's house, making Miss Gambee appear even more regal in her red velvet robe.

And the day kept getting better. Another Stonybridge tradition: the senior class president was allowed to ask the May Queen for a special treat at Assembly after the maypole dance.

We had all trooped from Miss Adams's house to the gym for Assembly. Miss Gambee took her place on the makeshift throne on the stage at the front. The rest of the faculty were on folding chairs behind her as she sat, facing the entire student body.

For the past however many years, the senior class president asked the May Queen for a "no homework" day. But I was the president of the Class of 1970. And we were special.

"May Queen, please may we have . . ." I hesitated for effect. "The day off school."

Pandemonium. Everyone cheered and stomped their feet on the floor. "The day off, the day off," the chant began.

Putting her hands up in the air to silence us, Miss Gambee paused for effect too.

"The May Queen grants your wish," she announced. "No school today."

Within two minutes the gym had emptied. And somehow, with the magical group ethos that had been bubbling all morning, Angel knew exactly the right thing to do next. She ran to her room in the dormitory that looked out onto the courtyard outside, grabbed an Aretha Franklin album, put it on the record player, turned up the volume as high as it would go, opened the window, and then sprinted back.

The entire senior class hopped onto the low wall above the courtyard. And we did another dance. We linked arms and danced our socks off as Aretha sang "Chain of Fools."

Chapter 64

2018
MAY 2

She was lucky. The weather was gorgeous. Her plane would be landing in a bright, sunny London.

There were times when it felt like the sun was an unidentifiable flying object in London, something people claimed existed but was actually fictional.

But now I was searching for my sunglasses for the drive to Heathrow. Maybe the sun was an omen. This was going to be fine. It might even be fun.

May 2, 1970, had been a beautiful day in Lenox too, and it was a Saturday, so we had, because of the Friday off, a three-day weekend to enjoy.

There weren't even any expeditions scheduled. We could stay in our rooms listening to music or go into town, drink coffee, and check out the record store yet again.

The combination of the mountain air, the sunshine, our perfect May Day, and the looming end of school had us all buzzing. Life was good. I remember feeling relieved that Karen, who had seemed surprisingly happy at the maypole dance and who had willingly joined in on our "Chain of Fools" dance, was still in a good mood.

She was at my table at breakfast, making comments about the lousy coffee. At one point she turned to me and described the infirmary. "At first I thought it was like the attic in *Jane Eyre*, but you know *Great Expectations*? It's like an antiseptic version of Miss Havisham's room—seriously, I should be in some old wedding dress scaring the shit out of Pip. Look, I know you won't talk to me, but that's OK, Abby. Everything is copacetic. That's a word I learned from Zoey, by the way."

I didn't understand where this good mood was coming from, but I didn't care. She was smiling, she was fine. It didn't matter that we'd all stopped speaking to her.

Of course I felt guilty for going along with the silent treatment. After she'd yelled at Cass for talking to her, though, I figured she wouldn't want me to try to change things either.

You're just a little pawn of Cassidy's. Fuck off is probably what she would have said.

She'd survive what had happened. I guessed she would have done well on the SATs and she'd go to a college where she could forget Stonybridge and flourish. That's what I thought as we all got up from the breakfast table. Karen would be all right. There were only a few weeks left of school. She was smart, she was funny, and she'd be absolutely fine once she left Stonybridge.

Most of us headed for the Senior Room after breakfast. I had a vague idea that we might get a group together for an afternoon walk in the Berkshires. I was sure I could find one of the teachers to accompany us. It would be good to be outside, smelling the spring.

As we walked down the hall, I saw Connie pick up one of the local papers that were always sitting on a table outside the dining hall. No one ever read them, and even now I can't fathom why Connie picked it up, but she did. When we got to the Senior Room, she sat down on the floor, lit a cigarette, and started to thumb through it.

The rest of us were splayed out. Angel was telling me what her plans for the summer were. I was listening but at the same time trying to figure out how I'd get chances to see Jimmy for a whole night over the summer. What lies I could tell to my parents that they might just believe.

"Shit!"

Connie said it so loud that everyone turned to look at her.

"I can't believe it. Jesus. Listen to this: 'Thomas Doherty of Lenox, Massachusetts, and Peter Finley of Pittsfield, Massachusetts, were apprehended on the side of the Massachusetts Turnpike on April 30 and charged with committing lewd and lascivious activities.'"

"What?" Cass rushed over and grabbed the paper from Connie's hands.

"No," she said as she read it. "No, no, no."

"He was arrested?" Angel went to Cass's side and peered over her shoulder. "No wonder he wasn't at May Day. He must have been in jail."

"Lewd and what?" Debby asked.

"Lewd and lascivious," Connie answered. "That means they were . . . you know . . ."

"Well, that proves me wrong. I'd always thought he was asexual." Zoey lit a cigarette. "Good for Mr. D. But he should have picked a better place. The turnpike? Not exactly romantic."

"He'll probably be fired."

"Shut up, Connie." Cass turned on her. "That's ridiculous. This is an all girls' boarding school. He was with a man, not a girl. It's not as if he would do anything bad to us."

"Yeah, but he'll have a record," Connie shot back. "That was my point, OK? He'll have a police record."

"Do you think he's still in jail?" Angel asked.

"Do they put people in jail for being faggots?"

"Maybe fags like being in jail with all those other guys there?"

"SHUT THE FUCK UP!" Cass screamed. "You're all privileged little spoiled fucking brats!"

She rushed out of the room.

"Christ. That was heavy-duty. I know she likes Mr. D., but she didn't have to yell like that" was Connie's comment.

I knew too that Cass liked Mr. Doherty, but I had had no idea she'd feel so strongly or go to such lengths to defend him. I'd never seen her be so passionate about anything and felt slightly annoyed that I was seeing a side of her I didn't understand, one she'd never showed before. She was as worked up as Jeb and Peter were when they argued with my father about Vietnam.

"I better go after her," I said.

But I couldn't find her anywhere.

Chapter 65

1970
MAY 2

Cassidy

The winding road seemed to go on forever, but it was probably only fifteen minutes before they made a left-hand turn into a long driveway.

She'd been lucky to find a taxi driver in town who hadn't asked her whether she was allowed to be doing what she was doing: going off campus without being chaperoned in any way. And she'd been even luckier because Mr. D. had once told her the name of his cottage and she'd actually remembered it: Pine Tree House.

"This is a pretty little place," the driver said when they pulled up in front of it. "I've always wondered who lives here."

"You need to stay and wait for me. I won't be too long."

"I'm keeping the meter running." He turned to look at her. "You better be able to pay for this."

"I have twenty dollars." She'd run to her room, found the twenty-dollar bill, and run out of the school, into the town, and found a cab outside the Café. No one had seen her. Or if they had, they hadn't stopped her.

I have to see him. I have to tell him it's going to be all right.

"Twenty bucks? Then you better be fast. I'll honk when I know you'll have just enough to get back. OK?"

"OK."

At first he didn't answer. She pounded on the door with her fist and called out: "Mr. Doherty. It's me. Let me in."

But he didn't. Maybe he *was* in jail. But she had to keep trying.

"Look," she yelled even louder. "I'm not going away, and if I have to stay too long, I won't be able to pay for the cab and I'll probably get kicked out and—"

The door opened. She was surprised because she expected he'd be a mess, but he was dressed as he always dressed, neatly and tidily in gray trousers and a white button-down shirt.

"You shouldn't be here, Cassidy."

"I know. But I am. I want to talk to you."

She barged past him into the little sitting room.

"So I take it that everyone knows?"

They were both standing in the middle of the room. He was staring at her, and she wanted to go over and comfort him, put her arms around him, but she wasn't sure if he wanted that and she didn't want to make him even more uncomfortable than he was.

"Yeah. But it doesn't matter. That's the thing you need to know. No one cares, OK? And they can't fire you or anything. We won't let them."

He turned away from her then. She could see from his shoulders that he was taking deep breaths.

"The thing is, Zoey's mother is on the board of trustees. She gives a ton of money to the school too. I can get Zoey to get her mother to make everything OK. You didn't do anything wrong. They can't fire you. I'm going to sit down for a second, if that's all right."

Which was what she did when he didn't respond. She sat in one of his leather armchairs. It was a little battered, like an armchair in a college professor's room would be.

"Everything is redeemable, right, Mr. D.? And what happened, you know, it wasn't anything bad or wrong. Everyone will forget it and it isn't important, it's not important at all, and you have to know that."

"I don't know anything anymore." He said it so softly she almost didn't hear the words.

"Look at me, Mr. D. Sit down. Please."

He did what she asked and sat down in the armchair facing hers. She could see the total devastation in his face. And it reminded her so much of her father, when her mother died, the way his face had collapsed then, as if there was nothing holding it together anymore, like someone had hit it with a sledgehammer and it had shattered.

He wouldn't look at her, not directly.

"No, listen. It's what you told me. Everything is redeemable. That's what that priest told you, and priests know, right? Especially a *Jesuit* priest. They know what's true."

He began to move his hands up and down his thighs as if he were ironing his trousers with them.

"If a priest says it, it's true. You have to listen to me."

"Cassidy. There are some things God doesn't forgive."

Finally his eyes met hers, and what was in them frightened her. Because it seemed as if he was sharing something in that look, that he was including her in it, in those things God didn't forgive.

"Don't say that. Please. You can't believe that. Not really. Please don't say that." She got up and went over to him, knelt in front of him. "Please. Please say it's going to be OK. Please say you'll come back on Monday and everything will be OK again.

"Please, Mr. D.?"

"You should go." He sat back in his chair and wiped his forehead. "I don't want you to get expelled. You shouldn't be here. But thank you for coming. It was very reckless and very kind of you."

"I'm not leaving until you tell me you're coming back on Monday."

She heard the cab honk.

"I have to go. But you have to promise me you'll come back on Monday. You didn't do anything bad. People do terrible things and get forgiven and they get to live their lives and be happy. You didn't do anything bad."

He took her hands in his. "Go back to school, Cassidy. Please. I don't want you to get in trouble for this."

"Then promise me. Promise me that everything will be OK. That you'll come back."

"Everything will be fine."

"Promise? I'm not leaving 'til you promise. I meant it when I said I love you, Mr. D. In the right way."

He sighed, squeezed her hands, closed his eyes. "Yes. I promise. And you should know I love you too, Cassidy. In the right way. Now go."

Chapter 66

2018
MAY 2

Her plane was arriving at Heathrow, Terminal 3. As I live in West London, it's an easy drive. "When you come out after you get your bags, go to the Caffè Nero and I'll be there waiting."

I'd met enough people enough times to know I didn't want to stand around the Arrival Hall continuously looking out for someone to come through those doors. I'd sit with my paper and have a cup of coffee.

There'd been no profile picture or information on Facebook; when I'd googled her, nothing had come up either. I had no idea what she'd look like and found myself wondering if she'd had plastic surgery or Botox and decided she wouldn't. Then I reminded myself never to make assumptions. People have a habit of doing the unexpected, something you'd never believe they could do.

"Hey, Abs."

Lost in thought, I hadn't seen her approach me. I was transfixed by her appearance. Long straight silver hair, way below her shoulders. No makeup. And she was wearing a white peasant blouse over a pair of blue jeans. Both her arms up to the elbows were covered in silver bangles, and she sported dangling silver earrings.

I hadn't seen that coming. An aging hippie?

"God." I stood up, hugged her. "Mary. So good to see you. How was the flight?"

"Fine. No turbulence. But not a whole lot of sleep."

"Wow—you packed lightly."

She had only a small black carry-on suitcase by her side.

"How long are you staying? Two hours?"

She laughed. The same throaty laugh. Suddenly I was a teen-ager again, sitting beside her in math class, passing notes.

"I'm here for five days. I always pack light."

"Here—" I held out a cup of coffee I'd bought for her. "You might need this—unless you're a health freak and no caffeine."

"Are you kidding? I mainline caffeine. Thanks, Abs. Does any-one call you Abs now?"

"No. Come on, let's get out of here."

Chapter 67

1970
MAY 3

Zoey

Miss Adams trying to be cool was tragic on one hand and helpful on the other. Setting up the Senior Room—that had been a trip. And at the beginning of the year she'd told the seniors they could go to any place of worship they chose to on Sunday mornings. Before that, they'd all been forced to go to the Episcopal church for services. Boring, tedious, boring.

With this new plan, they signed out for whatever place they wanted to go to, but they couldn't go alone and they had to write down a sentence about whatever sermon they'd heard at whatever church they'd been to. Not that there were a whole lot of choices, but still. At least it was different.

And Connie had had a brilliant idea. If they went to the synagogue, they could go on a Friday night and sleep in on Sunday. At first that had worked brilliantly. About a third of the class had joined in with Connie and gone to the synagogue on Friday and sat and listened to the Jewish service and come back and made stuff up about what they'd heard because they hadn't been able to understand it. But after a few weeks the people who ran the synagogue must have said something to Miss Adams, because she announced that this was no longer an option.

Well, hey, Miss Adams—you might want to think about letting in Jewish girls or Black girls to Stonybridge, right?

Had Miss Adams even considered it? Or was part of the Stonybridge tradition that no minorities were allowed?

Zoey had confronted her mother about that at least a hundred times. Each one of those hundred times her mother had changed the subject.

Anyway, for the past few Sundays she'd been going to the Baptist church with Angel. Angel wasn't a Baptist either, but she had convinced Zoey to go with her, saying she'd been there once with Becky and it had had the best after-service food. "The cookies are good. And they have great Sara Lee cheesecake."

She was getting dressed—you had to wear a dress to whichever service you chose to go to—and luxuriating in the pleasure of having the place to herself. Karen's banishment to the infirmary meant that Zoey had what all the other seniors wanted: her own room. Even rooming with Cass, she'd had times when she'd wanted to be by herself and not have to cope with the presence of another person. There was a limit to how much of another person's company she could put up with, which made her think yet again that marriage, that whole day-in, day-out routine, must be a real drag. You chose someone when you were young and then were stuck with them supposedly for your entire life?

Didn't people change? She'd seen the changes in all the girls in the four years she'd been at Stonybridge. Yes, maybe they were teenagers and teenagers were supposed to change, but was there some cutoff point? At twenty-three or whenever you walked down the aisle, you stayed that way forever?

And yes, she'd liked Lumberjack—a lot. It wasn't as if she didn't understand that it was possible to fall in love. But to give up your freedom and marry some man for forever? She was sure she'd never understand that.

Just as she'd chosen one of her black dresses and pulled it on over her head, she heard the school bell ring three times in a row. Which was the signal for the whole school to gather in the gym for an important announcement.

That had never happened on a Sunday before. In fact, she couldn't remember it ever happening on any weekend day—only on weekdays when something had gone wrong: once, the electricity had shorted or something and they'd had to cancel classes, another time it had snowed so much they had to announce that the food for that evening hadn't arrived so they'd been told to eat as much as possible at lunch.

She slipped on her flat black church shoes and started to make her way to the gym.

Maybe the Vietnam War had ended.

Maybe someone had been caught smoking dope.

Whatever it was, she was annoyed.

Normally she didn't care very much about food. But she'd been looking forward to that Sara Lee cheesecake.

Chapter 68

The ride to Mary's hotel had been uneventful. Flights from the West Coast got into London later than East Coast ones did, so we weren't stuck in rush-hour traffic on the M4. And it was a straight shot to her hotel in Notting Hill.

I had heard of the hotel: it had been a mecca for rock stars in the sixties and seventies, one of the first boutique hotels. It had kept its cachet and reputation, and the prices reflected its status.

"That's a smart hotel, you know," I commented as soon as Mary had told me the destination. "And a great area. You wouldn't believe how much house values there shot up after the movie. Anyway, I haven't asked you what you do or what you did. I mean for a living."

"I make documentary films."

"Wow. That's impressive."

"It's funny, I would have thought Zoey would be the one making films, but it turned out to be me."

"I feel remiss here. I don't know whether I've seen any of them. I don't tend to watch documentaries. Should I have heard of you? Are you famous?"

"As if. Besides, they're all based in America. Mostly about the inequities of the justice system. So it's very unlikely you would have seen one."

"That's even more impressive. A documentary filmmaker and a social activist. Meanwhile I don't work and never have, unless you qualify being a housewife and mother as having a career. People don't seem to be able to make up their minds about that these days."

"I saw on Facebook—four children and six grandchildren. That's definitely a career, more like two careers. So what you've done is impressive to me."

Straight shot down the M4. Straightforward conversation. I was beginning to really like Mary again.

"Do you have a partner?" I asked.

"I like how you phrased that—not sexually specific. Anyway, I was married for five years, but then my husband died. His name was Wade. We never had children. I never remarried."

"I'm sorry."

When was it? It must have been senior year. Of course it was, because we were in the Senior Room. Someone—was it Connie?—mentioned a boy called Skip she'd met at a dance and liked. Was it Zoey who had said: "How can you like any boy whose name is a verb?"?

"Thanks. It took me a long time to get over it, and I'm not sure I am over it even now."

"It must be so hard. Is that why I didn't see anything about you when I googled you? Do you use your married name for work?"

"Yes, old-fashioned of me, I know, but I do. Mary Howard. I only just set up that Facebook account in my maiden name. You're my first friend on it. Speaking of names, it's funny, I always remember Zoey asking Connie how she could like anyone whose first name was a verb. I told that to Wade when we first started seeing each other."

"I was just remembering that too. I wasn't sure it was Zoey, but you're right, it was her. Absolutely."

"It couldn't have been anyone else, could it?" Mary laughed.

We laughed together.

Like the good old days.

Except the good old days started to become dark, gruesome days all those years ago when we heard the three bells ring out. I remembered how we'd all piled out of the dorms, went to the gym, and took our seats. While we waited for Miss Adams to arrive, we speculated about what her announcement might be.

Someone had been caught taking drugs or drinking—that seemed to be the most likely.

Yet when the entire faculty filed into the gym and went to sit in their chairs facing us, the hum of whispering stopped. Whatever had happened, it was clearly serious. They all looked as if a bomb had dropped. I thought of the day JFK was assassinated. The teachers at my day school had looked stunned and ashen then too.

The last time the faculty had been facing us like this was two days earlier, on May Day, when I'd asked Miss Gambee for the day off. When I caught sight of her on the left of the stage, I saw her brush tears from her eyes.

Miss Gambee in on a Sunday when she should have been home? Miss Gambee crying?

I found myself grabbing the arm of Becky Powell to my right. She turned and made a "This is bad" face.

Miss Adams approached the podium and placed a piece of paper on top of it. She straightened, then put her hands on either side of it, holding on to it as if it were the wreckage of a ship, the only piece of wood she could find that might save her from drowning.

"I'm going to read a poem. Some of you might know it: it's by John Donne.

"'Death, be not proud, though some have called thee / Mighty and dreadful . . .'"

I tuned out to the words.

Someone had died.

Shit, someone had died.

When she'd stopped speaking, she looked out at us all.

"I have some very sad news to tell you. Mr. Doherty died last night. He was found at his home early this morning."

I turned in my seat to look at Cass behind me, two rows on the left. She was slumped in her chair, her head in her hands.

"I'm afraid I know what happens in situations like this at a boarding school," Miss Adams continued, her voice sounding more like her normal Miss Adams voice. "You will all be talking about this sad event, wanting to know the facts, imagining and gossiping. I'm going to stop any gossip right now. Mr. Doherty died by his own hand.

"I speak on behalf of the faculty and I'm sure the entire school when I say he will be much missed. This is a tragic event, and we will all mourn him in our own ways. We discussed canceling classes tomorrow, but in fact I know that Tom—Mr. Doherty—wouldn't have wanted that.

"He was dedicated to this school and to educating young women. So we will proceed as normal. I will give you more information regarding the funeral service when I know it myself. Now I suggest that you all go back to your rooms and have quiet time."

The faculty then filed out as they had filed in. The rows of girls began to empty after they'd left, starting with the freshmen at the front and continuing back to us.

We were all doing exactly as we were told, heading back to our rooms. I turned when I reached the middle of the quad and looked for Cass but couldn't spot her anywhere, so I ran back to the gym.

She was alone there, still slumped over, with her head still in her hands.

"Hey." I took the seat beside her and put my arm around her shoulder. "I'm sorry. I'm so sorry, Cass. I know how much you cared about him."

She shook her head.

"He promised," she said. "He promised me it would be all right."

The day before, when I hadn't been able to find her after that scene in the Senior Room, she'd finally come into our room. When I'd asked her where she had disappeared to, she said: "I went to see Mr. D. Everything's going to be fine."

"You went on your own?"

"Yes, Abs. I got away with it. No one noticed."

"But—"

"I had to tell him no one cared about what he'd done."

"Right." I nodded, expecting her to say more. She didn't.

There was no point in pressing her, I knew. She wasn't going to tell me any details. Whatever her relationship with Mr. D. was, it definitely wasn't anything bad. Besides, it had been such a great couple of days. The maypole dance, getting the day off school, dancing to Aretha Franklin. Nothing could ruin that, not even her reluctance to share with me.

But sitting in the gym with her, everything felt bad.

"He promised." She took her hands away from her face. I had been prepared to see tears, but there weren't any. What I wasn't prepared for was the anger in her voice. "He promised me. Why did he do it when he promised me? It's wrong. He loved me. How could he do that? Lie like that?"

"He loved you?"

"Shit. You don't understand. Not like that. For Christ's sake, Abby."

Now that anger was directed at me.

"OK. All right. You're right, I don't understand. But whatever he said to you, he was obviously really unhappy. Sometimes you can't fix unhappiness like that, I guess. Nobody can."

"What if God doesn't forgive him? What if everything isn't redeemable? Suicide is a mortal sin."

There was nothing I could say. I didn't believe in God. I knew she was a Catholic, but I'd never thought Cass took her religion seriously.

"We should go back to our room."

"You go. I'm going to the music room now. I need to be on my own there."

"The music room?"

The look she gave me then shut me up.

"OK."

We left the gym. I felt bewildered.

Mr. D. loved her? What did that mean? And why the music room? She didn't play any instrument.

It had never occurred to me before that weekend that Cass might have secrets she kept from me.

But she did. Which meant she didn't trust me.

I trudged back to our room, sat down on my bed.

I should have been thinking of Mr. Doherty. Instead, I sat there feeling sorry for myself.

Chapter 69

1970
MAY 3

Karen

She didn't feel guilty. Why should she? Mr. Doherty was always talking about truth, and that was all she'd done—told the truth. So he'd gone out and been lewd and lascivious: he'd probably done that tons of times before, only he hadn't been caught. The fact that he was ashamed of being known to be gay had nothing to do with what she'd told him.

His death wasn't going to interfere with the rest of her plan.

Anyway, even if she'd wanted to stop, she couldn't. It was in motion. Very soon the Leper was going to screw them all.

Chapter 70

Zoey

It was strange, this sadness she felt. It wasn't as if she had ever really thought about Mr. D. OK, Cass liked him, she knew. And the senior class had voted him May King. She'd been cool with that, but she'd never had a real conversation with him. So why did she feel so depressed?

Everyone had walked around all day with sad expressions. Sitting in the Senior Room, they talked in hushed voices, as if they were at a funeral. Zoey couldn't help but think some of the girls were faking it, that they thought if they laughed or looked happy, they'd be bad people. Which was all part of the hypocrisy of this school.

Still, she felt doleful. It didn't make any sense, not really, but she couldn't stop thinking how poor Mr. D. had had to fake it too, pretend he wasn't a homosexual, fit into society's norms.

He'd buried himself under the weight of other people's expectations.

It wasn't right.

Her father could go off with women decades younger than himself and no one batted an eyelash. Mr. D. got together with some guy on the side of a highway and he was arrested.

The world was full of hypocrites.

Whatever she ended up doing with her life, she wasn't going to be a hypocrite.

"Zoey—" Karen had opened her door and was standing on the threshold. "Don't panic. I'm not going to jump on you."

The whole not-speaking-to-Karen thing suddenly felt puerile.

"What do you want?"

"You look upset."

"Great observational powers." Speaking to her was one thing—liking her was another.

"Very funny. Guess what? I don't give a shit. I'm here to tell you to come to the infirmary after supper. There's something I need to tell you. And before you tell me to fuck off, you should know that Abby and Cassidy will be there too. It involves all of you."

"What if I don't choose to obey this summons?"

"No sweat." She shrugged. "But if you don't come, believe me, you'll regret it, because Cassidy will need you there."

Karen left.

Zoey wasn't depressed anymore. She was angry.

Chapter 71

<u>Cassidy</u>

Sitting in the music room, she had tried to remember every conversation they'd ever had. Had she missed something? A hint? Had he ever even mentioned the word "suicide"?

No, she was sure he hadn't.

Why had he lied to her? Had he already decided to do it when she came over? Was that why he was wearing nice clothes? So that he'd be well dressed when he was found?

Had he written a note?

All these questions swirled in her brain, along with the sickeningly familiar feeling of loss. People tried to comfort you when someone you loved died. But they couldn't, not really. Because the only person who could, the only person you wanted to talk to, was the one who had gone.

"What the fuck, Mr. D.?" She said it out loud, looking up at the ceiling. "You said you loved me too. I was fighting for you. So why the fuck did you have to do that?"

He had sat on this piano bench and told her everything was redeemable. He'd made things better for her. She hadn't been able to make things better for him. She hadn't saved him any more than she had saved her baby. They were both dead.

But there was Jeb. Their love was alive.

"I wanted you at our wedding. We would have made you godfather of our first child. I wanted you to share in our happiness. I don't believe you're in hell. You can't be. God wouldn't do that. You have to be in heaven. So, please, Mr. D. Listen to me. Please. Go find my mom. You'll love her too."

And then the tears that had been waiting ever since Miss Adams started reading that poem, when after the very first line she'd looked at the teachers and realized he wasn't there, when she'd known deep down what Miss Adams would say at the end of it, all those tears came crashing out in a tidal wave of grief.

When she'd finally cried herself out, she left the music room and went back to her own room, where Abby was sitting on her bed, reading a book.

"Are you all right?" Abby put the book down.

"Not really." She flopped onto her own bed. "I'm tired. I might just lie here. How long before lunch?"

"An hour. Do you want to talk about—"

"No. I can't right now, Abs."

"OK. Anyway, Angel came in and said you had a phone call. Some guy. I guess he didn't say his name."

"Right."

There had been quite a few times when Jeb had called without leaving his name, but luckily Abby had never been the one who took those calls.

The lying would end soon. She'd been worried about how Abby would react to the news of her and Jeb, but right then she didn't give a damn. All the other Madisons could hate her, she didn't care. She wanted the lying to be over and done with. She wanted her real life with Jeb to start, and that was all she wanted. To be with him and away from this school.

They'd live by the sea. Not the mountains. Their kids would play on the beach. They'd go to a normal high school and have a prom and be normal. They wouldn't be debutantes or have coming-out parties. The whole WASPy world she'd been so impressed and intimidated by was phony. This privileged school was full of miserable girls. All those visions of touch football and cocktails on the lawn and lobster dinners didn't count for shit, not when it came right down to it. It looked great in magazines, but it wasn't real.

"Cass—" Abby swung around on her bed so she was facing her. "Why didn't you ever tell me how close you and Mr. Doherty were? And what is it with the music room? I thought we were best friends. I thought we trusted each other."

She heard the hurt in Abby's voice and saw the pained expression on her face.

"I do trust you. With Mr. D., it was—I don't know, it was between us somehow. I can't explain it. It wasn't anything bad, it was good, but it was between us."

"OK." Abby looked away.

"You are my best friend. You know you are."

Abby's face was in profile. She could see tears on her cheek.

"Listen, I'm sorry. But I can't talk about this right now. Mr. D. helped me when I was first here. I don't know. I just can't talk about it. Not yet."

"All right, I—"

The door opened, and Karen stepped into the room.

"You both need to meet me after dinner tonight in the infirmary," she stated.

"Why?" Abby asked.

"Zoey will be there too. There's something you all need to know."

"Karen—"

"I'm not explaining it now, Abby. But if you both don't come, you'll both be sorry. Believe me."

And then she left.

"What the hell? Do you think we should go?" Abby asked.

"I don't know. I don't care."

Leave me alone. I want to be with Jeb. I can't be right now. So everyone else just leave me alone.

"But Zoey's going. That's freaky. And what could we all need to know?"

"I have no idea."

"I guess we should go. It must be *something*. I can't figure it out. She's been in a good mood lately. Why? And, you know, Karen's changed so much. I keep wondering if that's all my fault."

"We've all changed, Abs. This year has changed us all."

Cassidy turned her face to the wall and closed her eyes.

Chapter 72

Zoey

The infirmary was painted white and had two rows of iron beds against the east and west walls, two sinks standing side by side at the end, an exam table in front of the sinks, and in the middle of the room a table holding a thermometer, Band-Aids, Vicks VapoRub, and scissors.

The walls were bare, aside from one large round clock that ticked abnormally loudly.

There was an added feature—a small wooden desk with a chair pushed between two of the beds, obviously brought in when Karen was banished there to do her work. Her clothes were piled on an unused bed.

The lights overhead gave off a stark, striped effect, making the whole place even more clinical.

"So, what is this all about?" she asked when she entered. "Where are Cass and Abby?"

"You have to wait until they get here," Karen responded. She was sitting on top of the exam table. "They should be here soon."

"This is bullshit." Zoey didn't sit down but kept standing with her hands on her hips. "If they're not here in two minutes, I'm leaving."

"They'll be here."

"So where's Miss Rutgers? Does she leave you alone in here?"

"She comes to check up on me in the mornings and at lights-out at night, but she told me she and the other teachers are all meeting up at Miss Adams's for supper because of Mr. Doherty. She told me she trusted me not to take advantage of her absence in these circumstances."

"Right. Good chance for her to hit the booze."

Cass and Abby came in then. Zoey saw the smile on Karen's face. She didn't like that smile, not one bit.

"Groovy. Everyone's here. Take a bed, sit down. You'll need to be sitting, believe me."

"This is such bullshit," Zoey said, but she did sit on one of the beds. Cass and Abby sat on the two beds to her right.

"What's going on?" Abby asked. "What's this all about, Karen?"

"I'm going to tell a few secrets." Karen was still smiling. "And I'm going to tell you about some letters I've written. No, wait, I should say right now I've not only written them, I've sent them. You know, I used to hate the lighting in here. It's just so fucking bright. But right now, I love this lighting. Because I can't wait to see the expressions on your faces."

Chapter 73

2018
MAY 3

When I dropped her off at her hotel, Mary had thanked me profusely for the ride.

"I'll probably need a day to recover, but how about lunch tomorrow?"

"That sounds good to me. Do you want me to choose a restaurant around here?"

"Anywhere is fine. But some place we can actually hear each other talk. I'm not so great at noisy places anymore."

"Neither am I."

"Great—one p.m.?"

We exchanged numbers and I said I'd text her.

"Are you on WhatsApp?"

"Yes." I smiled. "I'll WhatsApp you then."

"Cool." She smiled too. "We're pretty tech-savvy for old people."

"And you're very hip staying here."

"Hip or groovy?" She gave me a goodbye hug. "Or—even better—far-fucking-out."

I'd found a small, quiet Italian restaurant on Kensington Park Road, not far from Mary's hotel. I'd messaged her in the morning, told her the name and said I'd meet her there at one.

It was another exceptionally beautiful spring day. People on the streets were dressed as if they were in the South of France about to head for a beach in the Med.

She was waiting for me at a corner table, a bottle of mineral water and a bottle of red wine in front of her.

"Hi," she said as I sat down. "I hope you don't mind, I ordered some wine, as you can see. Is red OK?"

"Yes, great."

"Listen, before we do anything else, I want to see pictures of your kids and grandkids. I saw a few on Facebook, but show me some more."

I dutifully got out my phone, scrolled through a few photos, pointed out my two sons and two daughters, my six grandchildren, then put it away.

"My mother always told me that looking at other people's children is boring. But there—you've seen them. And I'll give you the quickest possible rundown of where they all are and what they're doing—but I won't bang on."

"'Bang on'?"

"Sorry." I laughed. "It's an English expression. It means I won't go on and on about them. Boring."

So I did just that, gave her a quick rundown, expecting that at the end of it, she'd tell me about Wade, how they met, how he had died, her career. Instead she poured herself and me some wine, picked up her glass, and said, "To old friends. Cheers."

"Cheers."

We clinked glasses.

"So—did you tell your kids about what happened at Stony-bridge?"

"What?" I sat back.

"You know. Did you tell them? You must think about it."

"It was a long time ago, Mary. And no, I never told them. I didn't see the point."

"Right."

"Like I said, it was a long time ago. A different life."

"Do you keep in touch with anyone from then?"

"No. Do you?"

"I didn't, no. But then . . . the strangest thing happened. I was sitting out on my porch, which is where I do all my thinking. When it comes to my projects, I mean. I don't have much of a view, but I can see a sliver of San Francisco Bay from there, and seeing that tiny bit of water helps my brain function for some inexplicable reason. Anyway, I'd just finished a film about a woman who'd been falsely accused of killing her sister. It's a long story. The point is, it was over, done, and I didn't have a next project in mind and I was feeling old, you know. Like—what do I do next? Is there anything else I want to say?"

Mary took another sip of wine, smiled.

"Now I'm banging on."

"No, go ahead. I'm interested. Really."

"OK. Well, I was sitting there and my mind was wandering and then it came to me. Most of my films, the ideas for them, come from something I've seen on the news or a story I've heard. Or a letter or email someone has written to me. This was totally different. This idea came in the proverbial flash. Stonybridge. The killing. The unsolved killing. That deserves a film. All these years have gone by and no one knows what happened and I could try to find out. I could interview people, go back and look at the police files. Reexamine everything. There must be something they missed, right? Don't you ever think that?"

A film?

A documentary?

It was my turn to take a sip of wine before saying:

"No. Not really. Like I said, it was a different life. No, I don't think about it."

"Really? Never?"

"Well, sometimes. Yes, of course. Sometimes."

"So what do you think?" She leaned forward. Her bracelets clanked against each other. Her silver hair swished. "Do you have any idea who might have done it?"

"Whoa—Mary." I held up my hands. "Wow. That's out of the blue. Are you here to cross-examine me or something? Am I being interviewed? I have no clue who might have done it. I didn't then, and I don't now."

"But you wouldn't mind talking to me about it all, right? Sitting down for a few hours and going over it all again so I can get your perspective. I haven't talked to anyone else yet. The minute it came into my brain, you were the one I wanted to see first."

"Why me? I don't get it."

"Because . . ." She was staring at me intently. "Because we were friends once, Abby, and because . . . the thing is—what you said about that night—it never made total sense to me."

Chapter 74

1970
MAY 3

Karen

She had them right where she wanted them. How many times had she rehearsed this scene? Enough to know that whatever happened, it was going to be the best revenge in the world. A part of her wanted to wait, to hold on to this moment for as long as she possibly could, make them all sweat. Staring at Abby, she thought: *Your world is about to collapse. How will you like that? Are you going to cry? I hope you do. I hope you cry forever.*

"For Christ's sake, Karen. Get this over with, whatever it is, will you, or we're leaving," Zoey barked.

"I will. But remember—" She switched her gaze and stared at Zoey. "You asked for it."

Then she hopped off the exam table, went to the desk, picked up three pieces of paper, went back, and sat on the table again.

"These are copies of letters I've mailed. I think you'll enjoy hearing them. OK—here's the first: it's to the college admissions officer at Oberlin.

"'Dear Sir/Madam, A girl named Zoey Spalding is applying for admission to your prestigious college this year—she is now at Stonybridge

School for Girls in Lenox, Massachusetts. It may be of interest to you to know that Zoey's creative streak stretches far and wide. She put up a class list on the bulletin board asking for girls to put a star beside their name when they lost their virginity. So everyone in the class would know. She also arranged a secret abortion for a seventeen-year-old at her school. Is this legal? You tell me. Do you think I should inform the authorities? All my best, A Concerned Onlooker.'"

"Jesus Christ!" Zoey shouted. "What the fuck?"

"I've only just begun. This one's for you, Abby:

"'Dear Jimmy, Did your girlfriend, Abby, tell you that there is a class list up on the bulletin board at school? Well, there is. And if you have lost your virginity, you put a star up beside your name and a rating of how the sex was. One to five, five being the best. Anyway, a while after Abby came back from the February break, she put a star up beside her name. So congratulations, Jimmy. Except maybe you shouldn't pat yourself on the back too quickly. Because guess what? You only got a one. Now everyone in the senior class knows you're not exactly a hotshot when it comes to sex. What was the problem? Small dick? So sorry about that. If I were you, I'd think twice about having a girlfriend who spreads the news about your sexual prowess, or should I say lack of it? All my best, A Concerned Onlooker.'"

"You didn't send that," Abby said in a wimpy, pleading voice. "Please tell me you didn't send that."

"Oh, but I did. You think that's the worst of it, Abby? No such luck. Wait until you hear this one. Listen carefully, everyone.

"'Dear Jeb,'" she read from the top sheet, pleased that her voice was as strong and confident as she'd imagined it would be. "'Your girlfriend, Cassidy, killed your baby in February. She had an abortion in Canada. I, personally, think she should have told you she was pregnant. But she kept it a secret, the same way she kept it a secret from your sister that you two are together.

"'She's very good at keeping secrets. It makes me wonder if you can ever trust her again. It was your baby, Jeb. We'll never know if it was a boy or a girl, will we? All my best, A Concerned Onlooker.'"

She looked up, saw total shock and despair on all three faces. She'd never been athletic, but now she felt the kind of triumph a Wimbledon champion must have felt as he walked off the tennis court.

"Fuck. Karen—what the fuck? How? How did you find out?"

"You've all made me a leper. But the Leper can walk, Zoey. The Leper can follow you and stand outside the photography lab and listen in to your conversation. The Leper has ears. The Leper isn't so pathetic now, is she? So, Abby . . ."

She put down the copies of the letters, leapt off her table, went to stand in front of Abby.

"What do you think now? Cassidy and your brother. Is it all running through your mind right now? Are you thinking back, wondering when they got together? Realizing that the amazing Cassidy Thomas never gave a shit about you? Poor *Abs*. You thought you were best friends, didn't you? You and the perfect, beautiful Cassidy. You felt on top of the world, didn't you? You and the most popular girl in school were suddenly best friends. Nothing else counted. No one else counted. I wonder why Cassidy, your best friend, didn't tell you? If she liked you *so* much, why did she lie to you?

"Are you realizing now that she was only friends with you because of your brother? That she couldn't give a shit about you? When she got in trouble, who did she turn to? Not you. Not her so-called best friend. But to Zoey. She's been lying to you all along. Cassidy Thomas would have never been your best friend if it weren't for Jeb. She would have learned some Latin from you, sure. Used you, for sure. And then she would have ditched you because you're the pathetic one. The pathetic one with a best friend who doesn't give a shit about you, just like we were best friends but you didn't actually give a shit about me. And your so-called best friend killed your brother's kid. If you hadn't been so gullible in the first place and fallen for all that shit of hers, it wouldn't have happened, you know. You're as responsible as she is for that dead baby."

She was looking straight at Abby, staring her down. Finally, finally, she landed her stinger straight into Abby's heart.

Chapter 75

2018
MAY 3

A documentary? Jesus, she really had set me up. That was why she had made that account in her maiden name. If I'd known what she did for a living, I'd have avoided her. I would have ignored that Friend request.

I'd never have been sitting in a restaurant reliving that night forty-eight years ago when Karen taunted me about Cass's friendship, when she stood there, right in front of me, staring at me and gloating in her evilness.

I slapped Karen. Hard.

"Jesus!" She put her hand to her cheek, rubbed it. And then she smirked. "I'll report you for that. I'll tell Miss Adams you hit me. You're screwed. I'm going over there now to tell her. Forget a good college now, Abby."

"Don't you dare." Cass stood up too, moved toward her. "You've fucked up everyone's life already. Don't you fucking dare do any more."

"I'll do whatever I want to. You can't tell me what to do. And I'll tell you something else, Miss Perfect Cassidy. I told Mr. Doherty. I told him the truth too. All about the List—and your abortion."

Cass lunged at her, trying to grab her by the throat, but before she could get ahold of her, Karen turned into a mad whirling dervish, pounding her fists on Cass's chest, and a blow must have landed because Cass stepped back and Karen stepped forward, then Zoey was somehow there, trying to push Karen away, and Karen punched out at Zoey and I saw the scissors on the table beside me and then the scissors were off the table, glinting in the light, and they were in my hand and then they were in Karen's shoulder just as Zoey had pushed back at her and Karen cried out, staggering backward, falling, and she was on the floor.

She was lying there faceup on the floor with a pair of scissors sticking out of her shoulder, looking like a doll. Like some little boy was pissed off at his sister and her toys and had decided to maim her precious doll. Her eyes were closed. She wasn't moving.

No one was moving. I was standing there staring at her, panting.

"Shit." Zoey said it. "Shit, shit, shit. What happened? Shit."

"She fell backward."

"She didn't fall, Abby. You stabbed her with the scissors just as I was pushing her. Shit."

"She's OK. She's just knocked out." I knelt down, put my hand on her wrist, looked up. "See, she's breathing. I mean, she has a pulse. She'll be OK. She'll wake up in a second."

"I tried to strangle her." Cass was dragging her hands down her face. "It's all my fault."

"Jesus, Cass. I stabbed her. I stabbed her."

"You barely stabbed her." Zoey was standing beside me, staring down at Karen. "Look, there's hardly any blood. It's her shoulder, for Christ's sake, not her heart. The scissors have barely penetrated. I don't think—" Then she stopped.

She stopped so abruptly that I looked at her, followed her gaze. And I saw it.

The other blood, the blood coming out from behind Karen's head, spreading on the infirmary floor like a slow red tide.

Chapter 76

1970
MAY 3

Zoey

"Are you sure she's breathing, Abby?"

"Yes. I mean . . ." She saw Abby squeeze Karen's wrist tighter. "I think so . . . but it's kind of faint. We need to call an ambulance. But what's she going to say? I mean, when she wakes up in the hospital?" Abby was looking up as she asked, with terrified eyes. "She's going to say we attacked her. She's going to accuse us of trying to murder her. And . . ."

"And we'll go to jail," Zoey said, finishing Abby's sentence, wondering why she suddenly felt calm and removed, as if she were watching this all in a theater, as if it were one of her father's movies and had nothing to do with her.

"But if we don't call an ambulance . . . then what . . . what . . ."

"Finish a goddamn sentence, will you, Abby? If we don't call an ambulance, she may go into a coma or something."

Abby dropped Karen's hand, crawled to the corner of the room, propped herself against the wall, her knees up to her chest.

"I can't . . . I can't cope."

"We need to call an ambulance now." Cass had come up beside

her and was staring down at Karen too. "Oh shit. I think I'm going to faint."

"Come on—" Zoey took Cass by the elbow, led her to where Abby had collapsed against the wall, and sat her down. Then she sat down too, facing them both. "Take deep breaths, Cass. Put your head between your knees."

She waited while Cass sat there taking deep breaths and Abby sat there looking like a sandbag had just dropped on her head.

"Listen." She addressed them both. "We call an ambulance and then we get arrested and go to jail. That should be fun."

"What are you saying?" Abby was suddenly shivering from head to toe. "What are you saying?"

"I'm not saying anything. Only that maybe we should have a story to tell people. How this happened."

"She was *pushing* us." Abby's eyes locked on hers. "We can say it was self-defense."

"Yeah, with scissors sticking out of her?" Zoey heard herself snort. "That's a new kind of self-defense."

"I stabbed her. I'll tell them that. I stabbed her. But I didn't mean to hurt her badly."

"I know that, Abby. But Cass tried to strangle her, and I pushed her. We were all fighting her. She'll tell them that. So we all go to jail. Attempted murder."

"Is it true, Cass? About you and Jeb? And—"

"Seriously, Abby? Are you really asking that *now*?" Zoey pounded the floor with her fists. She could have throttled Abby. "We have to figure out what to do here. What we say."

No one spoke. Abby kept shivering, hugging her knees even more tightly to her chest.

They sat there, no one speaking, no one moving.

Think fast, Zoey said to herself. But she couldn't. Her brain had shut down.

She didn't know how many minutes had passed before she heard Karen's voice, heard her saying, "Let's do something fun for your birthday. We could go to the racetrack," and she saw Karen sipping her coffee and smoking and listening so intently to her that Thanksgiving afternoon and suddenly she wasn't watching a movie anymore.

"Fuck it, I'm calling an ambulance," she said, standing up. "Attempted murder—it's not as bad as murder, is it? And it's not as if we weren't provoked."

She headed for the door and the bank of telephones. But before she got there, she looked back at Karen. And she saw her face and she knew. She just knew.

Even as she walked over to her and leaned down and took her wrist in her hand, she knew.

There was no point in feeling for a pulse.

Chapter 77

2018
MAY 3

The waiter came to take our order. I hadn't looked at the menu, but I didn't wave him away; I told him to wait a second while we decided.

"I'll have the salad of roasted vegetables," Mary said, about one second after she'd picked up her menu. "How about you, Abs?"

"Give me a chance to look."

I pretended to peruse the menu while I tried to get my act together. She was making a movie?

Shit.

She was making a movie.

"Abs?"

"All right. OK. I'll have the spaghetti vongole."

"Excellent," he said. "Coming right up."

I wanted to ask him where he was from, anything to keep him there. Instead, I watched as he walked away. I watched, and I told myself to calm down. To look Mary straight in the eye and speak in an even tone.

"Why didn't what I said make sense to you, Mary? It made sense to everyone else. It made sense to the police."

"Yeah, OK, maybe, but . . ."

"But what?"

"But I don't believe the whole story."

"The whole story? Mary, this is ridiculous. Are you actually accusing me of lying?"

"No, Abs. I'm just saying there might be an alternative story."

"Like alternative facts? Have you joined the Trump brigade? What's going on? It sounds to me like you are accusing me. There's a police station around the corner. Should we go there after we eat or before?"

She laughed. "You're the one being ridiculous now. Chill out. I'm just trying to get the facts straight, that's all. Don't get so offended."

When I was pregnant with my first child, I read all of Proust's *Remembrance of Things Past*. I forced myself to finish it even though most of it bored me beyond belief. But there was one part that struck me then and stayed with me.

The main character had fantasies of a woman dying, wishing she would. I couldn't even remember why. Yet when she did die, he was completely distraught. The difference between wishing for something and the reality of it happening was a gulf he hadn't anticipated.

It was more than possible that I'd accepted Mary's Friend request, agreed to meet here, in order to come to this exact conclusion, that I had a subconscious desire to finally get the truth of that night in the infirmary out.

But now? The reality that this might happen?

It was unbearable.

Chapter 78

1970
MAY 3

Zoey

"She's dead."

"What?" Abby lifted her head. "What did you say?"

"Karen's dead. We let her die while we were sitting here doing nothing."

No one moved, no one spoke. They sat there like dumb animals until Abby finally said:

"I stabbed her. I killed her. I killed Karen."

She moaned, closed her eyes.

"You stabbed her, Abby, but we were all involved. And we all left her lying there. None of us called an ambulance. We sat here like zombies. For what? Ten minutes—maybe longer? Which means we're all guilty, all three of us. Which means our lives are screwed."

"I'll say I did it." Abby opened her eyes. "Jesus. Karen used to be my best friend. This is all my fault. I'll take the blame. I'll leave you two out of it."

"I *wanted* to kill her, Abs. You didn't." Cass dragged her hands down her face. "We can't let you take the blame for this."

"We can't, Cass?"

"No, Zoey, we can't. Or at least I can't—if you want Abby and me to leave you out of it, we will. You can go back to your room now."

So what exactly was she going to do? Let Cass and Abby go to jail while she went on and lived her life? Suddenly the thought of *The Three Musketeers* came into her brain. All for one, one for all. And then she thought of Mickey Mouse and how she'd always hated Walt Disney films. Why was that? she wondered. What kind of person hates Walt Disney films? She almost laughed. Karen's dead body lay about ten feet away and she was thinking of cartoons.

If she had to think about anything, it should be poetry.

Rage against the dying of the light.

Fuck Dylan Thomas.

Karen hadn't raged. She'd fallen down and hit her head and her brain must have bled out.

All those books were meaningless. No poem or novel was going to help now. No big words could help. Nothing she had read or thought was of any use. Wearing black clothes, being rude to her mother, trying to get her father's attention and love—none of it mattered.

The only thing that mattered was the life she wasn't going to get to have.

Maybe she *should* let Abby and Cass take the blame.

Fuck *The Three Musketeers* too.

But what were the odds of Abby keeping her mouth shut? As soon as Abby found herself being questioned, as soon as this became *real* and the police were involved, would she keep to her word? Abby had never been a friend. They'd competed for Cass's friendship. That was the sum total of their relationship.

Yes, right now Abby could be all self-sacrificing, but how long would it take before she said: *Zoey was there with us too.*

Maybe seconds.

Either they all went to jail, or . . .

"Wait." Zoey looked up at the clock. "What if none of us says any-thing? You heard Karen. Miss Rutgers might not check on her 'til to-morrow. All of the dorm mothers are at Miss Adams's house. We . . . we wipe off the scissors, wipe off our fingerprints from where we've been, and then . . . and then we stick together. Say we've been to-gether the whole time in the dorm. No one can prove that we weren't. How long have we been here? Look—it feels like years but we've only been here a half an hour. I'd bet anything no one has missed us. Ev-eryone's in their room. When we leave, we just have to be careful no one is in the hallway and sees us."

"But Karen . . ." Abby was gulping for air like a dying fish. "What . . . What happens to her?"

"She's dead. Nothing happens to her. If we're caught, our whole lives are ruined. We can't bring her back to life."

"But what if someone else gets blamed?"

"Who will get blamed, Abby? I bet everyone has an alibi. And anyone could have stabbed her with scissors. Becky Powell could have—and that's just one person. Karen was right—she was a leper."

"So Becky goes to jail?" Cass was shaking her head.

"No. Look, if someone gets charged, then we turn ourselves in. That's the deal. Come on, we don't know how much time we have. Nurse Rutgers might get back any time and decide to check on Karen tonight instead of tomorrow."

"I don't know." Cass looked over at Abby. Abby looked over at Kar-en's body, then quickly back.

"I don't know either," she said.

"What about your parents, your family, Abby? What will they do if you get caught? And Cass—your father? Hasn't he been through enough?"

"I don't know if I'll be able to lie like that."

"Cass—think of what Karen said to Mr. Doherty. I'm not saying she deserved to die, but it was an accident and . . ."

"The letters." Abby sat up straight. "Those letters she sent. People will find out. They'll think we killed her on purpose. We can't pretend we didn't do anything. Those letters."

"Shit."

How could she have forgotten about the damn letters? Dumb. She was the only one thinking straight, but she'd been moronic.

"Listen, we'll figure out something, make sure they don't get opened. I don't know . . . but there might be some way. We have to take the chance. Come on."

Neither of them moved, so she did. She took off her sweater and wiped down the floor around her. Then she made herself go over to Karen's body, lean down, and wipe off the handle of the scissors, using her sweater again.

Finally, she picked up the pieces of paper, the letters Karen had read out, and stuffed them between her waistband and her stomach.

"Wipe the floor around you, OK? Any surface you might have touched."

"Jesus," she said after a few seconds, when, yet again, neither of them had budged. "Do you have any idea what jail is like? We can't bring her back to life. Haven't you figured that out yet? This isn't a fucking movie. It's real, and we don't have enough time to sit around. If they find us here, that's it. There won't be anything we can do about the letters and we'll be charged with murder. Have you got that through your heads? Murder. Think of your families, will you? I for one don't want my mother or father visiting me in jail."

Abby took off her sweater, started wiping the floor around her with it.

Finally, Cass started to move too, taking off her sweater and copying Abby.

Zoey watched, willing them to hurry up. When they'd finished, they both turned to her and she said:

"OK. Now all we have to do is get out of here without anyone seeing us. Get behind me, and I'll open the door a crack. If there's no one in the hallway, we walk as quietly as we can to the staircase. Once we get there, we're OK—no one can say they saw us coming from the infirmary. Chances are everyone will be in their rooms anyway. We can make it up to your room and stay there. I'll wipe the door too—just make sure you don't fucking touch anything."

After she'd wiped the infirmary doorknob, she kept her sweater over it and opened it, a few inches.

"No one's there," she whispered. "Don't run—walk quietly, OK? Follow me."

She switched off the infirmary light, then led the way, on tiptoe, taking a look behind her halfway to the staircase to make sure they were following her. They were tiptoeing too. The three of them could have been children playing a game. She could see their shadows on the wall.

A few more steps and they were there at the staircase. No one had seen them. But now she had to turn around and put her finger to her lips and start gently creeping up the stairs. Because she'd been a moron again when she'd said back in the infirmary that they'd be safe at the staircase. If anyone saw them, they'd know they weren't in their rooms all night. They'd be dead.

No one was in the first-floor corridor. All the doors were closed.

Someone was playing Procol Harum; she could hear "We skipped the light fandango." Three more steps and they would have made it.

They took those steps. They made it.

They were in Abby and Cass's room. They'd made it.

"Why?" Abby sank down on her bed. "What was the point of all that, Zoey? She sent the letters. We're fucked."

Chapter 79

Cassidy

She'd gotten rid of her baby, and now she'd sat doing nothing while Karen died in front of her and she was going to go to hell. She would burn in hell. Forever. The only reason she'd gone along with Zoey and done what Zoey told her to was to save Abby. If Abby was caught and ended up in jail, the whole Madison family would fall apart.

She couldn't let that happen.

But it was going to happen anyway. Abby was right. Jeb would open the letter, and Jeb would know everything. Even if a miracle happened and he didn't open it, Jimmy would open his and the Oberlin person would open the other one and somehow it would all come out. Everything.

Everything was going to fall apart.

Everything had already fallen apart.

Every single thing.

"You could call Jimmy and tell him not to open the letter."

Zoey was still trying to fix it. She was sitting beside Abby on the bed, jiggling her foot crazily, thinking of a way out of this.

"And you could call Jeb, Cass. Tell him not to open his letter. Maybe whoever it is at Oberlin won't pay attention to that letter either."

There wasn't a way out. They were all going to hell.

Her mother was in heaven.

She'd never see her mother again.

"We're fucked." Abby said it again. "You can't tell someone not to open a letter. They'll want to know why. It doesn't work."

Jeb.

He'd know what she'd done, and he would hate her.

"She didn't sign those letters, Abby, remember? So no one has to know they're from her. Anyone could have sent them."

"How long before they figure it out?" Abby stood up, began to pace around the room. "The minute they find her . . . her body, people will . . . people will be looking for someone with a reason. It will be in the news, Zoey. You know it will. Sooner or later, someone will find out about the letters. They'll figure it out."

Cassidy could see it in Zoey's eyes then, the understanding that there was no way out, that it was over.

"I wonder how long she'd been planning this—how to wreck our lives," Zoey fumed. "Those fucking letters. What was I supposed to do?"

"Maybe you shouldn't have humiliated her. You didn't have to scream at her like that in front of everyone. Or stop everyone from talking to her."

"Oh great, Abby. You're telling me what I shouldn't have done? You're the one who started this whole thing. One nice word from Cass and you leave Karen in the dust. You're the one who treated her like dirt. You treated her like dirt because you wanted to be cool. You wanted to drop the whole tomboy studious routine and be friends with the most popular girl in school. But guess what, Abby? It didn't work. You're still a boring jerk."

"What about you? You dropped Karen the minute you got tired of being with her—or was it because . . . ? Because you and Cass shared that secret so you were friends again and you couldn't be Cass's best friend if you were still friends with—"

"Shut up!" Cassidy covered her ears with her hands. "We just let Karen die and you're talking about this shit? This best-friend shit? You're talking about me as if I were an animal you were hunting. Some trophy to show off. Stuff me and put me up on a wall, why don't you?"

They shut up. Finally stopping her pacing, Abby leaned against the wall, then slid down it in a heap.

Zoey began to rake her hair with her hands.

"You're not a trophy, Cass," Abby said in a little kid's voice. In Jennifer's voice.

Pumpkin pie is so gross. She could hear Jennifer saying it, she could see Jennifer in her ponytail. Jennifer and Jeb and all of them sitting around that table eating turkey.

I want to die.

But if I die, I'll go to hell. I don't want to go to hell.

"Wait!" Zoey sprang up from the bed. "Wait!"

She and Abby watched Zoey as she began to pace around the room.

"Wait, wait, wait. There might . . . I mean, it's Sunday, isn't it? It's Sunday, right?"

"Yes, it's Sunday." Abby shook her head. "So what?"

"The mailbag. You know, it's right under that revolting stuffed moose head."

"We know that, Zoey."

"That's what made me think of it. You, Cass, saying 'stuff me and put me up on a wall.' The mailbag."

"What about the fucking mailbag?" Abby was emphasizing every word, looking at Zoey as if she were crazy.

"What if . . . what if Karen put those letters in the mailbag yesterday? I mean, that makes sense. She puts them in the bag yesterday and she tells us today. She wouldn't put them in the bag today because it's Sunday and that mail guy Robert doesn't pick up the mail on Sunday."

"So what? He picked them up yesterday. They're gone."

"That's the thing. Some Saturdays he doesn't pick them up. I heard Connie complaining about that once—in the Senior Room, and Angel said, 'Yeah, I know, he skips a lot of Saturdays. I think he goes out and gets drunk as a skunk most Friday nights. He gets away with waiting 'til Monday because he's related to Miss Chase somehow. A cousin or something.'"

"You think he might not have picked them up yesterday?" Abby stood. "Really?"

"It's possible. Maybe he picked them up yesterday, maybe Karen sent them before yesterday—but it's worth checking out. If we can get to them before . . ." Zoey looked at her watch. "It's five past nine. If I go now—"

"But what if someone sees you?"

"We don't have a choice, Abby. It's our only hope."

"You'd do that? You'd go?"

"Right now, I'm the one who is thinking clearly, obviously. So I'll go. But when I get back, if I do find them and no one sees me, we have to make sure someone sees the three of us in this room together. So they'll think we've been here since dinner, OK? If I were in my room alone, I wouldn't have an alibi. I'd be screwed."

"OK." Abby nodded. "OK."

Jennifer was the same age Cassidy had been when her

mother died. She hadn't done anything wrong. She didn't deserve to go through hell if Abby were caught.

All her dreams of being with Jeb had vanished. There was no way she could lead a normal life now. But the Madisons could. They could still play touch football and argue about Vietnam and sit around a table. Being the Madisons.

"Go," she told Zoey. "Go."

Chapter 80

2018
MAY 3

Our lunch had turned into an interrogation the moment she'd said that my account of that night didn't make sense. I wondered whether she was taping me on her phone but knew there was no way I could ask to see it. *Oh, Mary—by the way, what kind of phone do you have?* Yeah, right. My only option was to let her talk and for my responses to at least seem innocent.

"I don't understand, Mary. What do you mean, what I said about that night doesn't make sense? We were in our room—the three of us. Zoey and Cass and I. We had no idea what had happened to Karen until the next morning."

"Yes, I know that's what you all said. But the thing is, Abs, at that point you and Zoey weren't friends. The opposite, if anything. Zoey and Cass weren't friends either, supposedly. So that's what bothers me. What was Zoey doing there with you two?"

"She knew how much Cass cared for Mr. Doherty. Remember—we found out he died that day. You must remember that. Zoey still liked Cass, she cared about her, even if they weren't best friends anymore. So she came to our room to help Cass."

"Yeah. OK. That's what I told myself at the time. It didn't quite scan that Zoey would do that, come to your room, but I figured anything's possible. But then . . . do you believe in synchronicity?"

"I don't know. I guess. What's that got to do with anything?"

"I didn't used to believe in it, but now I think maybe there really is such a thing. Because a few days after the idea came to me, to do a documentary on Karen's death, I was at a film festival—and guess who was there?"

"George Clooney."

"Ha. No, Zoey's father. David Spalding. I went over and introduced myself to him. I told him I'd gone to school with Zoey and asked him how she is, where she is. It turns out she's a lawyer and she's married with three children and living in the suburbs of Atlanta. I mean, Zoey? A lawyer? Married? Three kids? In a suburb? That's crazy, right?"

It was crazy. And profoundly shocking, in a way I couldn't allow myself to dwell on at that moment. I was too concerned with seeing where Mary was going with this.

"Anyway, he said he and Zoey barely speak now. And of course he was with a girl eons younger than him. He was still absurdly handsome for his age too. He's in his eighties, but he looks fifty—at the most. What is it with him? I mean, does he have super genes?"

"I guess he does." A deadpan answer, but I attempted a smile when I said it.

Where the hell was this leading to?

"Anyway, I could tell that his girlfriend was getting antsy so I said how nice it was to meet him and to give my best to Zoey when he did speak to her again. But then just as they were walking away, he stopped and turned back to me and said:

"'Whatever happened to that beautiful girl in your class? The stunning one who had an abortion?'

"Not too hard for me to guess who he was talking about. So I said: 'Cassidy Thomas?'

"And he said: 'Yeah. Cassidy. That's right. Of course. She paid me back. I never thought she would, but she did. What's happened to her?'

"I told him I didn't know what had happened to her.

"'Oh well,' he said. 'That kind of beauty is a curse, you know. I felt sorry for her then. A kid like that having to go to Canada and have it done. Thank God that's changed now. Anyway, I hope life has been kind to her.'

"Then he did walk away. I stood there thinking: Cass had an abortion? Jesus." She picked up a breadstick, put it down again. "Did you know Cass had had an abortion?"

"God—really?"

Synchronicity. David Spalding. Of all the gin joints . . . Shit.

"Yes, really. Clearly she had the abortion when she was at Stonybridge—and David Spalding paid for it. He must have known where she could go that wouldn't be a back-alley dive. Canada—it makes sense. Anyway, I went back in time, trying to remember. When could she have had it? What year? And then I remembered. She was different spring of our senior year. More low-key, quieter. Not her usual self."

"Are you sure that wasn't just the stress of the SATs?"

She raised her eyebrows. "Cass wasn't one to stress too much about exams. It's like she was diminished in some way for a while there that spring term."

Back came the waiter, this time with our food.

"Thank you," we both said.

"Anyway, when I realized Cass had had an abortion that spring, I thought: This makes what Abby said about that night make sense. If Zoey's father paid for the abortion, then Zoey must have known about it. Arranged it with him. Which means she and Cass were still friends. So it's not that surprising she was in the room with you guys."

"So now you're saying it makes sense that we were together. You said before it didn't. I don't understand what's going on, what you're getting at."

Mary speared a roasted carrot, devoured it.

"Motiveless malignancy," she stated.

"What?"

"Motiveless malignancy. Shakespeare. *Othello*. Did Iago have a motive to ruin Othello's life, or did he do it because it was in his nature to be malign?"

She speared an asparagus, devoured it.

"Don't look at me as if I'm crazy, Abs. No one was ever charged for Karen's death because there wasn't any solid physical evidence and no one had a motive. Except Zoey, possibly, because Karen was so obsessed with her, but Zoey had an alibi. She was with you and Cass all evening. Plus, in a way, even though no one had a motive, everyone had a motive. Karen was persona non grata, remember? By the time it happened, no one liked her."

"Except you."

"Except me." She nodded. "She was fucked-up at the end, but I always liked her."

I remembered her reprimanding me when we were on the playing fields on Friendship Weekend.

Mary had been the moral compass in our class.

Back then I resented her for it.

Now that morality terrified me.

"In any event, no one without an alibi had a motive, everyone had a motive—it was a mess, obviously. No wonder the police couldn't figure it out. And the scissors had been wiped clean and Miss Rutgers was such a shitty nurse, she never properly cleaned the infirmary, so there were fingerprints everywhere anyway from when that flu thing broke out in April."

I twirled some spaghetti strands around my fork. They slipped off, landed back in the bowl.

"Then—synchronicity, and I meet David Spalding and it turns out Cassidy had an illegal abortion. So I have to ask myself . . ."

She paused. I didn't prompt her. She took a huge swig of wine, finishing her glass, then refilling it and topping mine up.

"I have to ask myself, who had a real motive? And the answer is Cassidy Thomas. See, here's what I think . . ." She put down her fork, leaned forward. "I think that Karen somehow found out about the abortion and she was threatening to expose Cass. Cassidy couldn't take that. She stabbed her, Karen fell back, hit her head, and Cass left her there to die. Then she got you—and Zoey—to alibi her. She knew Zoey would probably be the first suspect, so she dragged her in too, to protect her."

"Oh please." I held up my hands. "You're Sherlock Holmes now? Miss Marple? No offense, Mary, but you're totally nuts. First of all, Cass could have had an abortion any time. Just because you thought she looked—what was the word? Diminished? Just because you think that, you've concocted this whole story to explain something even the police couldn't explain. Cass could have had the abortion after she left Stonybridge. You're trying to make this into a story that will work for your film. Find out how Karen died and get an Oscar or something. And you're accusing me and Zoey of covering up for her? You're accusing me of lying? Being an accomplice to murder? Honestly, Mary, it's ridiculous and offensive."

"Is it? Is trying to get the truth ridiculous, Abs? The point is, you would have done anything for Cassidy. I'll never forget how she turned you junior year."

"She *turned* me? What is this, now we're in a le Carré novel instead of an Agatha Christie one? You've got to be kidding."

"She did turn you. From someone who gave a damn about other people to someone who didn't."

"It was my choice to become friends with her. Despite what you think, I wasn't her puppet. Anyway, all of that has nothing to do with Karen's death. Your theory is bonkers."

"OK, I take your point about when Cassidy had the abortion, but it should be relatively easy to find out the truth. And I'm not accusing you, Abby. Maybe you didn't know. She was gone for a while and made up some story and you believed her. I'm just trying to put it all together. I'm just trying to find justice for Karen."

Mary leaned back in her chair. All those silver bracelets sparkled in the sun. We were in a table by the window, and I was beginning to sweat.

"You're trying to make a movie, Mary. That's what you're trying to do."

"Right now I have to try to find the bathroom." She stood up. "I'll be back in a minute."

I bet you will, I thought.

She didn't take her bag with her when she walked off. When she was out of sight I reached down, picked it up, and took out her phone. It wasn't recording. Gingerly, I put it back.

Justice for Karen?

Justice for Karen had eked out its last breaths while the three of us sat in the infirmary doing nothing.

Chapter 81

1970
MAY 3

Zoey

"Wait . . ."

Why was her brain the only one of the three actually working?

"If the letters are there in the mailbag and I get them, we'll have to hide them. And these." She pulled out the pieces of paper from her waistband. "Where are we going to hide these? We can't burn them. I don't think it's a good idea to tear them into pieces and throw them in the trash. What are we going to do with them?"

Even as she asked the question, she knew she was the one who'd have to figure out the answer. It was a joke, really. There was Abby, top of the class in all her subjects, probably acing her SATs, and she was sitting there like an idiot, looking hopeless, while Cass was sitting there mute.

"OK . . . We can't hide them here. They might search the rooms. Shit . . . let me think for a second. Maybe we could hide them in our homework, you know, in the middle of our papers somehow. But if they search our rooms, they might search our notebooks . . . shit."

"I'm sorry I didn't tell you about Jeb and me." Cass looked over at Abby. "We were going to tell everyone after I'd graduated."

"But why keep it a secret from me? Why couldn't you tell me?"

Girls. Idiotic girls. Now? Abby was whining. Now?

"For Christ's sake! You two can talk about Jeb Madison for the rest of your lives. But you'll be talking to yourselves in jail if we don't figure this out."

Would her mother or father visit her in jail? The thought of her mother visiting a jail was ludicrous. Would she write her letters? She couldn't picture her mother addressing an envelope to a jail either. She'd probably disown her. She was close enough to disowning her already.

"Wait." There it was—finally. Her brain had clicked. "What if . . . do you have an envelope in here?" Her eyes scanned the room, the top of the two desks. "A reasonably big envelope and a stamp?"

"I think so. Yeah. I have stamps."

"And a big envelope?"

"Yeah." Abby went over to her desk, rummaged around the papers on top, drew out an envelope and stamps. "Here." She walked over, handed them over. "I don't get it, though . . ."

"It's simple. I put all these"—she waved the papers in the air—"in the envelope. Then, if the original letters are in the mailbag, I put them in too. Get me a pen."

Abby went back to her desk, retrieved a pen, and handed it to her.

"I address the envelope to myself in New York and then, when we get out of here and I'm back home, I'll burn it."

They sat there like complete zombies.

As she stuffed the envelope Abby had given her with Karen's sheets of paper, she realized that if they got away with this, once they left Stonybridge, she'd never see Cass or Abby again.

It wasn't only that it might not be a good idea to spend time with each other after what had happened, it was that they had both shown their weaknesses. Up until now she'd always thought of Cass as a strong person. And Abby as a smart one. But they'd effectively fallen apart on her.

Her dreams of being a poetess or a photographer or anything to do with the arts now struck her as ridiculous. She wasn't a dreamer, she was a doer. She figured things out and got things done. She didn't want to be like her father or her mother. All she needed was the chance to do something, not rot in jail.

No—all she needed was a hungover mailman who hadn't done his job.

She wrote her name and address on the front of the envelope, stuck a stamp on it, filled it with the sheets of paper Karen had read out, and left without saying a word to either of them.

Chapter 82

2018
MAY 3

"Listen, Abby—" Mary was back at our table. "Honestly, I didn't mean to accuse you. I'm putting two and two together and—well, you know math was never my best subject. Just one more thing and then I'll drop it. Do you know who might have gotten Cassidy pregnant?"

"Jesus. I thought this was going to be a nice lunch. All you've done is barrage me with questions." I rubbed my hands over my face. "It was almost fifty years ago. Can we please move on?"

"Sure. Of course. I'm sorry." She put out her hand, covered mine with hers. "I have a tendency to go too far with things sometimes. People I work with call me a dog with a bone. I think they probably call me a bitch with a bone behind my back. Sometimes I don't know when to stop."

I didn't take my hand away. I'd been too defensive, I knew. It was time to be friendly.

"That's probably exactly what you need to be to get your work done."

"Yeah." She tilted her head to the side, let go of my hand. "Thanks, Abs. You know, I really wish we'd stayed in touch over the years. Anyway, would you like something for dessert?"

"No thanks. I'm fine."

"Lunch is on me," she stated. "No arguments. I'll get the waiter's attention."

As she put up her hand to signal for him, I looked at the peasant blouse she had on. This one was pale blue, a minor change from the white one she'd worn the day before. We all wore those back then. We all wore the same type of clothes when we weren't in the same uniforms. Except Zoey. Zoey was the only one who had her own style.

Zoey, who had appeared back in our room, had put her hands up in a hallelujah pose and said:

"The letters were there. Can you believe it? They were there. Sitting in the mailbag. Thank God for alcoholics. First Miss Rutgers and now the mail guy. And no one saw me. Jesus. We've done it. We've fucking done it. We got away with it."

She'd done it. She'd figured it out. Zoey had pulled it off.

And what did I feel?

Total relief. It meant I might not go to prison. It meant my parents, no one in my family, would know what I'd done.

I hadn't meant to hurt Karen badly, much less kill her. I hadn't even realized I was picking up those scissors. They were in my hand and then in her shoulder before I knew what I was doing. The way when you're driving a car and something comes out at you, you step on the brake without thinking about it.

She'd taunted me, I'd lashed out. Zoey had pushed her. A chain of events, none of which had been planned.

And we were all in shock afterward. That was why we didn't call an ambulance right away.

I kept saying that to myself. All that night.

And for the next forty-eight years.

Because Zoey was right. We did get away with it. But luck was involved. The mailman hadn't picked up the letters in the bag. No one had been sick that weekend, or if they had felt ill, they'd decided it was better staying in bed on the weekend than going to the infirmary with Karen.

Also, Miss Rutgers had gotten drunk that night at Miss Adams's house, so she hadn't even bothered to check on Karen when she got back. On Monday morning, she walked into the infirmary before breakfast and found the body lying there. At which point pandemonium ensued. An ambulance first, then police, then whispers, then screaming girls and a bewildered Miss Adams, who had no idea how to cope with the chaos. A student dead on her watch. When she was told, she fainted.

It didn't take long for the rumors to reach a boiling point. Karen hadn't had an accident. The fall was what killed her, but everyone focused on the scissors sticking out of her. Someone had viciously stabbed Karen.

There was a murderer in our midst.

Zoey had made us rehearse our stories for hours before she finally let us sleep and crashed out on our floor herself. She'd managed, meanwhile, to blast some music loudly, at around 9:30, which had made Angel come knock on our door to ask us to turn it down. Angel had seen the three of us together—another piece of luck, as no one would disbelieve the angelic Angel.

"We'll say I didn't want to be alone," Zoey had stated. "I'm the only one on my own in a room, so I'll say after Mr. D. dying, I needed company."

"We shouldn't use him like that," Cass had protested, but Zoey wasn't listening, and neither was I.

We'd come straight from dinner to our room, the three of us together. And stayed there all night.

"That's all anyone needs to know." Zoey sounded like a drill sergeant—but that was exactly what Cass and I needed. Total direction.

"We can't fuck it up now, not after I found the letters. We got lucky, OK? Karen's dead. There's nothing we can do for her now."

"A bunch of dead cells, is that it? Is Karen only a bunch of dead cells?"

"Cass—pull yourself together," Zoey barked. "We've been through all this a million times. It doesn't help anyone if we all go to jail. No one. It hurts people. That's all the truth would do. Hurt a lot of people."

Bowing her head, Cass murmured, "OK. All right."

It was such a simple story that it worked. No one had seen us go to the infirmary from dinner. No one had seen us leave the infirmary. Angel had seen us together in our room, with Zoey.

Zoey was the one who was most closely questioned. She was the one with the most obvious motive but Zoey could handle herself with the police. Zoey could handle anything.

They questioned every girl in the school, every teacher, every person who worked there in any capacity. I figured they'd call the seniors in first, but they didn't. They left us until last.

Weirdly, the interviews were carried out in the Senior Room. I suppose the police didn't want to haul a bunch of teenage girls one by one to the police station; instead, we tramped one by one and sat down where we used to sit smoking and laughing; where Karen had spent so much of her time after becoming friends with Zoey.

"What was your relationship like with Karen?"

I remember that was the first question asked by a red-haired detective with strangely blond eyebrows. He had introduced himself as Karl Pope.

"We were best friends for a couple of years." I knew he must have heard the whole story by then because he was interviewing the senior class alphabetically. "Then I became best friends with Cassidy Thomas so I didn't see Karen much anymore."

Most of his following questions were about Karen and Zoey's relationship. Which I answered honestly. When he finally asked me if Zoey had been with Cass and me all Sunday night, I answered honestly again.

"Yes, we were together all night. And Zoey slept on our floor. She didn't want to go back to her room and be alone."

He left it at that.

I had the feeling he was uncomfortable dealing with young girls, that a female detective would have done better. But back then there probably weren't any female detectives in the Lenox area.

Mary would have done the job brilliantly.

We had been told by Miss Adams, who, after her fainting fit, attempted to regain some sort of composure, that we were not to discuss Karen's death with each other, but there was no chance of that happening. We shared rooms, after all, and what else was everyone going to talk about? Or rather whisper about?

Who could have done it? Poor Karen. She'd been so intelligent, so funny, so kind.

Within a few days Karen had turned from a self-professed leper into a saint.

Meanwhile Stonybridge turned into another kind of jail. Because no one seemed to know what to do in this situation, we went on as usual in terms of going to classes, but we weren't allowed out, not even to play sports.

I'm not sure when exactly the parents started to complain, but they must have been bombarded with phone calls from stressed-out, frightened daughters, all begging to come home, and they began to put pressure on Miss Adams.

It was May anyway. The school year was almost over. The police hadn't come close to finding the responsible person. It could have been someone from the outside Karen had let into the infirmary that night. It was time to let us all go home.

My father was leading the fight to bring us home. And my father had a prestigious lawyer's clout.

So finally, on May 20, we were allowed to leave. There was no graduation ceremony. Parents arrived, picked up their daughters, drove away.

We hugged each other goodbye. Warily. All of us were so relieved to be getting out we skipped any "Let's keep in touch" platitudes.

Cass and I had barely been talking anyway. At nights we sat in our room silently. I'd tried a couple of times to get through to her, but all she'd say was "I can't think about it, Abby. I can't talk about it. I want to go home and stay there."

That morning as we finished packing all our things, she finally turned to me and said: "I'm sorry, Abby."

"So am I," I replied. "I should never have—"

"Don't say that. There's no point."

"But I'll see you, right? I mean, Jeb and you . . . you and I . . . I'll see you, right?"

"No." She put all her uniform clothes on the bare bed. "I'm going back home. I can't see Jeb now, not after . . . I can't keep lying. And I can't tell the truth. So it's better if I go home and stay there."

"But—"

"But that's it." She went over, grabbed the *West Side Story* album cover off the wall, threw it in the wastepaper basket, then came over to me, gave me a quick hug. "You've finished your packing. You should go now. I'm sure your parents are waiting. My dad won't be here for a while still. Go."

"Cass?"

"Go."

She turned away from me.

Chapter 83

"Abs?"

I saw Mary's hand waving in front of my face. "Where did you disappear to then?"

"I was remembering all of us leaving Stonybridge that May."

That was one of the very few honest sentences I'd spoken at lunch.

PART FOUR

Chapter 84

Zoey

Who named a girl Karen in 2018? Montana, Verona, Sunshine—any of the new age names would have been fine. But Karen? Why? Because that was Sarah's grandmother's name, Luke had said. "It's old-fashioned, but we like it."

Yeah, right, but I hate it, Zoey hadn't replied.

Her granddaughter was going to be called the same name as the girl she let die. How was that for irony? No, not irony. Karma. Karma had been a long time coming, but now it was kicking in—with a vengeance.

Almost fifty years and she'd never really thought about it. Occasionally it would crop up in her psyche, but she could stamp on it quickly, shove it to some mental basement, and leave it there in the dark.

When you were a partner in a big law firm and had a husband and three children, you had zero time to think about your teenage self. Even when that teenage self participated in a death. That was what she told herself when it came up from the basement of her soul. *I didn't kill her. I participated in her death. Only participated.*

But she ran the cover-up.

Karengate.

She handled it a hell of a lot better than Nixon handled Watergate.

She'd told them what to do. She'd dealt with the letters. And she'd talked them through everything all night, making sure they would stick to the story. They'd come from dinner straight to Abby and Cass's room and stayed there all night. Angel saw them when she came to ask them to turn the music down at around 9:30. And yes, it was not the right thing to play music so loudly that night, but they were in shock about Mr. Doherty and it felt right to play the Beatles' latest album at full blast.

No one could prove they were lying. Of course Zoey was the one with the biggest motive—that mud fight, that kiss. But everyone knew Abby Madison wasn't Zoey Spalding's biggest fan, far from it.

So why would Abby, president of the class, well-behaved, preppy Abby, lie to protect someone she didn't like?

Dealing with the detective's questions had been ridiculously easy. Yes, she'd once been good friends with Karen; yes, that had changed when Karen clearly began to have a crush on her; yes, she'd wanted her out of her room. But Karen *was* out of her room, in the infirmary.

And yes, she couldn't bear Karen. Absolutely. So why would she go to the infirmary and hunt her out? All she wanted was not to deal with Karen ever again.

Tell enough of the truth and the lies sound honest.

I should have been a criminal lawyer, not a corporate one.

The police finally had to let them all leave Stonybridge. All the parents were putting pressure on Miss Adams to get their children the hell out of there. They were worried, they were angry, they complained so much the police finally caved and let them all go. Another irony: Abby's father, a hotshot lawyer himself, was one of the leaders of the group of parents demanding they all be set free.

Almost fifty years later and she was so far from the girl she'd been those first few years at Stonybridge, it was hard for her to believe she'd ever cared about J. D. Salinger or Hermann Hesse or Emily Dickinson.

If someone had played a video of the 2018 Zoey, the Zoey sitting in her Atlanta house in the suburbs, looking out her kitchen window as a team of workers did her garden and pool, if someone had played that video to Karen back then and said, "See, this is the future Zoey Spalding," Karen would have been stunned and speechless.

Was it the prospect of her granddaughter being named Karen that had set everything in motion? Was that what had made what had been shoved down into the basement of her psyche take the elevator to the top floor?

She was dreaming about Karen. Terrible dreams, but not terrible as in scary. Karen wasn't begging for help to save her or jumping out of her grave shouting: "Murderers!"

In a way she thought she could have handled those better than the ones she was having. Because in the dreams she was having, Karen was sitting across a table from her, sipping coffee, smoking cigarettes, and saying, "What happened to you, Zoey? You're such a sellout. You've turned into a make-believe girl," and she was desperately trying to argue her own case: "I have a great career. I work hard. Just because I'm not a poet or photographer doesn't mean I've sold out."

"Yeah, right. Married with three kids, living in the suburbs, being a corporate lawyer. Sure, of course. No way have you sold out."

And Karen would sit there saying that with a god-awful smirk on her face.

That smirk stayed with Zoey when she woke up. It took hours to get that smirk out of her brain. And maybe not the next night, but the night after that or two nights later, she'd have the exact same dream with the exact same smirking Karen.

And maybe she could have gone to a shrink or a hypnotherapist and figured out a way to change her dreams without telling them precisely why she wanted to change them. Maybe that might have worked if there hadn't suddenly been reminders everywhere.

No one smoked anymore—except, it seemed, the guy who had come to paint her living room the week before, who took breaks, went outside, and pulled out his packet of Marlboros. It had to be Marlboros, of course. Marlboro Lights, but still. Marlboros.

Two days ago, she'd been at a charity lunch, and sitting beside her was a woman who started talking about guns and school shootings and then, out of the blue, said: "It's strange. Every time I hear about a school shooting, I remember this girl who was killed at her boarding school—it was in the next town over to where I grew up. She was stabbed and then left to die. I can't remember her name. Anyway, they never found out who did it."

Then she was back on guns and the evil NRA and that was it. But it was enough.

And now this.

A granddaughter who was going to be named Karen.

"I hate my name," Karen had once said to her as they were sitting in the Senior Room on their own. "I wish my parents had given me an interesting name."

"Like what?"

"Like Zoey—like your name."

Here we go again, she'd thought. *This copycat stuff never ends. It keeps getting worse. Jesus, now she even wants my name.*

She could remember it clearly: The scorn she had felt. How badly she'd felt like hitting Karen so many times. Her overwhelming sense of relief when Miss Adams had moved Karen into the infirmary.

And how easily she'd switched to survival mode, to getting them all off the hook that night.

How had Cass and Abby dealt with the past over these past decades?

There'd been times when she'd thought about trying to look them up, see where they were, but she'd thrown that idea into the basement too.

Did they dream about Karen? Was she haunting them too?

Because that was what it felt like now. Karen was always with her. Even this morning, when she'd opened the paper, she'd seen an article about the upcoming anniversary of Kent State by some left-wing journalist. The Monday in May 1970 when four students on the Kent State campus had been shot dead by riot police was the same Monday when Karen's body had been found in the infirmary.

If that night in the infirmary hadn't happened, Zoey would have been furiously railing against the government. As it was, all she could do was concentrate on not getting caught.

She'd prided herself on hating hypocrisy. She was the one who believed in equality and women's lib, who sympathized with Mr. Doherty's plight. Yet she was the one who went berserk when Karen kissed her in that mud fight. As if being kissed by a girl was, as Cassidy would have put it, a mortal sin. Her reaction had been shameful. So much of her past was shameful. Which is why she had tried so hard to bury it and keep it buried.

"What are you reading now?" Karen had asked her.

"A short story by Edgar Allan Poe."

"Why? Isn't he, you know, a mystery writer? I didn't think you liked mystery writers."

"He was a great writer. And a poet. His short stories are what I like best. This one especially."

She'd gone on to explain the plot. A guy murders an old man living in his house. It's not clear why exactly, but the old man has a terrible, scary eye. So the guy kills the old man, dismembers him, hides the body parts under the floorboards. The police come looking for the old man, and the guy says: "Oh, he's left. I don't know where he's gone." The police have no reason to doubt him.

But then the guy starts to hear a noise.

It's the noise of a heart beating, coming from under the floorboards. A beating heart, getting louder and louder until finally it drives him mad and he confesses.

"That's spooky," Karen said, making a face.

"It's called 'The Tell-Tale Heart.' It's brilliant. It's all about guilt. How guilt gnaws away at your psyche. Poe wrote it about twenty years before Dostoevsky wrote *Crime and Punishment*. I wonder whether Poe was translated into Russian, whether Dostoevsky had read 'The Tell-Tale Heart.'"

"God, you're smart. I wish I were as smart as you are."

She had secretly basked in that compliment. That was before Karen had turned into an annoyance, the wood tick burying into her flesh.

All these reminders now, they were that tell-tale heart beating.

It didn't mean she was going to follow in Poe's literary footsteps and go to the police and confess. It would be as pointless now as it had been all those years ago. Karen was dead. No confession could bring her back.

So she would live her life as she had been living it, in the big house in the suburbs, the house with a pool and two acres' worth of garden, live as happily as it was possible to live with a husband she'd been married to for forty years, have her three grown-up children and however many grandchildren over to visit, do her charity work, her yoga, her Pilates, and take her Labrador for walks.

Nothing would change.

Except for the fact that Karen was going to get what she'd wanted. She was dead, but her heart was still beating. And it wasn't going to stop.

Karen was now her *forever roommate.*

Chapter 85

2018

Julia Madison

It was one of those days when the rain wasn't going to stop. That didn't keep her from her routine, however. At 10:00 a.m., as always, she walked out onto the porch, grateful that she *could* still walk; not only that, but walk and hold a cup of coffee at the same time. At ninety-five years old, that had to be considered a triumph.

She sat in the wicker chair, sipped her black coffee, gazed out at a sea so dark it matched the sky. The older she became, the more she appreciated nature. It was easy and enjoyable to sit and simply take it all in. The sky, the water, the birds. All moving, all busy in their own way.

Just as Cassidy was busy inside, tidying up, washing dishes, doing laundry. Cassidy had her own routine every morning as well and always did the cleaning up after she got back from Mass.

Cassidy was the most religious person Julia had ever met, and that was a fact she would never have believed all those years ago when Cassidy Thomas first came into their lives.

She smiled, thinking of how naive Cassidy and Jeb must have

thought she and Teddy were. As if they didn't know from the beginning that those two had fallen for each other. They knew, of course, but they chose not to comment on it or confront them.

"Leave them be," she'd said all those years ago. "You have enough to argue about with Jeb. It's a fling. It will end when they both graduate."

"I misjudged them, Teddy. We both did." Talking to her dead husband was not, she had decided a long time ago, crazy. It was natural. "We both liked her—and obviously we understood Jeb falling for her, hard not to fall for such a beautiful girl. But we didn't think they had—what did we call it then?—staying power. How wrong we were."

The radio was on. Cassidy always turned it on when she cleaned. Jeb was singing along to some tune as he always did, and as always Julia's heart wept when she heard his voice. When he sang, he sounded like himself. Her son undamaged.

All those years ago, she'd thought Jeb and Cassidy wouldn't last, but not for the obvious reasons. Not because Cassidy was so young or from a different background, but because she had seemed so much more adult than Jeb. He was a dreamer, still a boy even when he was a senior at Yale. Happy reading his books, happy playing touch football on the lawn, but not ready to tackle the real world. Whereas Cassidy had always struck her as surprisingly mature and far older than her years. Added to that disparity was, of course, her phenomenal beauty.

Julia often asked herself back then what Cassidy would do with those looks. How would she handle all the attention she would constantly receive from men? More importantly, how would Jeb handle that as well?

He'd have to be a strong, solid, completely self-confident man to cope with that. One day he would have been, she knew. But not at the time.

So a part of her mother's heart was relieved when, after that terrible time at Stonybridge, Cassidy had gone back to Minneapolis and stayed there, telling Jeb their relationship was over.

She remembered how Jeb had come into the kitchen, admitted everything to her, and collapsed at the table in a flood of tears, uncomprehending. "Why won't she come back?" he'd asked. "She loves me. I know she does."

All she could do was try to comfort him. At the same time thinking: *This is probably for the best.*

It hadn't been for the best. It had been for the absolute worst. After graduating from Yale, Jeb came home and sat in his room supposedly writing the great American novel.

He'd never say what his story was about or how far he'd gotten in it, and Teddy lost all patience with him. That had been the most difficult time in their marriage. She kept telling Teddy to let Jeb be, he'd find his way, not to keep pushing him as hard as he did every day to get out and *do* something. Teddy would shake his head and tell her she was being too lenient and that Jeb was throwing away all the advantages life had given him.

Jeb must have heard them arguing.

It got to the point where even she was losing her patience with him. "You really should think about applying to grad school," she kept telling him, and he kept brushing her off. "Please—your father needs to see that you're doing something, Jeb," she'd begged. "You can't stay sitting in your room forever."

And then that night came. The night they'd sat in the living room and watched the draft lottery on the television and she had crossed her fingers and held her breath as they read out the birthdays and assigned the numbers. When Jeb's birthday came up and the number 4 was drawn, she hadn't been sure she would ever be able to breathe normally again.

Would he have acted differently if he were still with Cassidy?

Would he have saved himself, fled to Canada, or found some other way to dodge it? Instead he'd gotten up from the sofa and said: "OK, Dad. You win. I'm not fighting this. I'll fight for my country. Even though I don't believe in this war. Now I will really be doing something. You can stop yelling at me and Mom."

He wouldn't be budged. No amount of her pleading worked. His older brother had tried too, but to no avail.

"I don't get it, Mom," Peter had said. "Jeb *hates* this war. What the hell is he trying to prove? The idiot won't listen to me."

He wouldn't listen to anyone.

Julia should have been grateful that he didn't come back from Vietnam in a body bag. He came back alive. Yet the Jeb who came back wasn't the same person as the Jeb who had left. His eyes, which had always been so animated, were dulled and lifeless; he rarely spoke—when he did, he spoke so softly it was difficult to hear what he was saying; any loud noise, even a barking dog, would have him literally cowering.

Now they had a name for it: post-traumatic stress disorder. Then the only word she had to describe what had happened to him was "shell-shocked." His being, his personality, were absent. He didn't even read anymore. Instead he sat watching daytime soap operas and game shows on the television, staring blankly at the screen. He'd eat meals with them, but he *wasn't there*.

For a year they tried everything they could think of. They sent him to a psychiatrist, they got in touch with vet groups, they invited all his old friends to come around, but nothing changed those vacant eyes.

They were all at a complete loss, until Abby came up with a plan.

"I'm going to call Cassidy," she announced. "Cassidy might be able to get through to him. I'll tell her what's happened and how he is now. I know it's a long shot, but I have to try."

So Abby called Cassidy, and Cassidy came.

From the minute Cassidy entered the house, she devoted herself to Jeb entirely.

He didn't change overnight, and he never reverted to the old Jeb Julia had raised, but he got better. The first time she heard him laugh, when he and Cassidy were watching TV together, she had almost fainted.

A year later they were married in a family-only ceremony, in a Catholic church not far from the house. Cassidy's father and aunts and uncles came, and there was a small celebration afterward, but it was a modest and private event.

Was Jeb totally aware of what he was doing when he converted to Catholicism? She didn't know, but then again, she didn't care. He was as happy as he could possibly be. And all because of Cassidy.

Who was still beautiful, even now. Her hair was shorter, cut in a bob style, and her forehead was wrinkled, but she was a knockout even in her sixties.

The odd thing was that Julia had recognized, the minute Cassidy had walked back into their house, that Cassidy had lost something too. There had always been a sadness lurking; she'd sensed that when Cassidy first arrived at age sixteen and had understood that sadness was Cassidy's grief for her mother. At twenty, though, that lurking sadness had taken more of a hold of her. She wasn't just an adult before her time, she was old before her time, almost as if she had been in a war herself and was burdened by what she'd seen.

That burden wasn't due to Jeb's condition, though. The only time Cassidy was purely happy was when she was with him. It was something else, something Julia couldn't put a finger on.

Whatever it may have been, it didn't stop Cassidy from being the linchpin in the lives of the Madison family. Because Cassidy was taking care of Jeb, the rest of the family could all lead their lives without so much worry.

Peter was a lawyer in Seattle, divorced with two children and one grandson. Abby had moved to London, married a politician, and had four children who all had children of their own now. And Jennifer, who had finally been allowed to marry her long-term partner, Lucia, had become if not a famous pianist, one who earned a good living doing what she loved.

They'd all flown the coop. Or rather the coop had moved. She and Teddy had given Cassidy and Jeb the wedding present Cassidy had asked for: a house in one of the Thousand Islands off the coast of Canada.

"I know it's a lot to ask," Cassidy had said. "But I know we'd be happy there. I'll find a job, and I can take care of him there. We want to be by the sea. He needs to be away from everything, you know? He needs peace."

"We didn't know, did we, Teddy, that we'd end up here eventually too? That Cassidy would end up caring for you after your heart attack, caring for me after you died. Who knew? As they say now. Who knew she'd be the one supporting us in the end?"

"Would you like some more coffee, Julia?" Cassidy called out over the music.

"No thanks. I'm fine."

If only they'd had children. She'd never asked why they hadn't. It wasn't her business.

Nor had she ever asked why Cassidy and Abby weren't the

friends they'd been before. Abby and her family came over from England occasionally, once in a while for Christmas or Thanksgiving, but those two never spent time alone together, the way they had before. They were friendly to each other, in a strictly civil way.

Neither of them mentioned their days together at Stonybridge, not even once. And she was sure they never spoke of what had happened to that other girl, Karen.

It was as if Abby had, when she'd walked through the door with Cassidy that day, brought back a stranger to fix Jeb, not someone she'd been so close to.

None of that mattered, though. Jeb was the one who mattered and Jeb was singing "Sugar Pie, Honey Bunch" and Cassidy was laughing and it felt like the rain was laughing with them. This was a good place. A peaceful one. Tonight they'd watch *Top Hat* on DVD.

"Who am I to ask questions, Teddy? Especially when I'm not entirely sure I want to hear the answers?"

Chapter 86

Cassidy

This morning at church, she'd done what she always did—light a candle for the three babies she had miscarried and the one she'd aborted. And her mother. And Mr. D.

And Karen.

This time of year made the memories even stronger. They never went away anyway, but at the beginning of May it was hard to think of anything else.

Church was the only place she could be honest. So she went every day for Mass. She didn't even bother praying for forgiveness because she knew she wasn't going to get it.

When she was at home she concentrated on Jeb and Julia. She didn't have much time for reflection so those moments in church and afterward, when she took the long route home, were important.

After all the years, she'd only just begun to realize that she couldn't change history. Her thoughts would always take the same path. If she hadn't accepted Abby's invitation to help her with Latin. If she hadn't met Jeb. If she hadn't been paired with Zoey on Friendship Weekend. If she hadn't had the abortion. If they'd called an ambulance. If they'd confessed. If she hadn't gone home and left Jeb.

It is what it is.

That was a new expression these days. *It is what it is.*

It happened. There was no going back. She had kept her secrets and would continue to keep them, for Jeb's sake. But she had etched her guilt onto her skin. She'd had the letter *S* tattooed on her shoulder. Everyone thought it was a snake, and she wasn't going to correct them, tell them no, it stood for "Sinner": *I have branded myself a sinner, and I see this brand every single day. It is who I am.* Zoey was the only one who might have guessed that it was her Scarlet Letter.

Today, as she'd walked home from Mass, she had found herself thinking about Zoey. She could imagine Zoey having a ton of tattoos, but not the letter *S*. How did Zoey cope with her guilt? And what was she doing now? Was she demonstrating, marching on Washington, heading up a feminist group?

She had to be doing something like that. Zoey would never settle for anything less the way everyone else had.

It never ceased to amaze her how almost all of the hippies, once the war was over, stopped flashing peace signs to each other from their VW Bugs, traded them in for BMWs, traded acid in for cocaine, tie-dyed shirts in for suits, communes in for condos.

If there hadn't been a draft, would they have protested so strongly in the first place? Maybe if there had been a draft for every war the US had fought since then, there wouldn't have been any wars. Because the upper- and middle-class kids wouldn't want to fight them.

But what did she know? She'd never been political, and she

wasn't now. She'd spent most of her life teaching fourth and fifth grade at the local school. The politics there were all about friendships.

It was Stonybridge all over again—except these kids were nine and ten years old, not teenagers.

We should have known better. We weren't little kids in a playground. Why did it matter so much? Karen would be alive if it hadn't mattered so much.

Popularity was so crucial. And it was always the little girls. She'd see them getting into groups, shutting out other little girls—not talking to them, the way they'd all stopped talking to Karen.

She could put a halt to it when she was a teacher, but not back then.

People talked about the baby boomers, about growing up in the era of sex, drugs, and rock 'n' roll. You weren't there if you could remember it. Or something like that. But that whole hippie time of newfound freedom and exploration had passed her by. She'd spent her life since the age of twenty looking after Jeb.

She'd do whatever she had to do to protect him, even continue to lie about that night in the infirmary. There was no way she was going to upset his life any more than it had been already. She could deal with his depression, all the times he'd stay in the bedroom, not speaking until the cloud would lift and he'd come out again.

And she could deal with how he always talked in a whisper— how hard it was to hear what he was saying. Except when he sang.

She could deal with all the times he seemed to zone out, to disappear on her.

If they'd had children, maybe it would have been different. Jeb might have become more like the old Jeb again. But after three early miscarriages, she couldn't take any more. It was a sign. Her punishment.

So she looked at her tattoo every morning and went to church and lit candles and talked to God about her guilt.

And then came home to Jeb.

Nothing and no one else mattered.

Because the world still stopped.

Chapter 87

Mary's phone rang. She scrubbed in her bag, found it, pulled it out, and looked at the screen.

"Sorry, I just need to take this. I'll go outside and be back soon."

I nodded, then resisted the urge to put my elbows on the table and my head in my hands and cry.

Mary would hunt down everyone, the way she had me. I'd been easy to find, and Zoey would be as well. But I wasn't too worried about Zoey. If she was, as Mary had said, a lawyer, she wasn't about to confess and ruin her career; besides, out of the three of us, Zoey was the one with the sharpest brain, the one who would know how to stymie Mary effectively.

But Cass . . . Cass wasn't a liar. She'd probably confessed to her priest a million times by now. When I'd called her in Minneapolis all those years ago to tell her about Jeb and what had happened to him, all she'd said was "I'll be there. I'll call you back as soon as I get a flight and tell you when it lands."

When I'd picked her up at the airport, she'd climbed into my car and turned to me.

"I'm a mess, Abby. I'm here for Jeb. I've always loved him and I always will, but nothing else has been the same since that night. I won't say anything. I can't hurt your family. But I can't pretend with you. And that's going to eat me up. I think of Karen all the time. How we let her die there on that cold floor. And Mr. D. Karen telling him about the List and my abortion . . . I'm going to hell. But while I'm still alive, I'm going to do the best I can to help Jeb."

"He's really bad. I'm not sure even you can help."

"I have to try. It's . . . it's all so wrong. How did it all go so wrong?"

Her tears brought out mine. I sat with my head against the wheel of the car, unable to say a word.

"If only I'd told you about me and Jeb at the beginning . . ."

"If only . . ." I raised my head. "Do you know how many times I think, *If only*? If only we hadn't been in the infirmary . . . if only the scissors hadn't been there . . . if only I'd been nicer to Karen . . . if only I'd called an ambulance . . . there's no point, Cass. There are too many if onlys."

Cass was living pretty far off the grid now in Canada, but if Mary was determined to find her, she'd probably be able to.

Would Cassidy be able to tell bald-faced lies to Mary Greene? How much pressure would it take to crack her? Even if Cass didn't crack, would Mary stop searching for the truth? She'd know that Cass had married Jeb. Which meant she'd be close to positive that Jeb was the father of Cass's aborted child.

If she confronted Cass with that fact, how would Cass react? How would Jeb react if he found out?

The scariest part, though, was that at some point Mary would go to Lenox, dig up all the files. Reinvestigating cold cases— wasn't that a big deal now?

There had to have been something we missed, some way of tying us to that night they couldn't find then but they could find now.

Had the police kept Karen's clothes? There'd been that fight. All that pushing. We'd all been in contact with Karen. There could be DNA on her clothes.

If the police had kept Karen's clothes . . .

I could see Mary on the pavement outside the restaurant, gesticulating as she talked.

I could take all the blame, tell Mary now that I was the one who had stabbed Karen, and I alone had let her die. That would implicate Cass and Zoey, but only insofar as they'd been my alibi.

That would ruin my husband's career. It would be a scandal the papers would have a field day with. Wife of Shadow Cabinet Member John Wiley admits to killing a seventeen-year-old girl at a posh American boarding school.

He didn't deserve that.

And what would my children think? How would they cope?

So many lives ruined. Because I picked up those scissors. Because I couldn't stand Karen's taunts. That letter to Jimmy had enraged me, but that was nothing compared to the fury I'd felt when Karen had said Cass used me to get to Jeb, that that was the only reason she'd befriended me.

I picked up those scissors. Not to kill Karen, but to hurt her the way she'd hurt me.

Which was how it should have ended. Karen should have pulled out the scissors, reported me. I would have been expelled and that would have been that. It wasn't a deep wound; the scissors barely pierced her shoulder. We found that out during the time we'd stayed at school being questioned.

The fall was what had killed her.

No—the fact that we didn't call an ambulance was what probably killed her. We learned that as well. She would have had a chance of surviving if she'd been taken to the hospital immediately; at least that was what the police kept saying.

All we had to do was make that call.

All I had to do was make that call.

I knew I'd never be sure why I didn't. Was it fear? Self-preservation? Some sense of lingering anger toward her? Or just plain shock at what had happened?

I'd gotten away with it for close to fifty years. I'd figured out so many reasons to excuse my behavior, none of which actually worked to salve my conscience. Yet a bad conscience wasn't fatal. You learned how to live with it as if it were a secret limp, one that paralyzed you only when you were alone and awake in the early hours. Or when you heard the name "Karen" or saw someone resembling her. Or when a grandchild hugged a cute stuffed animal.

A guilty conscience could stay just that—a guilty conscience. As long as that guilt was a secret one.

Now my children, my husband, Jeb, my ninety-five-year-old mother, Cass, even Peter and Jennifer in their own ways would suffer the consequences of acknowledged guilt. As would Zoey Spalding.

Because I could sense it. I knew in my heart that Mary was bound to get justice for Karen. I couldn't put a tie around our wrists, bind myself to her, and live my life beside her to make sure she didn't find out the truth.

Her movie would be out there, and the whole world would know what we'd done.

The three of us would be spending years in separate jail cells.

As Mary made her way back to me, throwing her phone in her bag, she looked suddenly young again, and for the billionth time, I wished I'd listened to her in that field. Paid attention to Karen. Done what a good person should have done.

"You know that call I just took? It's funny, she's a good friend of mine, but we had a falling-out. I think we're OK again, but it reminded me of Stonybridge. Female friendships are so intense. Sometimes I think putting us all together like that at school meant something crazy was bound to happen. Sure, we had dances and saw boys occasionally, but it was all about our relationships with each other. You and Zoey were in love with Cass—"

"I wasn't in love with her. I had a boyfriend. Jimmy."

"You were in love with her, Abs. Not the way Karen was in love with Zoey—I'm not saying it was sexual or that you were obsessed the way Karen was, but you were in love. It was a girl-mance. I saw the way you were with her, remember? I was there. She was your world, you worshipped her."

"I—"

"Karen took it a step further with Zoey, but it's not surprising, really, is it? We were teenage girls with no real supervision. All those passions and all that jealousy—no wonder it exploded."

"Other girls went to boarding school, Mary. What happened at Stonybridge didn't happen anywhere else."

"No other school had Cassidy Thomas. That kind of beauty is dangerous. The thing is, everyone was in love with Cassidy. We all wanted to be her best friend. You have to remember, think about back then. When Cass was best friends with Zoey, it was OK: Zoey was different; in her own way she was as apart from the rest of us as Cassidy. So it made sense. No one felt bad. But when you and Cass got together, well—then everyone was jealous. Angel, Connie, everyone. Why had she picked you? You weren't that different from everyone else. Why were you the chosen one? The whole dynamic of our class shifted then. And sorry, but it was a bad shift. A bad shift that became a toxic shift with that fucking List."

"Toxic?"

"Yes. Toxic. I know what happened to Karen at that dance, Abby. How do you think that played out in her psyche? How did the List play out in any of our psyches? You score points for getting laid? Jesus, I hate to think of the long-term effects that List has had. The rot set in when that piece of paper was posted on the bulletin board. We were a fun, great class until then. It turned sordid and squalid and demeaning."

Jimmy. The low number I'd put up beside his name. If I'd found out he'd done something like that to me . . . ?

"The List was Zoey's idea."

"Who cares whose idea it was? The point is, no one stopped it. I include myself in that."

"You've thought about this a lot."

"It was a long flight. Listen, I'm at fault for not tearing that List down too. We're all to blame for going along with it. And I know I blamed you for ditching Karen the way you did, but the truth is I bet Karen would have done the same.

"If Cass had chosen her instead of you? I bet she would have been in heaven. All her dreams would have come true. The reason it all became as crazy as it did is that Cass happened to find you—the person who was best friends with the weakest, most insecure person in the class. Other girls might have been able to handle it better. Not Karen."

"You should have been a shrink, not a filmmaker."

"Yeah, right. The point is, like I said, female friendships are intense at that age. The interesting thing is, they still are. It doesn't matter what age you are, women can still get jealous of each other, all that crap. Maybe it's because female friends tell each other everything. We make ourselves so vulnerable to each other. Anyway, like I said, all I want is to try to get justice for

Karen. Sorry to be like that dog with a bone. But it feels right, you know?"

She waved to the waiter, signaling for the bill.

"Isn't it strange how time works?" she asked.

"What do you mean?"

"Well, think about it. These days Mr. Doherty could be a teacher happily married to a man and walking proudly in parades; Karen could kiss Zoey and be open about her sexuality. Even if Zoey didn't reciprocate, Karen wouldn't be shunned. She'd be able to find someone who returned her feelings. She'd be able to find happiness. Cassidy could be on the pill. Or she could have a legal abortion. Society has moved forward, thank God.

"Anyway, enough about the social fabric. Can I call you tomorrow? Maybe we could go to a museum or something. I promise I won't talk about the past anymore. I'd like to catch up with you properly. Hear more about your life now."

I wasn't sure whether I believed her; my guess was she'd bring it all up again somehow, but it didn't matter, not really. Whatever I said or didn't say, the end result would be the same. She was right, society had moved on, but Mary wasn't about to move on from Karen's death. She had a story to chase, and she would find a way to chase it to the end.

"That sounds great. But I'll have to check my diary when I get home."

"Of course."

The waiter arrived with the bill, she paid for it, and I thanked her. We went out, onto the pavement.

"Do you want a lift to your hotel?"

She laughed that throaty laugh of hers.

"Abs, it's about a five-minute walk. And it's a beautiful day. Oh, look—across the street. Isn't that the bookstore from the movie *Notting Hill*? I want to go in there."

Before I could say, *It's not*, she stepped off the pavement.

Looking the wrong way, to the left. Looking the American way.

I was looking the right way.

I saw the bus heading straight for her.

All I had to do was reach out, grab her wrist, pull her back.

Acknowledgments

Massive thanks to my editor, Lucia Macro, and my agent, Charlie Viney, for believing in this book and for all their wise and perceptive help.

Thanks too to Asanté Simons and copyeditor Andrea Monagle for all their hard work.

For all sorts of much needed support, I'm indebted to Clare Bowron, Keith Barnes, the Colegrave and Feige families, and Maggie Blake Bailey. A special shout-out to Violet, Aya, Arturo, and Santiago.

And, of course, I couldn't have written this without my female friends—far-out and groovy survivors of the dance floor.